THE COUNTESS

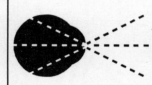

This Large Print Book carries the
Seal of Approval of N.A.V.H.

THE COUNTESS

LYNSAY SANDS

THORNDIKE PRESS

A part of Gale, Cengage Learning

GALE
CENGAGE Learning

Detroit • New York • San Francisco • New Haven, Conn • Waterville, Maine • London

GALE
CENGAGE Learning

LIBRARY OF CONGRESS CATALOGING-IN-PUBLICATION DATA

Sands, Lynsay.
   The countess / by Lynsay Sands. — Large print ed.
     p. cm. — (Thorndike Press large print romance)
   ISBN-13: 978-1-4104-3919-2
   ISBN-10: 1-4104-3919-4
   1. Brothers—Fiction. 2. Widows—Fiction. 3. Large type books. I. Title.
PR9199.3.S2195C68 2011
813'.54—dc22   2011014054

Published in 2011 by arrangement with Avon, an imprint of HarperCollins Publishers.

Printed in the United States of America
1 2 3 4 5 6 7 15 14 13 12 11

THE COUNTESS

CHAPTER ONE

"My lady?"

Christiana remained curled on her side in her cocoon of blankets. She merely opened one eye to peer at the older woman bent over her. Grace, her maid. "Hmm?"

"Your sisters are here." Those four words and the urgency behind them brought her other eye open at once.

"What? My sisters in London?" Christiana rolled over, thrusting the blankets and linens away to sit up. "And here at this hour? There must be some sort of emergency for them to be calling so early."

"That was my thought when I saw them getting out of the carriage," Grace admitted as Christiana got out of bed. "So I hurried up here to fetch you. If you're quick we can have you dressed and downstairs before your husband sends them away."

"Dicky wouldn't send them away," Christiana said with surprise, and then tacked on

7

an uncertain, "Would he?"

"He's done so with others."

"Who?" Her horror and surprise came muffled from inside the cloth of her nightdress as the maid dragged it off over her head.

"Lady Beckett, Lady Gower, Lord Ollivet and Lord Langley . . . twice." Grace turned away to trade the nightdress for a pale blue gown that matched Christiana's eyes. As she began to help her don it, she added, "And I can tell you Lord Langley didn't like it the first time, but was absolutely livid the second."

"I can imagine," Christiana said with a sigh as the dress dropped to cover her body. The Langley estate bordered her childhood home, Madison Manor. Robert, the only son and heir, had grown up with her and her sisters. He was like family, the big brother she'd never had. He wouldn't have appreciated being sent away like some sort of undesirable. "Why didn't you tell me?"

Grace snatched up a hairbrush and began to drag it through her hair before saying, "What good would it have done?"

"None," Christiana admitted unhappily. Her husband had every right to turn away whomever he wished from his door, while she, as she'd come to learn, had few to no rights at all in this marriage. She sighed, and then grimaced as Grace tugged at her hair, pulling it into the tight, matronly bun Christiana had worn since marriage, a style she absolutely abhorred. Aside from being ugly, having her hair pulled so tight all day resulted in terrible headaches, but Dicky insisted it gave some sophistication to her unruly person.

"What could have brought my sisters here?" Christiana asked worriedly.

"I do not know, but it must be something important. They did not send word of their arrival in the city ere arriving," the woman pointed out, and then stepped back. "There. I have finished with your hair."

Christiana barely managed to swipe up her slippers before Grace took her arm to urge her to move. "Come, we must hurry. Haversham will have found and fetched Lord Radnor by now. Let us hope we were quick enough and your husband has not yet sent them away."

Grunting in agreement, Christiana hopped on first one foot and then the other to get her slippers on without the necessity of stopping as the woman rushed her to the door.

Christiana could hear both Lisa's and Suzette's high anxious voices from the entry below as she hurried along the upper hall and immediately frowned at the rudeness of keeping her sisters in the entry rather than showing them to the parlor. She couldn't blame Haversham, however, the butler would only be following Dicky's orders regarding guests.

Dicky's voice sounded next, loud and pompous as he announced, "I fear *my wife* is still sleeping. You really should have sent a messenger around with a card had you wished to see her. *I* could have responded with an appropriate time for such a visit. As it is, I fear you shall simply have to return to your father's townhouse and send that card now."

"Can we not just slip up to speak to her, Dicky? We *are* her sisters and it's important." Suzette's tone was a combination of desperation, anger and something like shock. The anger was no doubt at Dicky's pompous words. Probably the shock was as well, Christiana acknowledged and knew the man her sisters now faced was a far cry from the one they'd encountered prior to the wedding. She had no doubt they were just as confused and startled by the change in him as she herself had been for the first six months of their marriage. However, it was the desperation that worried her. Something was definitely wrong.

"It's all right, husband. I am awake," Christiana called out as she reached the stairs and started down.

Dicky immediately turned to peer up at her, his face like thunder. Whether his anger was over her sister's words or her own, she didn't know. Dicky preferred to be obeyed, and promptly; he wouldn't appreciate Suzette's insistence. However, he also wouldn't be pleased with her arrival before he could send Suzette and Lisa away as he apparently had others.

Forcing a soothing smile to her lips, Christiana stepped off the stairs and moved to his side. The man had a terrible temper and could say the cruelest things when angered. She had to live with the insults and criticisms, but her sisters shouldn't have to face the rage she found so frightening. It wasn't the anger itself that unsettled Christiana so much as the depth of it. Fury swirled around him at all times like a dark cloak. When provoked, his face flushed red and twisted into a tight, cruel mask, and he would begin to snap and snarl with such rage and venom that spittle actually flew from his lips, and gathered at the corners of his mouth like a rabid dog. He also tended to tremble with the depth of his feelings as if they were barely contained and might explode at any moment. It was that explosion Christiana wished most to avoid. He was a strong man and she didn't wish ever to see the wreckage his anger would leave in its wake were it completely unleashed.

"Good morning, Dicky," Christiana breathed nervously as she reached his side. She leaned up to kiss his cold, hard cheek as if all were well and she wasn't fighting the urge to flee the seething fury she could sense simmering in him.

Dicky did not even respond to her greeting, snapping instead, "I was just explaining to your sisters that it's quite rude to arrive uninvited so early in the morning."

"Yes, well, family is allowed some leeway, aren't they?" Christiana said, and winced at the pleading she could hear in her own voice. There was no mistaking that she was begging him not to make a scene and she could tell by her sisters' expression that they recognized it, which was just humiliating. Even more humiliating was that Dicky chose to ignore the plea.

"*My* family would never arrive uninvited and without any warning," he snarled, sneering at her sisters as if they were beneath contempt.

"Of course your family wouldn't. They're

all dead," Suzette snapped in response and Christiana glanced at her with alarm. Her gaze then darted worriedly back to Dicky, who was sucking in air through his teeth and puffing up.

Recognizing the signs of an approaching explosion, she quickly took his arm and tried to urge him away, saying, "Why do you not go enjoy your breakfast and leave me to deal with my sisters?"

Dicky didn't move. Feet planted solidly, he ignored her tugging and scowled at Suzette who merely glared defiantly back.

Christiana closed her eyes briefly and fought the urge to slap the stupid girl. Oh yes, Suzette was being brave enough, but then she had little to lose in this battle. Dicky couldn't hit her or even penalize her in any way. It was Christiana he would punish for the girl's bravery . . . and probably in several different ways. It wouldn't be enough for him to rant and rave at her for half an hour about her unruly and uncouth family. He would also most likely insist Suzette was a bad influence and order Christiana not to see her again. Then he would add various other little unpleasantries to the punishment such as ensuring that all meals served were ones she disliked, having her woken early with some excuse or other, and then either insisting she retire early when she was curled up with a good book, or keeping her up late when she was exhausted. Where Dicky had started to leave her to her own devices lately, he would probably force her to suffer his company for the next several days as he ranted and raved about everything and everyone in London in a manner sure to leave her disheartened and depressed, and then he would insist on taking her out to aid him in purchasing some item or other, only so that he could announce that her choices were poor ones and select something else instead in a show of how little taste she had. All of which were petty punishments, but when added together and carried on for long periods of time would leave her exhausted and despairing of a life of such steady, small tortures.

On top of all of that, Dicky would also be spouting criticism after criticism of her looks, her dress, her speech, her comportment, her family members, her intelligence, her naivety, her friends or her lack of them. It would be a steady trickle of abuse that slowly eroded every last vestige of self-esteem she possessed until she longed for nothing but the escape of sleep. There was no other escape available to her. Suicide was out of the question, as was divorce.

"Where is your father?" Dicky barked suddenly, drawing her attention back to the matter at hand. "What kind of man leaves two young unmarried women to gallivant about the city without his escort?"

"Visiting us is hardly gallivanting about the city," Christiana protested quickly to forestall Suzette doing so. "Please husband, your breakfast will be getting cold. Why do you not —"

"*Our* breakfast," Dicky corrected sharply and then smiled in a way that made her sigh inwardly. He had thought of a way to punish someone. "But you're right. It *is* getting cold while we waste our time on *uninvited* guests."

Christiana found her hand suddenly caught up in his as Dicky began to drag her up the hall, "Show my wife's sisters to the parlor, Haversham. We shall attend them after we have enjoyed the breakfast Cook has worked so hard to produce."

Christiana cast a glance that was half apologetic and half warning to her sisters and then she was in the breakfast room and Dicky was slamming the door closed behind them.

"Your father should be ashamed of raising three such unruly creatures," Dicky snarled as he led her to the sideboard and the food waiting there. "A little discipline would have gone a long way toward making better women of you all. But then he has little discipline himself, does he not?"

Christiana remained silent, merely picking up a plate and beginning to select food from the offerings. She had learned long ago that to try to argue her case merely ensured an even longer, more furious rant, so simply chose a piece of toast and some fruit and started to turn away.

"You will eat a proper breakfast, wife," Dicky snapped, bringing her to a halt. "Give me your plate."

Christiana bit her tongue as he snatched the china away, and managed to swallow the sigh that tried to escape as Dicky began to pile kidneys and kippers on her plate. She hated both kidneys and kippers and he knew that. It seemed the punishment was starting already.

"There. Now you may sit."

A glance at the plate Dicky shoved under her nose showed that he'd added scrambled eggs to the kidneys and kippers. She preferred boiled eggs, but merely took the plate and turned to take her place at the table. But she was wishing the whole while that she had the nerve to toss the plate, food and all, in his face. Unfortunately, she never did anything so bold, ever. She might have, had he dared to treat her like this before they were married, but he had been all charm and compliments then. This behavior hadn't started until after the wedding, and Christiana had been so startled and taken aback by the sudden transformation in his attitude that she'd been slow to stand up for herself. It had left her feeling as dazed as if someone had hit her in the head. By the time she'd got over the shock and even considered standing up for herself, it was too late, the criticisms and abuse had already taken effect and rather than argue, she'd found herself wondering if perhaps the dress he was criticizing *wasn't* cut too low, or that the shade *might* clash with her coloring. Her self-confidence had been shaken, and as time had passed it was shaken more. Now rather than even consider that he might be wrong, she simply tried to appease him, soothe his temper and please him if possible. Somehow she had become a slave with less rights than the servants who worked for them.

"You're not eating your breakfast," Dicky said as he joined her at the table.

Christiana cleared her throat. "I am not very hungry."

"I don't care. You're too skinny. Eat,"

Dicky said firmly, and then added, "Your diet is atrocious. You don't eat enough meat. Eat your kidney and kippers."

Christiana bowed her head and began to eat, doing her best not to taste what went into her mouth. That was impossible, however, and she was more than grateful to finish the last bite and stand up.

"What are you doing?"

Christiana stilled, her eyes shooting to her husband. "I am finished, Dicky. I thought I would go see what my sisters —"

"*I* am not finished." When confusion covered Christiana's face, he snapped, "Is it too much to expect my wife to keep me company while I breakfast?"

She settled reluctantly back in her seat, but resentment and anger were stirring within her again. They never breakfasted together. From the first morning of their marriage he had either risen early, breakfasted and left the house before she had even stirred, or he slept later than her and took his breakfast in his room alone. At first Christiana had worried over that, thinking a wife and husband should breakfast together, but after a while she'd been grateful for the respite. Now she was just annoyed with the man, knowing he was simply using the demand for her company as an excuse to

18

make her sisters wait longer.

Dicky took his time about finishing his meal, but finally pushed his plate away and rose. He then insisted on walking her to the parlor and did so at a pace that snails could have outstripped. Christiana was gritting her teeth by the time he paused to open the parlor door.

"Chrissy!" Suzette started to her feet with relief when Christiana entered, but stopped abruptly when Dicky followed. She then watched with obvious frustration as he ever so slowly walked Christiana to a seat and saw her settled.

"So?" Dicky arched an eyebrow as he took up a position on the arm of Christiana's chair where he could loom over her like a bird of prey about to pounce. He then eyed her sisters like they were naughty children. "What was so urgent that you had to arrive here at such an ungodly hour?"

Suzette's gaze slid to Christiana and then to Lisa before she forced a cool smile and sweetly lied, "Nothing at all. We just missed Chrissy terribly. It has been more than a year since your marriage and you have not brought her back to visit *as you promised.*"

Christiana could feel Dicky stiffen at the chastisement and sighed inwardly. Here was more he would punish her for later.

"I am an Earl, girl, an important man who is far too busy to waste time gallivanting about the countryside when there is work to be done here," Dicky said stiffly.

"Ah, well, we are seeing each other now," Christiana murmured to forestall her sister saying anything else. "And I am very happy to see you. You must tell me everything that has happened since I left home."

Much to her relief, Suzette caught the hint and immediately launched into tale after tale of life back on their country estate. She actually seemed to begin to enjoy the endeavor, devilment sparkling in her eyes as she recounted who had married, who hadn't, and every bit of gossip she had heard no matter how trivial. As for Lisa, she sat silent, her worried gaze remaining warily on an increasingly impatient Dicky as Suzette babbled on. It was a relief to all of them when he suddenly stood to announce, "I shall leave you ladies to your nattering then. I have more important issues to attend to."

On that pompous note, he left them, moving much more swiftly than he had allowed her to on entering.

"Thank God," Suzette moaned when the door closed, her gay, trouble-free facade dropping away. Anger immediately replaced

20

it and she sat forward to demand, "What the devil is going on, Chrissy? Does he act like that all the time? My God he was nothing like that when he courted you. He —"

"Hush," Christiana hissed. Standing, she moved swiftly to the door and knelt to peer out the keyhole. When all she saw was empty hall, she released a relieved breath and moved back to her sisters.

"How bad is your marriage?" Suzette asked quietly as Christiana settled on the couch between her sisters. "You look tired and miserable. He's not treating you right, is he?"

"Never mind that," Christiana said wearily. There was little anyone could do about her situation and discussing it would merely bring her misery to the surface. It was easier when she simply didn't think about it. "What is going on? Why are you two here?"

Suzette and Lisa exchanged a glance and then Lisa finally spoke up for the first time since their arrival and announced, "Father has been gambling again."

"What?" Christiana gasped with dismay. "But he promised never to gamble again after Dicky paid off his last gambling debts."

It was how she'd ended up married to the man. Her father had landed them in hot water with one aberrant night of drinking and gambling. He'd raised what money he could by selling family heirlooms to meet the debt, but it hadn't been enough, and he'd been at a loss as to how to pay the rest. The creditors had been knocking on the door when fortune had seemed to smile on them in the form of Dicky. He'd arrived at Madison Manor with an offer of marriage for Christiana, and on hearing of their dire straits had offered to clear the remainder of her father's debts in exchange for Christiana's hand in marriage.

To her father's credit, he'd refused the offer until Dicky had convinced him that he loved Christiana. Dicky had claimed to have seen her at the local fair that summer and spoken to her briefly, which she hadn't recalled at all. He'd also claimed he'd been fascinated and found out all he could about her and that everything he'd learned he'd found pleasing.

His words had been convincing and her father had been swayed, but despite his dire straits, had insisted that while he would give his blessing to the union, it was only if she was willing. Unfortunately, Christiana had been easy enough to persuade. Dicky was handsome, well off and an Earl. Any girl would be flattered to be courted by such a man. And what a courtship! He'd been the sweetest of men, calling her his little rosebud and romancing her with touching poems and declarations of undying love. It had all been rather heady to a simple girl who had spent her life quietly in the country with only her sisters and one neighbor boy for company, and in no time at all he'd swept her off her feet and gained her agreement.

Christiana grimaced at the thought of the naïve idiot she'd been, and now saw that she should have questioned his motives and insisted on more time to make her decision. But her father only had two weeks to pay off his gambling debts, and she'd foolishly believed every word Dicky had said to her. She'd been sure he must love her and that there could be no other purpose for his rapturous courting. After all, what other reason could there be? It was not as if he knew about the outrageously huge dower that her mother's father, Baron Sefton, had bestowed on herself and her two sisters in his will. That was a family secret.

Of course, once they'd married and his behavior had changed so dramatically Christiana had begun to suspect he'd known about the dower after all and that gaining it had been the true target of his courting. She just didn't know how he could have learned about it.

"Father said he didn't mean to," Suzette said unhappily, drawing Christiana's mind back to this new problem. "He feels horrible about what's happened and has been scrambling to try to figure out a way to pay off his debts, but can think of nothing."

Christiana grimaced. He'd felt horrible the last time too. "When did it happen? And how? He has not even been to London and there is nowhere near Madison for him to —"

"He has been in London this last month," Lisa corrected quietly. "Didn't you know?"

"No," Christiana admitted with dismay. "Why didn't he come to see me?"

"He did," Suzette assured her. "In fact it was his original reason for traveling to London. He was worried because Dicky hadn't brought you home to visit, and we weren't getting responses to the letters we were sending."

"I haven't received any letters, and I have been writing faithfully every week," Christiana said quietly, anger beginning a slow burn in her stomach. Not getting responses to her own letters had left her feeling even more lonely and depressed. Now it seemed Dicky had somehow been ensuring none of her letters went out and that she didn't receive any in return. What else had the man been doing? She wondered grimly.

"The bastard," Suzette snapped, looking ready to smack someone.

"You say father came here?" Christiana asked, returning them to the topic at hand.

"Aye," Lisa murmured, her worried gaze on a still furious Suzette. "Dicky said you were out at the dressmaker's."

"He didn't tell me," Christiana said unhappily.

"Apparently Dicky welcomed him and took him to the club for a drink . . . and then on to a gaming hell," Lisa said.

Christiana sat back with dismay.

"Father was supposed to return home two weeks ago," Suzette continued the explanations in a quiet voice. "When he did not arrive and we heard no word we began to worry. I sent messages to the townhouse but got no response, and then finally decided Lisa and I had best come to London and find out what had happened."

When she fell silent, Lisa picked up the tale again. "We arrived in London at dawn and went straight to the townhouse. We found father there in the library. He was in his cups and sobbing."

Christiana let her breath out on a sigh and asked with resignation, "How bad is it?"

"Worse than last time," Suzette said tightly.

"Worse?" Christiana could feel the blood rush out of her face.

"He owes less than last time," Lisa said quickly. "But the estate is still recovering from his first misstep and there is no ready cash or even much to sell. If father cannot come up with the money, he may be forced to sell the family estate to pay off the debt."

Christiana sucked in a horrified breath. This *was* worse than last time.

"We shall be ruined once this gets out," Lisa pointed out solemnly.

Christiana bit her lip, knowing that was true. "How long does he have to find the money?"

"Two weeks," Suzette answered.

"Two weeks," Christiana breathed with dismay. Her mind raced around like a rat in a larder for a moment and then she straightened her shoulders determinedly. "I shall talk to Dicky. We will have to take some money from my dower and —"

"No. You paid last time. It's not fair that you should pay again," Suzette argued, and then added grimly, "Besides, it appears that you are still paying for father's last misstep."

Christiana waved that away, knowing Suzette was referring to how Dicky treated her.

Not wishing to discuss it, she instead addressed her suggestion, "Suzette, you cannot pay. You cannot claim your dower without first marrying."

"True," she agreed. "So I shall marry."

"In two weeks?" Christiana shook her head. "You cannot find a suitable husband in two weeks."

"Who says he has to be suitable?" Suzette asked dryly. "Dicky was supposedly suitable and that hasn't turned out very well, has it?"

"But —"

"Do not fret, Chrissy," Suzette interrupted. "I have a plan. I just need a little help from you to make it work."

"What kind of plan? And what help?" Christiana asked worriedly.

Suzette sat eagerly forward and took her hands. "There are always Lords who are land and title rich and yet in desperate need of funds. I intend to find one who is desperate enough that he will strike a deal with me. In exchange for marriage and access to three quarters of my dower, he must agree to allow me access to one quarter of it to use as I wish, as well as the freedom to live my own life." She smiled widely. "All I need is for you to sponsor our coming out . . . immediately. You have to get us to balls and teas and soirees and anything else where I can meet and assess the men available. I will do the rest."

Christiana stared at her sister. Her plan seemed sound enough. Three quarters of Suzette's dower was still a fortune, and certainly the arrangement should leave Suzette happier than she herself was in her own marriage. In fact, Christiana actually felt a moment's envy that her younger sister would manage such an arrangement. As for Suzette's request, sponsoring her for a coming out was little enough to ask, and certainly much easier than trying to convince Dicky to allow Christiana access to her funds. While the man was pleased to waste money on food, wine, and his own pleasures, when it came to giving her anything as small as pin money, his fist suddenly spasmed and closed tight. Of course, Dicky did seem pleased to say no to her when it came to anything, so convincing him to sponsor her sisters for a coming out might not be all that easy either, she thought worriedly.

"Chrissy?" Suzette asked anxiously. "You can do that, can you not?"

Christiana's gaze returned to her younger sister. Seeing the worry and desperation on her face, she straightened abruptly. "Cer-

28

tainly I can. I shall make Dicky do it . . . somehow," she added in a mutter as she got determinedly to her feet.

She would confront him at once, Christiana thought firmly as she crossed the room, and found she wasn't afraid for the first time in a long time. It wasn't just because she was angry about Dicky's part in her father's gambling either. Somehow just learning that her family had tried to write her and that she wasn't as alone as she'd felt this last year was resurrecting her spirit, as was this short time basking in her sisters' company. The old Christiana was awakening inside her as if from a long sleep, and she was ready for a fight.

"What if he says no?" Lisa asked worriedly, bringing her to a halt as she reached the door.

Christiana paused just long enough to force a smile to her lips, and then glanced back to say lightly, "Then I shall just have to kill him, won't I?"

CHAPTER TWO

Christiana usually knocked before daring to enter Dicky's office. This time, however, she was angry and ready for a fight. She did not knock, but thrust the door open, and sailed determinedly inside, her voice sharp as she announced, "We have to talk, Dicky."

Christiana thought it a very strong start. It was just a shame that Dicky wasn't there to hear it. The room was empty. She started to turn away with a scowl, intending to hunt the man down, but paused mid-turn as she saw someone sitting in one of the chairs by the fire. Recognizing her husband's dark hair above the chair back, Christiana glared briefly, awaiting some sort of acknowledgment that he'd heard her. When none was forthcoming, her scowl deepened and she strode forward.

"You will not ignore me, Dicky. I know you have been withholding my family's letters from me, and you have somehow been preventing my letters from getting to them as well. And now I find out that you took my father to a gaming hell of all places? How could you when you know what happened the last time? You have treated me most shabbily since our marriage, but I never imagined you would do something so —"

Christiana had been building up a nice head of steam as she crossed the room to stand before him, but stopped now as she got a good look at the man she was berating.

Dicky was leaning back in the chair, eyes closed and fingers resting on his chest as if he'd meant to loosen his cravat but had dropped off before he could. No doubt Dicky had nodded off after returning here on escaping Suzette's "nattering," she thought grimly.

And the liquor probably didn't help, Christiana decided as her gaze shifted to the empty glass next to the half-empty bottle of amber liquid on the table beside him. She recognized the carafe, it was very fine, very expensive whiskey that he usually only opened when celebrating something.

Wondering what on earth he could have to celebrate, Christiana bent to shake his shoulder. "Dicky, you — Oh!" she gasped and leapt back when he suddenly slid from his seat and landed in a heap on the floor. Christiana was about to bend down and rouse him from his stupor when a rustling from the door drew her attention to the fact that Suzette and Lisa had followed and now stood in the open door.

Suzette peered at Dicky and then raised her gaze to Christiana and said wryly, "I thought you were just teasing when you said you'd kill him."

"Very funny," Christiana muttered, not appreciating her sister's sense of humor. "He's drunk. Close the door before one of the servants sees the state he's in."

"Does he often drink this early?" Suzette asked, crossing the room to join her as Lisa quickly closed the door.

"Not this early, no," Christiana admitted. "But he does start earlier than he should and drink more than he should on a regular basis. It's given me hope that he'll fall down the stairs and make me a widow sooner rather than later," she added dryly and then grimaced, knowing how bitter and unkind the thought was.

"I think he has," Lisa said quietly as she joined them around Dicky's prostrate form. "Made you a widow I mean. I don't think he's breathing, Chrissy."

Christiana glanced doubtfully back to Dicky. He'd slid onto his knees, and slumped forward over them so that his head landed on the rug in front of the fireplace. While it didn't appear that his back was moving or expanding with the inhalation of breath, it was hard to tell for sure with him crumpled the way he was.

Christiana knelt beside him and with a little help from Suzette managed to lay him out on his back. They then both stared at his chest for a moment. It wasn't moving. Hardly believing what she was seeing, Christiana leaned forward to rest her ear above his heart. There was no steady thump, no thump at all.

Eyes widening, she sat back on her haunches again and simply stared at the man, finding it hard to believe he was dead. Dicky just wasn't thoughtful enough to do something so kind.

"He *is* dead, isn't he?" Lisa asked.

Christiana glanced to where her youngest sister still stood by the chair and said uncertainly, "It would seem so."

"What do you think killed him?" Lisa asked with a frown and then suggested, "It was probably his heart. I noticed how flushed he got when Suzette argued with him. He seemed a very passionate man."

Christiana didn't comment, instead she let her gaze drift over the man she'd been so eager to be free of and let a sad sigh slip from her lips. She'd thought herself in love with him when they married, but the man she'd loved hadn't existed, he'd turned into someone entirely different once the ceremony was over. That man had smothered every last drop of her love over this last year with his controlling and critical attitude. Still, she felt a tinge of grief stir within her. It was probably for the man she'd thought he was and the life she'd hoped for, Christiana acknowledged. Despite everything, she'd still held on to a drop of hope that something would happen to turn him back into the wonderful Prince Charming he'd been when he'd courted her, and that she could yet have the happy ending she'd expected on their wedding day.

Christiana hadn't been foolish enough to think there was *much* hope for that, but there was absolutely *no* chance for it now. She was a widow . . . and had every intention of staying one. There was no way she would ever entrust herself into another man's hands again, not in this lifetime. Christiana had learned her lesson well.

Shoulders straightening resolutely, she said, "I suppose I should have the servants call a doctor to —"

"No," Suzette interrupted. "If he's dead you will have to go into mourning and cannot give us our debut. We will be expected to join you in mourning too and will have absolutely no chance of saving ourselves."

Christiana recognized the truth in Suzette's words, but said helplessly, "What can we do? He's dead."

As Suzette glowered at the hapless Dicky, Lisa suggested, "Perhaps we could just put him in his bed and tell the servants he is feeling unwell. Even a couple of days may be enough for Suzie to choose someone desperate enough to accept her offer. The moment she settles on someone and heads for Gretna Green you can pretend to discover Dicky dead in his bed."

"A couple of days wouldn't even be enough time for Suzie to start her search for a husband," Christiana argued sensibly.

"It is," Suzette insisted. "Tonight is the season opening ball at Lord and Lady Landon's. Everyone will be there. You and Lisa can gossip with the women to find out who is rumored to need money, and I can assess those men and find out which seem the most desperate and amenable to my needs."

"Everyone will be there *who has been*

invited," Christiana corrected dryly. "And we weren't."

"You were," Suzette argued. "Lady Landon told us so."

"When could she have told you that?" Christiana asked suspiciously. "You only arrived in London this morning."

"Lord and Lady Landon were at the last inn we stopped at on the way to London," Lisa said with a wide smile. "They're both very nice and were kind enough to share their table with us. While talking, Lady Landon said she had sent you and Dicky an invitation and would be pleased to extend the invitation to include the two of us."

"Dicky never mentioned an invitation to the Landons' ball." Christiana glanced to his body.

"What a surprise," Suzette said with disgust and glowered at the man. Her foot also moved sharply in his direction before stopping abruptly and Christiana raised an eyebrow, sure the girl had just stopped herself from kicking the corpse.

"Lady Landon also mentioned the Hammonds' ball is the night afterward," Lisa announced. "She said it is a crush, and everyone attends it as well. She said she knew you had also been invited to that. She and Lady Hammond are apparently good friends and Lady Landon promised to send a message to Lady Hammond telling her how delightful we were and suggesting she extend your invitation to include us as well." Lisa beamed with satisfaction. "Between those two balls, Suzie should find someone so we only need the two nights and then you can claim you found Dicky dead in his bed."

Christiana stared at her with disbelief. "He is dead *now,* Lisa. After a couple of days . . ." She didn't finish, it was just too gruesome to say that the man would start to smell.

"We can open the bedroom window and let the cold air in," Suzette said at once. "It will slow down decay. We could even make a trip to the ice house to get ice to pack around him and —"

"Dear God," Christiana leapt to her feet with horror. "I cannot believe you are suggesting this. He is a man, not a slab of meat."

"Well, it's not like he was a *good* man," Suzette said with irritation. "From the little we've seen, it appears he treated you abominably."

"And he *is* the one who took Father to the gaming hell and started this latest ruination," Lisa pointed out solemnly.

Christiana was silent, her thoughts torn. She peered from the man on the floor, to Lisa's worried expression, to Suzette's desperate one and clenched her hands. "Two nights," she said tightly. "We cannot risk any more than that."

"Two nights," Suzette agreed on a breath of relief.

Christiana shook her head. "We are mad."

"The mad Madison sisters," Suzette said with a sudden grin.

Christiana didn't smile, she was too busy considering the problem of how to get her husband up to his bedroom. Then there was the small matter of how they were going to keep his valet — not to mention the rest of the servants — away from him. Another problem was how to fetch back the ice to keep him cold enough that the smell alone wouldn't give away the state he was in, and then they had to find the invitations and arrange for appropriate gowns for the three of them in very short order.

Dear God, she thought, this couldn't work, and they truly were mad to even consider it.

"Take his feet, Lisa."

Christiana glanced to her sisters as they moved to either end of the man on the floor. Eyes widening with alarm, she asked, "What are you doing?"

"We have to get him up to his room," Suzette said sensibly. "You go make sure there is no one in the hall."

"But —"

"Move," Suzette grunted impatiently as she caught Dicky under the shoulders and hefted his upper body off the floor.

Christiana narrowed her eyes and propped her hands on her hips. "See here, miss, I may have had to take that kind of bossy nonsense from Dicky this last year, but that was only because he was my husband. I'll not have you ordering me around like a servant in his place now he's dead."

Lisa had just grabbed Dicky's feet, but dropped them to the floor with a thud and hurried to her side to pat her arm soothingly. "Now Chrissy, I don't think Suzie meant anything by it. We're all just a little overexcited at the moment."

Christiana rolled her eyes. Lisa always had been the peacekeeper, forever trying to soothe hurt feelings and prevent the outbreak of battles. Shaking her head, she glanced to Dicky. He really was a good sized man, and was not going to be moved easily or quickly. "Well, we can't take him like this."

"What do you mean?" Suzette let Dicky's

upper body drop.

Christiana winced at the thud of his head hitting the wood, but explained patiently, "Even if there is no one in the hall now, someone could come out while we are carting him up the stairs. Then what would we say?"

Suzette frowned and peered down at Dicky with dislike. "Even dead the man is a pain."

Christiana actually felt her mouth twitch with amusement and knew it must be hysteria. There was absolutely nothing funny about any of this. Her eyes slid over him again and then settled on the rug he half lay on and suddenly she knew what to do. "We shall roll him up in the rug and cart that upstairs. That way if anyone comes along they won't see him."

"How do we explain why we're dragging a rug around?" Suzette asked doubtfully.

"We shall say the rose room is chilly at night and you, Suzie, are going to stay in it and we are hoping the rug will help keep it warm for the few nights you are here," Christiana announced with satisfaction. It was nice to have an issue she *could* solve for once. It made a change from constantly banging her head against a wall trying to sort out how to fix her marriage.

"That may work," Lisa said slowly.

"It will," Christiana assured her. "Now come, help me roll him onto the rug."

With the three of them working together it was a quick job getting him positioned on the end of the rug and then rolling him up in it.

"Now what?" Suzette asked as they straightened.

"Now we carry him upstairs," Christiana said firmly. "Suzie, you take that end, Lisa you take the middle and I shall take this end." She knelt at her end of the carpet and waited for her sisters to position themselves, and then said, "On the count of three. One, two, three."

The last word was almost a grunt as Christiana tightened her hold on the rug and pushed herself to a standing position using only her legs.

"Gad, he's heavy," Lisa complained as they started to walk slowly toward the door.

"The added weight of the rug does not help," Suzette panted as they paused at the door.

Christiana merely grunted in agreement and jutted out her hip to help hold up her end as she reached out with one hand to quickly open the door. It was a very fast maneuver, even so the rug started to slip from her hip and she barely caught it in time to keep from dropping it. Sighing her relief, Christiana started out into the hall, only to come to an abrupt halt as she spotted Haversham approaching.

Unfortunately, Lisa and Suzette were not expecting her to stop so abruptly and there was a soft curse and a bit of stumbling about behind her that nearly jerked the rug out of her hands as the weight increased. Just managing to keep her hold, Christiana glanced over her shoulder to see that Lisa had lost her grip on the rug and it was sagging in the middle. Even as she saw that though, the younger woman quickly caught it up again.

Sighing, Christiana turned back and forced a smile for Haversham as he paused before her. She would say this for the man: he was well trained. The butler didn't even bat an eyelash at the sight of the three women dragging a heavy rug about.

"Is there some way I may be of assistance, my lady?" the man asked politely.

"No, no," she said quickly. "We're just taking Dicky up to warm the rug. I mean we're taking Dicky's rug up to warm the room," she corrected herself quickly in a strangled tone and then, because she couldn't lie worth beans, babbled, "The guest room.

The rose one that's so chilly. Suzie will be staying there. In the room. And it's chilly so we're going to warm it with the rug. Dicky's already warm. With a fever. He's up in his room fevering so he won't need his rug you see," she ended almost desperately, unable to miss the exasperated sigh from behind her. Probably Suzette, she thought unhappily. It sounded like one of her "my sister is a big dolt" sighs. Christiana had suffered them often while growing up. But surely there should be an age limit to such obnoxious sounds? She felt certain they shouldn't be allowed after a person had married.

"I see," Haversham said slowly. "Would you like me to carry it up for you?"

"No!" The word exploded from her mouth like a ball from a cannon. Forcing herself to calm down, she added, "I need you to do something else."

Haversham nodded politely, waited, and then prompted, "And that would be?"

"That would be what?" Christiana asked uncertainly.

"The something else you need me to do, my lady," Haversham explained patiently. "That would be what?"

He was speaking slowly as if to a particularly dull child, but Christiana could hardly blame him for that when she had apparently

43

turned into an idiot. She really had not been made for cloak-and-dagger activities, she decided wearily as she struggled for some errand to send the man on.

"I need you to send one of the servants out to buy a chicken," she said at last.

Haversham's eyebrows rose. "A chicken?"

"For Dicky. He's sick," she reminded him of the lie. "And they do say chicken soup is good for such things."

"Yes, they do," he agreed solemnly. "Should I go upstairs first and see if Lord Radnor desires my assistance undressing and getting himself into bed? I fear his valet is under the weather as well and incapable of aiding him."

"Freddy is sick?" Christiana asked with surprise. That was a spot of good luck for them. It solved the problem of keeping the valet away from Dicky.

"Deathly ill. I shouldn't be surprised if he is unavailable for days," the butler said solemnly, and then added, "I, of course, will make myself available to Lord Radnor to fill in for Freddy in the meantime."

"Oh no," Christiana said at once. "I mean, ill as he is, my husband is not likely to need assistance dressing. He'll no doubt rest abed until he is recovered. I'm sure he won't need you."

"Hmmm." Haversham nodded. "Then I shall arrange for someone to go purchase a chicken and leave you ladies to your endeavors."

"Yes, you do that," Christiana said with relief. She waited until he disappeared through the door to the kitchen, and then muttered, "Let's go," and immediately started forward again.

"Thank God," Suzette gasped as Christiana headed for the stairs at a hurried pace. "I thought he'd never leave. And really, Chrissy, you cannot lie at all."

Christiana grimaced but could hardly argue the fact, so merely picked up the pace as much as she could, eager to unburden herself of her dead husband. By the time they reached the top of the stairs, they were also sweaty and exhausted, but continued forward without resting. They had reached the door to Dicky's room and Christiana had just jutted out her hip and released one hand-hold on the rug to open the door when the next door down opened.

Christiana immediately glanced around with alarm. Unfortunately, the slight movement was enough to dislodge the bundle from her hip. She felt it slip off and drop toward the floor, but this time wasn't quick enough to stop it. Worse yet, Suzette and

45

Lisa were taken by surprise and lost their own holds on the rug. The whole length of it thudded to the floor and then unrolled, spilling a very dead Dicky at the feet of Christiana's maid as the woman paused in the hall.

All four women stared down at the man and then Grace lifted her eyes to Christiana and murmured, "Finally killed him, did you? It's about bloody time."

CHAPTER THREE

"I must say, Lady Radnor, while Suzette has your father's dark hair, all three of you have your mother's features. She would be proud at how lovely you all turned out."

"Thank you, Lady Olivett," Christiana said, a smile tugging her mouth wide and bringing on a small ache that merely made her beam. The ache was because she'd smiled so much this evening, something she hadn't done much of this last year. She was enjoying the ache as a sign that things had changed for the better, and oh how they'd changed. She hadn't enjoyed herself so much since . . . well, since she'd married.

Christiana had spent the last hour since arriving at the Landon ball enjoying her newfound freedom and chattering away with the other married women. She was doing her duty and gaining gossip about Suzette's dance partners as expected, but that still left plenty of time to just converse and laugh and enjoy herself. It was lovely, and she vowed never to allow herself to be so controlled and beaten down by anyone ever again. Truly, she could hardly believe she had allowed Dicky to do so in the first place and supposed it was only because no one had ever treated her like that before, and she had never been without the support and love of her family prior to that either. The combination had worked against her, leaving her feeling alone and frightened. But that was before, now she was a widow, had her sisters back, and intended to enjoy every minute of it.

"The music is coming to an end. Who is Suzette's next dance partner?" Lady Olivett asked curiously.

"Danvers, I think," Christiana answered, smiling at the woman. Lady Olivett had been a dear friend of her mother's while she lived and had immediately taken Christiana and her sisters under her wing when they arrived, which was very generous of her considering how shabbily Dicky had treated her, turning her away when she'd tried to visit Christiana and welcome her to London.

"Yes, I think you're right. There he is approaching her and Willthrop," Lady Olivett commented.

As Christiana turned to glance toward her sister, the lady continued, "Danvers isn't a much better prospect than Willthrop, but at least he is young and good-looking. Still, caution her not to get too interested in him. He is in financial difficulties and a bit of a bounder to boot."

"I will," Christiana assured her, turning her gaze to search the other side of the dance floor where Lisa was ensconced amongst a giggling gaggle of single young ladies. Danvers was one of the names Lisa had been supposed to find information on. They had split the names on Suzette's dance card in half, Christiana and Lisa each taking every other one, in the hopes of making it less obvious they were seeking information on the men. Now, she was curious to see which prearranged signals Lisa would give Suzette. However, her gaze never found her youngest sister. Instead, it halted abruptly on a man just entering the ballroom. After a year of marriage, she'd recognize the man anywhere. Dicky . . . alive and well, and looking very, very angry.

"Lord Radnor! Your wife said you were ailing and wouldn't be able to come tonight, but you've made it after all."

Richard Fairgrave, the Earl of Radnor,

paused and turned, relaxing a little when he recognized his host, Lord Landon, approaching. But then the man's words sank in.

"My wife?" he asked, his gaze sliding in question to his best friend and the man who'd saved his life and brought him here, Daniel, the Earl of Woodrow. Daniel merely shrugged helplessly.

"Yes," Landon said cheerfully and glanced around. "She's here somewhere. Lady Radnor and her sisters were among the first to arrive. There she is," he said with triumph, pointing toward a small group of women gathered at the end of the ballroom.

Richard peered to where a petite blonde stood in a circle of several much older women. The older women were all chattering away while the woman who was apparently his wife listened, or didn't listen. He couldn't tell. Her eyes were locked on him with something like horror. He felt his eyebrows rise, but looked her over slowly, noting that she was overly thin, pale to the point of sickly, and not particularly pretty.

"As I say," Landon continued, turning back to face him, "she told us you had taken to your bed with a malaise and wouldn't be attending tonight. You look fine to me, though. Still, she does appear to be surprised to see you."

"I'm sure she is," Richard said quietly.

The jovial smile on the man's face faded briefly and he said in more solemn tones, "I'm glad to see you here. You've kept too much to yourself since your brother's death. It's good to see you rejoining society. You were missed."

"Thank you," Richard murmured, oddly touched by the sentiment.

Nodding, Landon thumped him on the back in a manly manner, and then cleared his throat and glanced around. "Well, I suppose I should see to the rest of my guests. Go assure your wife you're well. She must have thought you at death's door to be so shocked now," Landon said with a laugh. "I fear you must have overplayed it a bit, boy. Next time you want to slip out to see your mistress, just give a sniffle or two and a cough. There's no need to act like you have the plague." Laughing, Landon slapped him on the back again and then turned to disappear into the crowd.

"I had no idea," Daniel assured him solemnly. "I was on my estate and out of the way of society and its gossip until your letter arrived, and then I was busy making arrangements to sail to America to hunt for you."

51

Richard nodded silently, not taking his eyes off the blonde across the ballroom. She hadn't moved but still stood, face pale and eyes and mouth round with horror, staring at him as if he were the devil himself.

"What do we do now?" Daniel asked grimly. "You can't confront George for the greedy, murderous, bastard of an imposter he is if he isn't here."

Richard frowned as he realized the truth to those words.

"Worse yet," Daniel continued. "You'll have completely lost the advantage of surprise once he hears you were here at the ball. He'll know you're alive and take measures to try to stop you from taking back everything he stole. He — Where are you going? Richard?"

Richard was now crossing the ballroom to approach his "wife," detouring only to collect a healthy glass of whiskey along the way. The depth of the woman's horror, and the fact that she couldn't seem to snap out of it, suggested to him that more was amiss here than even he knew about, and he wanted to know it all. Knowledge could be a deadly weapon in the right hands and Richard intended it to be in his.

"Why Christiana, I thought you said Dicky was sick," one of the older women trilled as he reached the group.

"He looks hail and healthy to me," the woman beside her said firmly, eyeing him with suspicion. No doubt because Christiana, as the woman had called her, was still gaping at him like a fish out of water.

Richard took a moment to glance at the gaggle of women about them, his look enough to make every last one of them mutter about seeking out refreshments or friends and move away. Once left alone, Richard turned back to Christiana. Her eyes had grown wider as he approached. Unattractively so, he decided as he took in the way they almost bulged out of her head, and the woman appeared to have lost her powers of speech. She simply stood staring at him looking so pale he feared her fainting or simply dropping dead on the spot.

Frowning, he held out the glass of whiskey. "You look quite overset, my lady. This should help you regain some color."

He expected her to take a mere sip of the potent liquid so was rather startled when she took the glass he offered and tossed it back as if it were water. It certainly did the trick, however, just more so than he'd hoped. Her pallor washed away under a sudden rush of red that was really no more attractive than the pallor had been, and she gasped as if her breath had been taken with the pallor. She then bent forward hacking and coughing in a most violent manner.

Grimacing, Richard took the now empty glass with one hand and patted her back with the other. "I suppose I should have warned you to sip it."

Either the words or the sound of his voice brought her upright and she suddenly shrank back from his touch as if he were some unclean beast.

"You're alive," she gasped, and the whiskey's rasp in her voice did not hide her displeasure at the fact.

It seemed obvious the woman knew of her husband's perfidy. Richard didn't know why but he'd assumed that she would have been innocent in all this. However, it appeared she was aware of the fact that George, his younger twin by several minutes, had hired men to kill him in a bid to steal his identity, title and wealth. She obviously was not pleased to learn it had failed. For some reason the knowledge that the woman had known about it disappointed him.

"You could at least try to hide your horror at knowing I yet live," Richard said coldly. "It will hardly do your case much good to show so openly how little my survival pleases you."

"I — no, I — you —" she struggled briefly, and then took a deep breath and said, "It is a bit of a surprise, my lord. We were sure you were dead when we left the house tonight. You were so still and cold in the bed . . ."

Richard felt his eyebrows rise on his forehead as he realized that she couldn't be talking about him. He had been nowhere near this woman earlier tonight. It couldn't be he who had been still and cold in a bed. Was George — ?

His thoughts died as a strangled gasp sounded to the side of them. Turning, he found himself staring at two younger versions of the woman who was supposed to be his wife; one blonde and one brunette. Both looked just as horrified to see him as "his wife" was.

"But you're dead," the younger blonde breathed with a horror that could not be feigned. Turning to Christiana, she added with confusion, "Wasn't he dead, Chrissy? We packed ice around him and everything."

"The ice must have revived his cold dead heart," the brunette said grimly, apparently recovering more quickly than the other two. Richard's eyebrows rose when she added grimly, "More's the pity."

"Suzette!" Christiana gasped. Glancing

55

nervously at him, she moved closer to her sisters and murmured, "Perhaps we should go out for some air. Lisa looks ready to faint and you, Suzie, obviously need some time to cool yourself. Perhaps so much dancing has overheated you."

"Allow me."

Richard glanced to Daniel as he moved to step between his "wife's" sisters and take each by an arm. The man had obviously followed him and he was grateful for it. It was now urgent that he speak to the woman who had thought she'd married the Earl of Radnor and find out whether his brother was dead or alive. Packed in ice? Dear God.

"I shall see the ladies outside so the two of you might talk." Daniel turned Suzette and Lisa firmly away despite the fact that it was obvious neither was particularly amenable to the idea. He then glanced over his shoulder to suggest meaningfully, "You might consider somewhere more private for this discussion."

Richard took a moment to note that while none of the other guests was presently near enough to hear properly, they were trying, and they were certainly watching. Mouth tightening, he took his wife by the arm and began to lead her in the opposite direction to the one Daniel was leading her sisters.

Christiana went no more willingly than her sisters had accompanied Daniel. However, where her sisters had seemed reluctant to cause a public spectacle, "his wife" apparently didn't care. He'd barely dragged her half a dozen feet before she planted her feet firmly and yanked her arm from his hold in a way that anyone watching would have noticed. She also planted her hands firmly on her hips and glared at him in a way that almost dared him to try to force her from the room.

Richard glanced briefly around, frowning when he saw that they weren't going without notice. Mouth tightening, he turned back to his "wife" and said firmly, "We need to go somewhere more private to talk."

"No."

His eyebrows rose in surprise at the blunt refusal. "No? But —"

"I have had quite enough of your 'talk' during this last year of marriage, my lord," she said grimly. "And I have no intention of being the docile little wife I have been to now and follow you to some empty room so that you can berate and insult me. I also have no intention of leaving this, *the very first ball* I have ever attended."

Richard tried his most charming smile, "I don't intend to insult or berate you, and this can hardly be your first ball."

"You know it is," she said at once.

He shook his head, not believing her. "I'm sure you attended many during your season. You —"

"You know I had no season," she interrupted, confusion flashing briefly across her face. It was quickly replaced with anger. "I do not know what game you now play, Dicky, but I have no intention of leaving this room with you."

Richard hesitated briefly, wondering why she hadn't had a season, and if that were the case how she had come to meet and marry his brother, but then decided that wasn't important at the moment. He needed to know if his brother yet lived or not, and since she wouldn't leave the room with him, he had to find another way to gain them some privacy. His gaze slid over the people milling about the ballroom and then he became aware that the strains of a waltz were starting. Nodding to himself, he glanced back to his "wife." "Then perhaps you would do me the honor of dancing with me?"

Her eyes narrowed. "You don't dance. That has always been one of your excuses for not attending the balls during the season. You would not even dance at our wedding."

Richard managed to keep from grimacing. He'd forgotten that George had always seemed to have two left feet. Their dance instructor had done his best when they were children, but George simply hadn't been able to manage any sort of grace on the dance floor and had finally refused lessons. Managing to hold on to his smile he said, "Yes, well, I am willing to give it my best effort now. Will you not dance with me?"

He held his hand out and she stared at it briefly as if it were a snake, but then sighed and placed hers in it with little enthusiasm and a muttered, "Very well."

Afraid she might change her mind at any moment, Richard ushered her quickly onto the dance floor. He found it ironic that she was so obviously less than pleased to dance with him. As a wealthy and titled member of the peerage he had always enjoyed a certain success with women, but it appeared Christiana was less than enthralled with him, and *she* was supposed to be his wife. It made him wonder what the devil his brother had done to the woman.

Once in the center of the dance floor, Richard took her into his arms for the dance. She was stiff and awkward in his hold, her face turned away as if she couldn't even bear to look at him. Richard gave her a moment, hoping she would relax, but she continued to move like a wooden doll, her jaw tense and eyes darting about as if in search of escape. He finally decided just to get it over with and asked, "So am I to understand you thought your husband dead?"

He didn't realize how he'd framed the question until the words were out, but Christiana didn't seem to notice his saying "your husband" rather than referring to himself in the first person. Her head whipped around, her wide eyes meeting his with dismay, but then she seemed to forcibly calm herself and merely turned her face away again, muttering, "You did seem to be."

"And your response to that death was to attend a ball?" he asked carefully.

He saw the flush of shame that rose up her neck, but when she turned her face back to him it was mitigated by anger and she scowled. "Well, what was I supposed to do, Dicky? We couldn't risk having to go into mourning. Suzie has to find a husband, and it's *your* fault she does. You are the one who took Father to that gaming hell. Now he's apparently gambled his way to the edge of ruin again and Suzie has to find a husband

and claim her dower to pay off his debts and avoid scandal." Hurt bewilderment covered her face and she asked, "How could you take him to one of those places when you knew what happened the last time?"

Richard had no answer for her. He had no idea why George would have done such a thing. His instinct would be to say greed had led to it because that seemed to ever be George's motivation. However, Richard couldn't see how ruining Christiana's father and family would increase his own riches. He also had no idea what had happened to Christiana's father "the last time" but it obviously wasn't good. Sighing, he said the only thing he could and offered a quiet, "I apologize. It was not well done to take your father somewhere like that given his history."

Christiana was so startled by her husband's words and the apparent sincerity behind them that she stumbled in her step and fell against him. Dicky immediately caught her against his chest to keep her upright.

"Are you all right?" he asked, holding her close and tilting his head to try to see her face.

Christiana nodded and took a deep breath to steady herself, but it helped little. With everything that had occurred that day, she hadn't eaten since breakfast and was now feeling the effects of the drink she'd so precipitously downed. Her thoughts were slowing and growing a bit muddy even as the tension eased from her body. It left her more relaxed, which she didn't necessarily think was a good thing at the moment. Especially when they were dancing so close now that she was inhaling his scent, and finding it surprisingly heady, a spicy male aroma that made her want to inhale again. She had never noticed him smelling this lovely before, but then was rarely as close to him as this.

"Christiana?"

She reluctantly lifted her eyes, confusion and vulnerability swirling inside her.

"You're quite lovely when you aren't frowning," he said suddenly as if surprised at the revelation.

Christiana felt her lips part slightly with surprise. This was the very first compliment she'd heard from the man in the year since their wedding. It was so rare and so unexpected, it quite took her breath away. Or perhaps that was the whiskey, she thought. For surely it was the whiskey that made her forget how horrid the man was and notice only how handsome he looked in his formal garb. Of course, she had always known Dicky was a handsome man, at least on the surface. His features were strong and sharp, but suited his face perfectly, and he had short, dark hair that looked so silky it made a girl want to run her fingers through it. She had always found him incredibly attractive physically. However, at the moment he was eyeing her with a concern she had never seen before and it seemed to increase his attractiveness tenfold, making him darned near irresistible.

"If you continue to look at me like that I may be tempted to kiss you," he said in a husky voice.

Christiana's eyes widened slightly and for a moment she almost wished he would, but then she recalled this was her husband and abruptly turned her head away with a little, "Oh dear."

"What is it?" Dicky asked with a small frown.

"I believe that drink you gave me may be affecting my good sense," she muttered, thinking it the only excuse for how she could find this man attractive after having suffered under being his wife for a year. Besides, she was beginning to feel a little off balance, her thoughts a little slow and confused. Of course, she was also finding it suddenly overly hot and a touch airless in the room, but suspected that was from being in Dicky's arms. At the moment, they were as close as lovers, his body brushing against hers with each dance step, his one hand at her back, his arm encircling her, the other hand clasping her suddenly sweaty one . . . and his smell just kept wafting up her nose, sliding through her body, making her want to lean into him. That drink was definitely affecting her, she decided grimly.

"Perhaps I should take you outside for a breath of fresh air."

"No!" Christiana said at once, instinct telling her that would be a very bad idea indeed. She was already terribly confused and flustered and it was difficult enough being this close to him in public, but out on the dark terrace, with the sparkly stars overhead and torchlight the only thing chasing back the shadows . . . No, Christiana felt sure the best thing she could do was put some distance between them so that she could start thinking straight again. Unfortunately, she would have to wait until the end of the waltz to do that.

"Are you sure?" Richard asked, pulling back to look at her. "You are quite pale. Perhaps some air would make you feel better."

Christiana stared at him silently, her gaze moving over his handsome features with bewilderment. He was like a different person. His expression was kind and concerned instead of the cold mask she was used too, and certainly his behavior was nothing like the man she had been married to this last year. It was more like the man she'd thought she'd married, and was stirring up feelings Christiana had thought long dead.

"Why are you being nice to me?" she asked with confusion. "You are never nice to me. Why are you being nice now?"

Dicky reacted as if she'd struck him, his head jerking back as if under a physical blow, and then anger briefly crossed his face. He said quietly, "I apologize if my behavior has been less than kind this last year. All I can say is I haven't been myself." He glanced away, frowned, and then continued, "At the moment, I can't explain what has been occurring, but I can promise you things will be different from now on and I will do everything I can to protect you and make this last year up to you."

Christiana stared at him with something like wonder. His words could have been plucked from one of the many hope-filled dreams she'd had this last year. They were words she'd longed to hear ever since the wedding and his horrid change in behavior and she had the sudden urge to pinch herself to be sure she wasn't dreaming now. But before she could, Dicky urged her closer against him to continue the dance. While she allowed him to lead her back into the rhythm of the music, her mind was awhirl with confusion. This was not the man she'd lived with this past year, but it was the man she'd thought she'd married, and his words were making hope rise within her foolish heart. Hope that perhaps there was an explanation for his previous behavior and that whatever had caused it was now over. Perhaps she could have the marriage she'd hoped for.

Or perhaps she was deluding herself, and would get her hopes up, only to have them dashed again, Christiana worried. Unfortunately, it mattered little either way. He was alive and was her husband. That meant that at the moment all she had was the hope that things would be different and her life would not continue as it had been since her wedding.

Christiana was distracted from her thoughts when Dicky's hand moved up and then down her back in an almost unconscious, soothing caress. At least, she suspected that was how he'd intended it, but it had an entirely different effect on her. Rather than soothe, it sent shivers up her back to her neck. Confused by her body's reaction, she instinctively stepped back to try to put some space between them and bumped into someone.

Richard pulled her closer again and murmured, "I apologize. It has been some time since I danced. I am a little rusty at leading."

Christiana glanced over her shoulder to offer an apology to whomever she'd bumped, and then glanced sharply back to Richard. The small accident had been her fault for moving, yet he was taking the blame. That was completely unheard of prior to this. Dicky simply did not take blame for anything. In fact, Christiana usually caught the blame for everything, even if it had nothing to do with her.

"No, it was me," she admitted, not one to allow others to take the blame for her mistakes.

Dicky lowered his head and said with amusement, "My dance instructor would disagree most stringently with that. It is always the man's fault. He is the one leading, the one who is supposed to be steering you safely around the dance floor."

67

Christiana bit her tongue and said nothing. Confusion was rife within her and it wasn't just because of the complete about-face in his attitude. He had spoken the words into her ear, his breath brushing the outer shell and sending startling shivers through her. She was also suddenly very aware of just how close he'd pulled her after the small accident. She was now plastered to him, her breasts against his chest, and his legs and hips brushing against her with every step. He had also let his hand slip lower on her back so that it now crested the upper curve of her behind. All of this was stirring the oddest sensations in her, making her shiver and long to press herself tighter still against him. She even had the quick mad thought to wonder what it would be like if he slipped his hand a little lower, and pressed a little tighter so that their hips met more firmly.

Even when courting she hadn't experienced these physical reactions to him and it was quite unsettling.

Richard found himself repeatedly stealing glances at the woman in his arms. It seemed obvious from their brief exchange that she had no idea what George had done, and that the man she lived with and thought was her husband was actually an imposter. It also seemed obvious that this last year of the sham marriage had not been a happy one for her, that his brother was treating her poorly. Christiana was as much a victim of George's machinations as he was and the revelations about to come out would not be pleasant ones. Scandal would follow as it was realized that the wedding had not been legal, that she wasn't actually married at all since George was an impostor.

The thought made Richard angry all over again. It also made him want to do what he could to protect her. From what he could tell, Christiana deserved none of this. She had married in good faith, but would now be ruined by it unless he could find a way to prevent that.

His gaze slid over her troubled features. Had he really thought her unattractive? Richard now decided it had merely been her expression of shock on seeing him. She had certainly grown more attractive as they'd danced. The first burst of anger she'd had earlier had put a natural bloom in her cheeks and a spark in her eyes that was almost arresting. The confusion and hurt that had followed as she'd reprimanded him for taking her father to a gaming hell had made him want to comfort and hold her closer. Now she appeared a touch flustered. Hectic color had bloomed in her cheeks, and she was nibbling her lower lip in a rather adorable fashion. However, she was also much more relaxed in his arms, her body almost fluid rather than the stiff wooden woman he'd first led to the dance floor. The swift changes were fascinating to him and he found himself wondering what she would look like under the influence of other moods and passions. For instance, how would she look in his bed, with desire making her sloe eyed, and her lovely blonde hair spread out on a pillow?

These thoughts coursing through his mind, Richard almost without realizing it let his hand slide a little lower to curve over her behind and urge her tighter against his hips. The effect was rather startling. Christiana didn't pull back, but gasped and shivered, her eyes dropping closed as their hips met and they both became aware of the hardness he hadn't realized had grown between them.

"Husband?"

The word was a breathy sigh, and Richard smiled and lowered his head, deliberately allowing his breath to brush her ear as he said, "Yes?"

"I — Oh," she paused as he nipped at her

ear, and then said a little shakily, "I think . . ."

"What do you think?" he asked, nipping at her ear again and enjoying the shudder it sent through her. It made him grow even harder.

"I think the music has stopped," she managed to get out in a strangled tone even as her hands tightened on his hand and shoulder.

Richard stilled, released the earlobe he'd captured between his teeth, and then straightened to glance around. The music had indeed stopped and most of the dancers had left the dance floor while others were still flowing past them to leave it as well. His gaze shifted back to Christiana, noting how flushed she was and the way she was nibbling at her lips. She hadn't pulled free of his embrace, however, and he had a sudden urge to nibble on those lips himself, so was about to suggest again that they go out on the balcony for some air when someone suddenly appeared beside them.

"I believe I was promised the next dance."

Richard stared blankly at the man who had approached them. He recognized him at once. Robert Maitland, Lord Langley. They had attended school together and been friends then, though they'd drifted

71

apart afterward. The way Langley was looking at him now, however, was not friendly at all.

"Oh, yes, I'd almost forgotten," Christiana said in a voice that was high and strained and slipped from his arms to move to the man's side. He almost caught her arm to stop her, but then refrained. If the man was on her card for the next dance, she would have to dance it with him. It was considered the height of rudeness to do otherwise.

Nodding stiffly, Richard stepped out of the way and merely watched as the couple moved a little further away on the dance floor. His eyes narrowed slightly as he noted how comfortable the woman appeared to be with Langley as she went into his arms for the dance. She was also smiling at the man with a combination of relief and what could only be described as affection. It made Richard wonder about their relationship. It also caused a small, surprising, pang of jealousy to slip through him. Ridiculous, he told himself as he turned to move off the dance floor. She was nothing to him. While he found himself wanting to protect her, that was all. Other than that, he didn't even know her.

"You looked like you needed rescuing."

Christiana smiled weakly and lifted her eyes to Robert as he moved her around the dance floor. He wasn't wrong there. She had been falling under her husband's spell, her body being assaulted by completely alien desires and wants. In fact, she'd been half a breath away from suggesting she did want to seek out the fresh air on the balcony after all when Robert had appeared. The problem was it hadn't been fresh air she'd been hoping to find. Christiana had hoped Richard might take her in his arms and kiss her there. That drink she'd had was obviously having some strange effects on her. She'd never felt this way toward Dicky before, even on their wedding night.

"Yes, I rather did need rescuing. Thank you," she murmured vaguely and glanced to where Richard now stood on the edge of the dance floor, following them with burning eyes. She thought she could actually feel a trail of warmth slide along her body as his eyes skated over her and quickly turned her head back to Robert as he spoke.

"I was surprised but happy to see that he finally let you attend a ball."

Christiana didn't comment. Dicky hadn't exactly let her attend. However, she simply couldn't explain the events of that day to him. She couldn't even explain the events

73

of the last few moments to herself. How had her general dislike and loathing of her husband turned to desire on the dance floor?

The combination of whiskey on an empty stomach and exhaustion from the day's events must have conspired to confuse and befuddle her, she reasoned . . . and she *was* exhausted. It had been a very stressful day all told, and had simply grown more stressful when Dicky appeared here at the ball. Christiana had just begun to adjust to the fact that she was free of him and had enjoyed those precious hours of not worrying about what Dicky would say and do. Yet now here he was alive and well and she was suddenly attracted to him in a way she had never been before. Christiana hadn't even felt this way toward him during their courting. She'd never once wanted him to kiss her or pull her close then as she'd wanted during the waltz. In fact, she had come to realize that her feelings for the man during their courting had been more of a child's daydream than a woman's wishes. The courting had been all hearts and flowers, leading to a child's light fluffy dream of happy-ever-afters. However, the attraction she'd felt just now on the dance floor was much more raw and physical and left her bewildered and even a little scared. She had never experienced that with him before, but then while he had been ever charming before the marriage, he had never shown kindness and concern until now. There was something different about him tonight and she wondered to herself if his brush with death had somehow changed him. If perhaps that's what he'd meant by things being different now.

"Chrissy, there is something different about Dicky."

Christiana blinked and peered up at Robert with surprise. It was as if he'd read her thoughts.

Before she could say so, he added, "I have felt it for some time now. He's not the man I attended school with."

Christiana frowned. Robert wasn't talking about his being different tonight then. "How so?"

"Did you know I have been to see you three times the last few months and he has turned me away each time?"

She grimaced apologetically, and admitted, "I only knew about two occasions and found out about those just this morning. I'm sorry. I hope you know I consider you like family and would never —"

"It doesn't matter," he interrupted. "The

point is that the Richard Fairgrave I knew was nothing like the pompous ass who took such delight in sending me away. It was more like his brother, George."

Her eyebrows rose at mention of her husband's brother. George Fairgrave, the younger of the twin brothers by moments, had died in a fire just months before she had married Dicky. She tilted her head to the side and frowned. "Oh?"

Robert was silent for a moment, appearing uncomfortable, but finally met her gaze and asked uncomfortably, "Does he have a birthmark?"

Christiana raised her eyebrows. "Not that I've seen. Should he?"

He nodded grimly. "It's a small strawberry on his left buttock."

Her eyes widened and then she flushed. "Oh, well, he may have one then, but I have never seen him without clothes."

"You have not seen him . . . ?" Robert's voice died and he now flushed as well, as he apparently realized what he was asking.

Aware she was blushing furiously, Christiana glanced around to see if anyone was listening. Much to her relief Robert had steered them to a relatively open area on the dance floor and no one was near enough to hear. Still, she scowled and murmured,

"I think we should change the subject. It really isn't proper to discuss —"

"No it isn't proper," Robert agreed quietly. "And despite how close we have always been, I wouldn't have brought it up, but it is very important. Please, trust me on that. If I am right, you could be in danger."

She frowned at his words and glanced away, but then admitted, "He has simply never disrobed in front of me."

"Not even on your wedding night?" he asked.

"On our wedding night he did not even take off his cravat," she admitted with embarrassment and then with some annoyance said, "And you are not his wife so how did you see this birthmark?"

"A group of us used to go skinny-dipping in a nearby lake back at school. He and I were among that group," he explained, and then asked gently, "He didn't even take off his cravat?"

She shook her head with irritation. It felt like her face was on fire now and she'd really rather not discuss this. It just wasn't done.

"And he hasn't at any time since either?" Langley prodded.

"There hasn't been an 'any time since,' " Christiana admitted in little more than a whisper. That was her shame. Her husband found her so wanting that he had not visited her bed since her wedding night. She'd often wondered if she'd been terribly bad at it and that was why Dicky had suddenly gone cold on her and begun to treat her so poorly. Unfortunately, she hadn't had her mother to explain the matter of the marital bed to her and had been completely ignorant of what to do or expect so had lain in bed, unmoving and practically not breathing until it was done. Fortunately, it had been quick. Perhaps had she known what to do things would have been different.

Or perhaps it would have been different had she experienced those feelings and sensations then that she'd had tonight while they were dancing, a little voice in her head spoke up. Christiana didn't think she'd have lain holding her breath and unmoving had she felt even a little of what she had tonight in his arms. She'd wanted to touch and kiss and do all sorts of things to the man she'd danced with.

"Can you try to see if he has the birthmark?" Robert asked quietly, drawing her from her thoughts.

Christiana grimaced at the suggestion and admitted, "I'd really rather not."

"You don't have to actually . . . erm . . ."

He hesitated and then said instead, "If you were to enter his room while he was dressing or undressing you could see if he has it without . . . er . . . an 'any time since.' "

Christiana wrinkled her nose at the suggestion. Dicky did hate it when she entered any room he was in without gaining permission first.

"It is important," Robert assured her.

She glanced to him silently, and then said, "You suspect he doesn't have the birthmark, which suggests you believe he isn't Dicky at all? You think Dicky is really George?"

Langley nodded apologetically. "I began to suspect it the first time I came to visit and he turned me away, but the second time just convinced me more." He scowled and shook his head. "I could just kick myself for not being there when he was courting you. If it *is* George and I'd spent any time around him back then I would have known at once. I could have saved you from all this misery. I —"

"Your father was dying, Robert. Of course you spent those last weeks at his side. Never blame yourself for that, marrying Dicky was my choice," she said firmly.

"Dicky," Robert said the name with disgust. "Richard hated that name. George is the only one who called him that."

Christiana frowned at this news. It was Richard, or the man they'd thought was Richard, who had insisted they all call him Dicky. She preferred Richard herself.

"George was always a pompous little ass," Robert informed her grimly. "He was not well liked at school and was only ever included in things because he was Richard's brother, which just made him act worse. He was envious of how well liked Richard was and bitter that as the older twin Richard would gain the title on their father's death." He sighed and then admitted quietly, "I suspect it was Richard who died in the fire and George just took his place."

Christiana shook her head and pointed out, "But if it really was Richard who died in the fire, George had no need to impersonate him. He would have gained everything anyway."

"That's true, but . . ." Robert shook his head. "I suspect that wouldn't have been enough for George. He would have still been George. Titled or not, and holding all the wealth or not wouldn't have made anyone respect or like him better and I think he envied that most about his brother. Everyone liked and trusted Richard. Being heir to the title and estate never affected Richard. He was naturally kind and considerate and everyone knew and appreciated that."

Those last words resonated through Christiana's head. Richard was naturally kind and considerate and everyone knew and appreciated that . . . like she had on the dance floor just now. The man she'd just danced with had been surprisingly kind and considerate, and she had appreciated it. But he'd shown precious little of either attribute this last year. Was the man she'd married Richard Fairgrave, the Earl of Radnor, or his twin, George? And if it was George, what would that mean to her? Would their marriage be legal?

"Try to see if he has the birthmark," Robert said quietly. "If he doesn't, come to me at once no matter the hour. I shall handle everything after that."

Christiana nodded unhappily and thought how much simpler life would be had her husband just had the good graces to stay dead . . . If he was her husband.

CHAPTER FOUR

"If you glare at her any harder she's like to burst into flames."

Richard glanced to the side at that comment from Daniel and scowled. "She is avoiding me by dancing with seemingly every man in the room."

"Not every man," Daniel said with amusement, and then proved he was aware of what had been going on by adding, "Just Langley and his chums. Langley is apparently a longtime family friend. No doubt he has enlisted his friends and associates to keep her away from you."

"Why? I am her husband," Richard pointed out dryly, and then added, "Or at least I am as far as they know."

"That's apparently why," he explained wryly. "According to her sisters, I should be ashamed of claiming you as friend as you have treated her horribly."

Richard raised his eyebrows and Daniel

nodded.

"Apparently the best thing you have done for her was to drop dead. Both sisters bemoan your unexpected resurrection."

"Hmmm." Richard peered back to his "wife." The music had ended and her present partner was leading her off the floor. He could see her tensing as she neared the edge of the dance floor and then she suddenly relaxed, a smile curving her lips as Langley stepped up to claim her for another dance. Apparently, he had run out of friends and was risking raised eyebrows by dancing with her for a second time. Gaze narrowing, Richard asked, "A family friend, huh?"

"Like a brother according to Suzette."

Richard grunted and turned his attention back to his wife and Langley. The man was holding her at a respectable distance, but his protectiveness of her was obvious in the way he peered down at her and the gentleness of his hold. Like a brother or not, Langley was far too proprietary with another man's wife. "Did you find out anything else?"

"You mean other than the fact that your brother apparently collapsed in his office this morning and is most likely dead?" Daniel asked dryly. "I should think that would be enough to concern you at the moment.

If he is dead it complicates things somewhat."

Richard managed to drag his attention away from "his wife" again as he considered the ramifications. He'd been rather looking forward to confronting his brother, forcing a confession from him and plowing a fist into his face. Actually, he'd planned to beat the man senseless for all he'd put him through, but that would be out of the question if he was dead.

"There may be some difficulty proving who you are if he's dead," Daniel pointed out, drawing a sharp look from Richard.

"What do you mean?"

"Well, this last year everyone has thought it was George who died in the townhouse fire. The man now apparently lying packed in ice in your room has been pretending to be you all that time. There will definitely be some confusion. They might think you are George, survived the fire, and are merely trying to claim to be Richard to ensure you inherit all without the necessity of waiting for his will to be validated. Or they might even decide you are merely your father's byblow, fortunate enough to look like the twins, and greedily trying to claim their wealth and title now they are both dead. After all, George was supposedly buried over a year ago."

Richard grimaced. The man buried in the family vault was one of the criminals who had been sent to kill him. The man had been about his height and size. Found on his bed and charred to a cinder, no one had been able to tell any different. They'd all just assumed it was him, but Richard knew different and removing the vermin from the family vault was only one of many things he wanted to do once installed safely back in his rightful place. If he managed to get there, he thought grimly.

"We shall have to prove your identity . . . somehow," Daniel said in a tone that suggested he was concerned about their ability to do it. "And then there is the scandal that shall befall everyone. Lady Christiana married who she thought was Richard Fairgrave, the Earl of Radnor, over a year ago and has been living with him since that time."

"But it wasn't me," Richard pointed out quietly.

"No. It was George, but he signed your name on the license and contract."

Richard frowned. "The marriage wouldn't be legal. She is married neither to myself nor George."

"Exactly. The scandal shall surely be the

85

ruin of her . . . as well as her sisters. They won't escape it either . . . which is a true shame when they are already working so hard to avoid the scandal their father has tipped them into with his gambling."

"Christiana mentioned something about that," Richard said on a sigh, his gaze sliding back to the woman in Langley's arms. "Suzette needs to find a husband quickly so she can claim her dower and save them from their father's gaming debts. Christiana seemed to think I, or George, really, caused it all by taking their father to a gaming hell."

"Hmmm."

Something in his tone made Richard glance Daniel's way again and he raised an eyebrow at his sour expression. "What?"

"After leaving the women, I took a moment to ask around before returning to you and there is some interesting gossip floating about."

Richard narrowed his eyes. "What kind of gossip?"

"Apparently the Earl of Radnor has become quite chummy with a few unsavory characters about town; the owner of a certain gaming hell, for instance, one that is suspected of drugging the drinks of certain unwary lords and fleecing them of all that they own."

"Christiana's father?"

"That would be my guess. And it wouldn't have been the first time. I suspect George was behind the first supposed losses as well, and did it deliberately to force the man to the edge of ruin so that he could offer for Christiana's hand," Daniel said grimly, and then explained. "Christiana and her sisters are the granddaughters of Lord Sefton."

"Old moneybags?" Richard asked with surprise. The Baron had been rumored to be richer than the King.

Daniel nodded. "He apparently divided his estate into three parts and put it in trusts for the girls, to be turned over on their marriage. However, he arranged it all so that it would be a secret. He had no desire to have his granddaughters hunted by fortune seekers."

"Then how do you know about it?" Richard asked dryly.

"Because Suzette just explained it to me," he admitted with wry amusement.

Richard narrowed his eyes. "Why on earth would she do that when the two of you just met?"

"I'll explain that later," Daniel muttered, glancing away. "Right now, the important thing is that Suzette thinks Dicky somehow found out about the dower and married

Christiana to get it."

"I could see that being the case," Richard said dryly.

"Really?" Daniel asked with a frown. "I did wonder, but he gained so much wealth when he got rid of you and took your place that he shouldn't have needed to marry for more."

"All the money in the world would not be enough for George," Richard said grimly. "He always wanted more of everything. It was like he was trying to fill the hole where his soul should have been with things." He scowled at the thought of his brother and then glanced back to Daniel and said, "I can see him having taken Christiana's father to this shady gaming hell the first time to force him to the edge of ruin and gain her fortune, but why would he take him there again now? He had already married one sister. He couldn't claim the dower of either of the others, and all he accomplished was possibly bringing scandal down on everyone. Christiana would not have avoided the scandal, which meant it would taint him as well. What profit is there in that?"

Daniel frowned and shook his head. "I have been wondering that myself, but have not yet come up with anything. He must have had some plan in mind, but I cannot see what it might have been."

Richard scowled with displeasure at the mystery and glanced back to the woman in Langley's arms. "So to reclaim my name and birthright I shall have to ruin a woman who has already been sorely mistreated by my brother."

"And probably battle in court for months or even years to prove you are Richard Fairgrave, or a Fairgrave at all," Daniel said quietly. "And then even if the courts eventually decide in your favor, there will still be those in the ton who think you an imposter."

"Damn George," Richard breathed wearily. "As usual, he has made one hell of a mess."

"There is an alternative," Daniel said tentatively.

Richard glanced at him narrowly. "Do not even suggest I forsake everything and slink back to America. While I have no desire to ruin Lady Christiana and her family, I also have no desire to give up my rightful title and place. It is all I have."

"I wasn't going to suggest that," Daniel assured him.

"Then what is the alternative?"

"You could simply take up your place again as if you'd never been away," he said quietly.

"What?" Richard asked with amazement.

"Well, you cannot gain justice from George, he is apparently dead," Daniel pointed out. "So, revealing what he did will only succeed in hurting innocents. Besides, by merely stepping in and taking up your position again, you can avoid a long drawn-out battle to prove you are who you are. It will be as if your stay in America never happened . . . except that it did and you would now have a wife."

"A wife who hates me," Richard muttered, his gaze returning to the woman in question. She was laughing at something Langley had said. With her face alight and softened by amusement she almost looked pretty, he decided, and recalled their dance. She hadn't seemed to hate him by the end of the dance. In fact, he was quite sure if he'd managed to get her out on the balcony she wouldn't have fought off his kisses.

"She hates George not you," Daniel corrected quietly. "And who could blame her. The man was a bastard as we both well know. But you are a different kettle of fish. With a little time I suspect she will let go of that anger and come to trust you. The two of you might even make a good match of it." He was silent for a moment and then added, "Whatever the case, it would make reclaiming your title and position that much easier and would prevent Christiana and her sisters from further hurt by your brother's actions."

Richard frowned. The suggestion was not without merit. He had no desire to destroy Christiana, nor did he wish a long drawn-out court battle simply to claim his own name. However, while there was a bit of hope in their response to each other on the dance floor, it was little to gamble his future on. He didn't know the woman and was reluctant to take such a step blindly.

"What if it turns out she is a shrew?" he asked quietly. "Or a bitter ice maiden? Or a spoiled brat with whom I cannot bear to deal?"

"Hmm." Daniel peered at the woman in question. "She does not seem to be any of those things, but then few reveal their true faces in public." He considered the matter for a moment and then suggested. "Well, we could keep George's body for a couple of days while you find out her true nature and if you find you cannot stomach the idea of being married to her, we can just drop George back in your bed to be found dead, and go the legal route after all."

"George's body." Richard's eyes widened as he recalled that little problem. Oddly

91

enough, he hadn't considered it when Daniel had first made the suggestion.

"Yes," Daniel said dryly. "If you decide to take a day or two to find out, we shall have to be sure to leave before the ladies, make our way to your townhouse, and snatch his body from the bed before they see it is still there."

"We should get it done now," Richard announced and began making his way around the ballroom toward the doors.

"So, you're going to give it a try?" Daniel asked, hurrying after him.

"What choice do I have? I would prefer not to ruin an innocent if I can help it, but I also don't want to land myself in a miserable marriage just to make up for George's sins. We'll do as you suggested, and remove the body for the next day or two while I see if I could stomach being married to her. If not, we will replace him and go to the courts."

"And if you find you are willing to be married to her?" Daniel asked. "What will we do with the body then?"

"I haven't the foggiest notion," Richard admitted dryly. "But we will worry about that if and when the time comes."

"He just left with Woodrow."

Christiana gave up searching the ballroom for Dicky and glanced back to Langley. "Did he?"

He nodded solemnly and then asked, "Will you be very upset if it turns out that Dicky is George?"

Christiana glanced away with a frown, those few moments in her husband's arms on the dance floor the first thing to come into her mind. Any other memory of this last year would have had her saying, no she wouldn't be upset at all, but that one . . . Sighing, she simply said, "The scandal will be horrendous."

"Yes, well, we might be able to mitigate that," Langley murmured as he turned her around the dance floor.

"How do you mean?"

Robert was silent for so long that she began to think that he wouldn't answer, but apparently deciding it was unavoidable, he said reluctantly, "I knew one of George's old mistresses and she said he could not . . ." He paused and looked embarrassed, but then said, "I am sorry to ask this, Chrissy, but was the marriage properly consummated?"

Christiana's eyes widened incredulously at the question and he grimaced and began to speak quickly.

"I really am sorry to ask it, but if George was incapable of the task as his mistress suggested, then it makes all the difference in the world."

Christiana stared at him blankly. "Well . . . I — he — I think it — I don't know," she admitted, now scarlet herself. She shrugged helplessly and confessed, "I'm not quite sure what the consummation includes. Father simply said 'Just do what he says and your husband will manage the rest.' I did as he said and assumed what Dicky did was the consummation."

"Of course," he muttered, avoiding her eyes briefly, then cleared his throat. "You said he didn't even take off his cravat on your wedding night, but did he take off anything else?"

She considered the question briefly, and then offered, "I think he took off his shoes."

Langley grimaced impatiently. "What about his pants? Did he take them off or at least open them or pull them down?"

"I don't think so," she said slowly.

"You don't *think* so?" he asked incredulously. "Were you even there? How could you not know if he took off his pants or not?"

Christiana scowled, half angry and half embarrassed, and then glanced around to be sure none of the other dancers were listening in on the conversation. Reassured that no one appeared to be paying them any attention, she glanced back to Langley and hissed, "I was bathed and powdered, dressed in a gown and propped in bed and then he came in and put out the candle. There was a thud and then another I assumed was his shoes hitting the floor and then he climbed on top of me, rocked about a bit as if riding a horse, then rolled off and said, "There. It is consummated." I have no idea if he took anything else off but his shoes, but it didn't seem to me he had time to disrobe further between putting out the candle and climbing on top of me."

"You were under the blankets?" Langley asked sharply. When she nodded, he asked, "And he was on top?"

Christiana bit her lip at the growing excitement in his expression. "That was wrong, wasn't it? I did wonder, but Dicky said it was consummated, and I had no one to ask, so . . ."

"Dicky," he muttered with disgust. "It's no wonder Richard hated that name. I do as well." He let his breath out on a little huff and then suddenly smiled. "That doesn't matter. However, what does is the fact that, from your description, the marriage cer-

tainly hasn't been consummated. We can take you to a doctor now this very night. He can examine you, proclaim you still a virgin, and we can have the marriage annulled at once. There would still be a scandal, but not much of one compared to the alternative."

"The alternative being proving he doesn't have the birthmark and is really George masquerading as his brother, which would mean the wedding wasn't valid and I have been living with him without benefit of marriage?" she asked quietly.

Langley's smile faded, but he nodded.

"You do realize that if he is George and has taken his brother's place . . . Well, we simply can't allow him to get away with it," she pointed out gently. "We would have to tell someone."

"At the expense of you, Suzie and Lisa suffering a maelstrom of scandal?" Langley asked grimly.

She hesitated, but then nodded.

"You always did have an implacable belief in justice," Langley muttered with frustration.

Christiana smiled faintly, but then sighed. An annulment would certainly be less scandalous than possible murder, stealing a man's name and living in sin. But if the man she thought she married really was George Fairgrave, he was even more dastardly than she'd thought, and should be stopped and brought to justice. Still, she would rather do so with as little damage to herself and her family as possible and there was really no rush for justice.

"Why do we not find out what is what before we worry about anything else," she suggested quietly. "I shall see if he has the birthmark or not. If he does, he is Richard, I will be examined, be proven a virgin, and I will simply go for an annulment. If he doesn't and he is George, I will still be examined, be proven a virgin, and go for the annulment, but then, once the dust has settled, we can see about reporting him to the authorities," she suggested. "That little bit of distance might be enough to protect Suzie and Lisa, or it would at least give them the chance to find husbands before the scandal hits . . . husbands who hopefully have powerful families who can help protect them."

Langley was silent for a moment, and then nodded reluctantly. "I would prefer you were away from him at once. However, doing it your way may cause the least damage all the way around."

"I think it's for the best."

"Aye, well, be as quick as you can about seeing if he has the birthmark, Chrissy. Do it tonight if you can manage it. I have a bad feeling that you might be in danger and the sooner you are away from him the better I will feel."

Christiana smiled gently and squeezed the hand holding hers as they danced. "You always were a good friend, Robert. I have missed you this last year."

He nodded acknowledgment of the praise, then drew them both to a halt as the music ended. They both took a moment to survey the people in the room. Christiana had just assured herself that her husband was not back when Langley murmured, "Your husband hasn't returned, more's the pity. If he had I would do my best to get him drunk so that he passed out the moment he returned home. Then you would merely have to take a quick look and rush out while he snored off the drink."

"Dicky rarely does things in a convenient manner," she said dryly as he led her to an empty seat along the wall. Christiana was grateful to drop into it. She had been dancing nonstop for some time and was ready for a break. But she hadn't forgotten her responsibilities and peered around now for her sisters. "I wonder where Suzie and Lisa are."

"I shall take a look about for them," Langley promised. "Would you like me to bring you back a beverage? You have been dancing quite a bit and must be thirsty."

"Yes, please. A drink sounds delightful." The effects of the earlier drink appeared to have dissipated as she'd danced. Besides, he would bring her punch, which probably wouldn't have much alcohol, if any. At least it hadn't at the few country events she'd attended.

"I'll be back directly," he assured her and moved off.

Christiana immediately began scouring the crowded ballroom for Suzie, Lisa or her husband. Finding all three of them would be a good thing. While moments ago she would have been glad did Dicky not return, she was now rather hoping for it. If he did, and Langley did get him drunk, it would certainly make it easier for her to see if he had the birthmark or not. If that didn't happen, Christiana hadn't a clue how she was supposed to get a peek at his behind.

She suspected that was not normally a problem in a marriage and that were she to ask any other married woman in here if their husband had a birthmark or any other distinguishing feature on their bottom, they *would* know the answer.

"Finally, you've stopped dancing!"

Christiana gave a start as her sisters suddenly appeared before her. Eyebrows rising, she asked, "Finally?"

"Yes, it was beginning to look as if you might dance until dawn and we are both exhausted and ready to leave."

"You're joking," she said with surprise and reminded Suzette, "You planned to stay to the end in a bid to find a likely husband."

"I've found him," Suzette announced with satisfaction.

"Already?" Christiana asked with disbelief.

She nodded. "And I've proposed."

"Well who is it?"

"Lord Woodrow. Daniel."

Christiana blinked at her with confusion. She'd never heard the name. "Who is Daniel Woodrow?"

"The fellow who walked us out for some air so you and Dicky could talk," Lisa explained and Christiana blanched in horror.

"Dicky's friend?"

"He is not Dicky's friend," Suzette assured her solemnly.

"Are you sure? He seemed to be with him."

"I'm sure. When we got outside I berated him for being friends with Dicky and he said, 'I assure you I never have and never will be friends with your sister's husband. In fact, I think he's a despicable creature who should be taken out in a field and shot.' " Suzette beamed. "He really doesn't seem to like him at all, Chrissy, which at least shows the man has good taste."

Christiana shook her head slightly, but then admitted, "I have never heard Dicky mention Woodrow and he hasn't been to the house. In fact, I have never seen him before tonight so I suppose he could be telling the truth. It's just that he seemed to be helping Dicky when he took you two outside."

"He said he was trying to prevent anyone else hearing what he had overheard," Lisa explained.

"And he's perfect," Suzette assured her. "He's land rich, but poor as a church mouse when it comes to the money to run those lands. And he's titled," she added and then frowned and admitted, "I'm not yet sure what his title is. He may just be a Baron, but —" She shrugged indifferently.

"And you say you proposed to him?"

Christiana asked.

"Yes," Suzette said, beaming with pride at taking her own future in hand.

"Well, what did he say?"

"He is taking this evening to think about it," Suzette answered with a little sigh, and then shifted impatiently and said, "I don't know about you two but I am exhausted. It has been a terribly stressful day. Why do we not head back to the townhouse and get some rest?"

Christiana bit her lip. "Are you sure you wouldn't rather stay and consider a couple more men before we leave? If Lord Woodrow says no —"

"Nay," Suzette interrupted firmly. "We have weeded out all the candidates here tonight and Daniel was the only one I was interested in. The rest are either unattractive, pompous or older than Father. I can always choose one of the others, or maybe find another at tomorrow night's ball if Daniel says no, but otherwise . . ." She grimaced. "Frankly I have no interest in shackling myself to an old man. I want children and would rather be at least attracted to the man who helps me make them. Besides, Dicky isn't dead so the urgency has been removed. I have two weeks now to find a husband."

"Oh, of course," Christiana murmured and got wearily to her feet.

"You found them."

Christiana turned to Langley as he approached with two glasses in hand.

"Yes. Well, actually, they found me, and are quite ready to go," she admitted, and then reached for the nearer glass he held and asked, "Is that for me?"

"Yes," he murmured sounding distracted as he glanced to Lisa. He then frowned and glanced back to her with surprise and said, "No!"

It was too late, however, Christiana had already taken the glass and quickly gulped down its contents, barely tasting it in her effort to finish it off so they could leave. She was already lowering the glass when she realized the liquid she'd swallowed was burning a trail down her throat and splashing into her stomach like liquid fire. Whiskey again, she realized and drew in one long gasping breath as the air seemed to be sucked out of her. That breath was then followed by a deep, nasty fit of coughing.

"I'm sorry," Langley said thumping her back with his free hand. "That was whiskey for me. The other glass was for you."

Gasping for breath as she straightened, Christiana took the glass of punch, quickly

103

drinking that down now in the hopes of clearing her throat. Her eyes widened incredulously as a second wave of heat poured down her throat.

"Oh dear," Langley muttered.

"Oh dear, what?" Suzette asked grimly, eyeing Christiana with concern.

"That was the Regent's punch," Robert said on a sigh, taking the glass from Christiana as she burst into another round of coughing.

"Regent's punch?" Lisa asked, rubbing Christiana's back.

"Rum, brandy, arrack and champagne with some tea, pineapple syrup and a couple other ingredients thrown in for flavor," he explained dryly.

"Well, judging by Christiana's reaction there was precious little of those other ingredients in it," Suzette said dryly.

Robert grimaced. "Lady Landon usually has her staff make it stronger as the night goes on. She is sure it is the reason her balls are always so well attended and such a success."

"Brilliant," Suzette muttered.

"Are you all right, Chrissy?" Lisa asked with concern when Christiana's second round of coughing finally began to subside.

She nodded, her breath still too raspy to

respond, but she wasn't at all sure that was true. The two drinks seemed to be hitting her hard. Dear God, her head was spinning and spots were floating before her eyes, though whether that was from the whiskey or her coughing fit she couldn't tell. She took another moment to regain her composure under the concerned gazes of Suzette, Lisa and Langley, then forced a smile and suggested, "We should be going."

"Are you sure you are all right?" Langley asked with a frown. "You are still quite flushed."

Christiana grimaced, but nodded and turned carefully in search of the exit. "We are all tired. A good night's rest will do us good. Besides, I have something to look into if you'll recall?"

"What's that?" Lisa asked even as Langley suggested, "Perhaps you should leave that for another night now, Chrissy. You are not used to liquor and it may go straight to your head."

Christiana shook her head. "The first glass didn't affect me that badly, and this hasn't either except to steal my breath. It will be fine. I shall let you know what I find out."

"What are you two talking about?" Lisa asked impatiently, concern tautening her expression.

"Nothing you need worry about," Christiana assured her, beginning to lead the way out of the ballroom. "Just something I need to check with Dicky about."

CHAPTER FIVE

"The window is open. That's a bit of good luck."

Richard stopped climbing at Daniel's murmured comment and peered toward the window in question. It had taken some poking about, but after climbing several trees and checking the windows of several rooms, they'd deduced this was the master bedroom. At least they hoped it was. Richard didn't have a clue. His own townhouse had burned to the ground in the fire that was supposed to have killed him, and he didn't know the layout of this new one George had purchased afterward.

"They probably left it open to keep the body cool," he said as he continued to climb, pulling himself up branch after branch until he reached the large thick one that stretched toward the open window.

"Do you see anyone in there?" Daniel asked as he joined him on the branch a moment later.

"There's someone in the bed," Richard muttered, craning his neck in an effort to see as much of the room as he could. "But I don't see anyone else."

"Is it George in the bed?"

"I can't see him well enough to be sure from here, but who else would it be? The girls are at the ball and the servants would hardly be sleeping in the upper chambers."

Daniel grunted and then asked hopefully, "I don't suppose you can tell if he really is dead then?"

"No," Richard said with exasperation and began to ease his way further out along the branch, wishing that he'd thought to change before trying this. Aside from the fact that his clothing kept catching on branches, he feared his white shirt would be very visible to anyone who happened to glance their way in passing. The thought was enough to make him use more speed than caution getting to the window and he nearly paid for his haste with a tumble from the tree. Fortunately, Daniel reached out quickly to steady him when his knee slipped off the branch, catching him by the back of his breeches and unfortunately, yanking them up his backside in a most uncomfortable manner.

"While I appreciate the aid, please release

my breeches," Richard said finally once he was sure of his position.

Daniel chuckled in response, but released his hold. "We'd best get out of this tree before we're seen."

Since that's what he'd been trying to do, Richard merely grunted and scooted along the branch as fast as he dared. After one last quick glance inside to be sure no one had yet entered, he swung himself over the ledge and into the room. Aware that Daniel was following, Richard straightened to move swiftly out of the way and suddenly found himself standing at the bedside, staring down at its occupant. It was like looking into a mirror, Richard thought, except of course that he wasn't wet and gray with death like his brother.

"I'd say he's definitely dead," Daniel murmured coming up beside him. "Other than that he looks healthy enough though. He hasn't gained weight or become dissipated since I last saw him. I wonder what killed him?"

Richard shook his head. He had no idea and was too troubled by an unexpected surge of emotion to consider the question. This was not the reunion he'd expected tonight, and while part of him felt cheated of the confrontation he'd intended, another part seemed to actually be experiencing some grief for the loss of his twin. While George had proven himself a bastard with his efforts to have Richard killed so that he could take his title and lands, they hadn't always been enemies. As young children they had been close friends. It was only once George had grown old enough to understand that he was somehow considered less simply because he hadn't fought his way out of their mother's womb first that he'd grown bitter and allowed jealousy to twist his thoughts.

Even so, the man had been the last family member Richard had. Their father had been an only son and their mother had lost her family in a house fire while still a child. That was how George had got away with his plans. There had been no family members to recognize the trick, and he'd apparently kept his distance from the few good friends Richard had made over the years. Everyone had assumed he was grieving the supposed loss of his twin, George, and had left him alone to sort it out. Including Daniel, until he'd received Richard's letter. And thank God for Daniel. Without him Richard would still be in America.

"How the devil are we going to get him out of here?"

Richard blinked at the question and then turned to peer toward the window and the tree beyond it.

"Oh, no," Daniel said at once. "There is no way we are going back down that tree dragging George's corpse between us."

Richard ran a hand through his hair as he turned back to peer at George. "I guess we'll have to take him down the stairs then."

"And just how are we to manage that without getting caught?"

"Most of the servants are probably abed by now," Richard pointed out. "If we are quick we should manage it all right."

"Right," Daniel said dryly.

"Come on." Richard moved to the top of the bed. "The sooner it's done the better."

Richard bent to slip his hands under his brother's armpits, intending to sit him up, but the action put his face close to George's and he paused.

"What is it?" Daniel asked, at his side at once.

Richard straightened and stepped back. "See if you smell anything by his mouth."

Daniel raised an eyebrow, and then bent to inhale close to George's mouth. "Whiskey," he said at once and then frowned and added, "And bitter almonds?" He now straightened slowly and turned a frown on

111

Richard. "Poison?"

"That was my first thought," Richard admitted grimly.

Daniel blew out a low whistle. "Murder. That's a wrinkle I hadn't expected. Although I guess I should have. We know you aren't the only one he has crossed."

"No. He crossed Christiana, and poison is a woman's trick," Richard said grimly. "A man would have met him at dawn with swords or pistols."

"Now don't go hanging the poor woman already," Daniel cautioned. "I don't think George would have agreed to a duel. Or he may have agreed, but then he would have sent riffraff out to kill his challenger in his bed. He wasn't the sort to risk his own hide and he had no honor to speak of." He shook his head. "George also didn't much leave the house from what I was able to learn tonight. Poison may have been the only way to ensure he died. Besides, I just don't see Lady Christiana poisoning him."

Richard peered at him curiously. "Why are you so quick to defend her?"

"I like her," Daniel said with a shrug.

"You do not know the woman. You didn't even speak to her," Richard pointed out with exasperation.

"I talked to her sisters though," Daniel

argued at once. "And they were both lovely young women. I'm sure she is too. They grew up in the same family."

"So did George and I," Richard pointed out dryly.

Daniel frowned. "Good point."

Richard shook his head with disgust. "Come on, we need to get him moved. We can worry about who killed him after we have him safely away."

Richard moved back to try to shift George into a sitting position, but paused with a curse when he found the man stiff as a board.

"Hmmm, he's been dead a while," Daniel pointed out quietly.

"Right." Richard scowled at George as if he were deliberately being difficult and then said, "You take his feet, I'll take his shoulders."

Daniel nodded and moved to take the man's feet so that they could heft him off the bed.

They had both seen the ice packed around the body, but neither had considered that some of it must have melted until water began to drip from George's sopping clothes in a steady stream.

"Back, back, back," Richard said sharply, quickly hefting his end back over the bed.

"Damn," Daniel breathed as they released their burden. "We will leave a trail of water through the house taking him as he is."

Richard scowled briefly, but then stepped back up to the bed and began to work his brother's frock coat off his shoulders. It appeared the women had dumped him in the bed without making any effort to undress him. "Find a dry blanket."

"Where?" Daniel asked, glancing around the room.

"Try that chest at the foot of the bed," Richard suggested as he finally freed the jacket and tossed the sodden cloth to the floor.

"Got it," Daniel announced a moment later and reappeared at his side. He slung the blanket over his shoulder, leaving his hands free to help finish undressing George. Once they had him naked, Daniel laid the blanket out on the floor and they quickly shifted George from the bed to the blanket. This time he only dripped a little.

"I think your bed is ruined," Daniel said wryly as they straightened from rolling George up in the blanket.

Richard glanced to the bed. The mattress was swollen with water and likely to grow more so as the remaining ice melted. Not that he particularly wanted to sleep on a mattress his dead brother had occupied anyway.

They lifted George up together, each taking an end of the blanket and then moved quickly to the door with their burden. Richard then set down his end to open the door, only to discover it was locked.

"Probably to keep the servants out," Daniel suggested quietly.

Richard grunted and glanced to a second door on the adjacent wall, this one leading to Christiana's room, he suspected. Hopefully it wouldn't be locked. He picked up his end again and nodded toward the door. "That way."

Daniel immediately began to back across the room. Both of them sighed with relief when he set down his end, tried the doorknob and it turned. He then started to push the door open wide, but stopped abruptly and instead pulled it closed.

"What is it?"

"There's a woman sleeping in a chair by the fire," Daniel hissed.

Richard hesitated and then eased the end of George he was holding to the floor and moved over to ease the door open and look for himself. Sure enough, a middle-aged woman was slumped in a chair by the fire, snoring softly. Probably Christiana's lady's

115

maid, Richard thought. Grimacing, he eased the door closed and briefly leaned his forehead against it.

"What do we do now?" Daniel asked.

Richard straightened and turned back to his blanket-wrapped brother. Bending, he caught the stiff body around the waist and lifted him. He then straightened, hefting George a little higher against his chest so that his feet didn't hit the floor.

"Are you going to be able to carry him like that?" Daniel asked in a concerned whisper.

"I've been working a farm the last year, Daniel, I'll be fine. And this will be faster than the two of us dragging him about. If we're quick and quiet we should get through the room without waking the maid." Richard wasn't sure that was true, but he was hoping. Fortunately, Daniel didn't argue the point, but helped him lift George even higher until he clasped him around the upper legs just below his bottom. It left Richard's legs free to move without bumping into George every step. Once he was sure he had a good grip on George, he said, "You'll have to get the doors."

Daniel nodded and moved to the door to the connecting bedroom again. He eased it open just enough to peer inside, then apparently finding the maid still sleeping, he pulled it wide and gestured for him to hurry.

Richard took a deep breath and started forward at once with his burden. He didn't breathe again, however, until they'd crossed the room and Daniel opened the door and ushered him out into the hall.

"Dear God, Richard, for a minute there I thought we were done for," Daniel gasped once he had the door safely closed.

"Now we just have to make it out of the house," Richard muttered, starting forward. He was eager to get out of the house before they encountered anyone else, and had just reached the stairs when the front door suddenly opened below. Heart stopping, he immediately backed up, crashing into an unsuspecting Daniel. Fortunately, the man kept his feet and quickly turned to get out of the way. The two scurried back up the hall until Daniel had the sense to try one of the doors. Finding it open, he waved Richard in with his burden and followed, then pulled the door closed and stood with his ear pressed to it.

Richard waited in the darkness, his brother's blanket-wrapped body pressing to his chest, and finally asked, "Do you hear anything?"

"They're talking," Daniel whispered. "I

think they're still in the entry."

Richard shifted closer, stepping up behind Daniel to better hear what was being said.

"I swear he was dead, Chrissy. He was growing cold when we left tonight."

Christiana grimaced at Lisa's distressed words, but concentrated on putting one foot in front of the other, and merely muttered, "He must have made a deal with the devil to come back."

"Hush, one of the servants will hear," Suzette cautioned as she closed the front door. The words had barely left her lips when Haversham appeared at the end of the hall, hurrying toward them.

Christiana waved the man away. They didn't need help. Besides she didn't want him to witness her in this shape. Those drinks she'd had were rather having an effect now.

"Are you all right, Chrissy?" Suzette asked, taking her arm to steady her. "You are not at all steady on your feet."

"I'm fine," Christiana answered, but wasn't all that sure she was. While she hadn't noticed much amiss during the short ride home, when she'd risen to alight from the carriage, the world had suddenly tilted a bit and she'd nearly tumbled out of the contraption. Fortunately, the coachmen had been there to catch her arm and steady her much as Suzie was doing now.

"I fear those drinks Langley gave her may have affected her after all," Lisa said with concern, taking her other arm as the world tilted again and Christiana stumbled in her direction.

"Surely two drinks wouldn't affect her this much," Suzette protested.

"Two drinks on an empty stomach might," Lisa reasoned.

"Three drinks," Christiana muttered.

"Three?" Suzette peered at her with surprise. "When did you have a third one?"

"A firsht one," Christiana corrected and paused to frown at the slur. She spoke with more care as she explained. "I drank Dicky's whiskey earlier." She frowned when *whiskey* came out as "whishkey," but then decided it didn't matter and admitted, "It's okay though, I actually feel good."

"Oh dear," Lisa said.

Suzette merely shook her head. "Well, at least she feels good, probably for the first time since marrying that odious man. No doubt he *did* make a deal with the devil to return."

" 'S what I said," Christiana pointed out, stopping to wave her finger at Suzette.

Unfortunately, Suzette's grip on her arm prevented it.

Lisa sighed pitiably. "What are we going to do, Suzie? We can't let her stay married to him."

"Oh don' worry. I'll fix it," Christiana assured her, wondering why they were still standing there in the entry.

"How?" Lisa asked dubiously.

"I'll get to the *bottom* of it," Christiana answered blithely, and then burst out laughing at what to her seemed a very clever play on words. Her sisters were less impressed and merely watched her cackle, and then exchanged a worried glance.

"Perhaps we'd best get her to bed," Lisa murmured. "She appears to be getting worse."

"Aye," Suzette said dryly and they urged her to and up the stairs.

"Never fear, Chrissy," Lisa patted the arm she held as they reached the upper hall. "We will see you tucked safely in your bed so you can sleep off the effects."

"I can't sleep," Christiana protested, tugging on her arms. "I need to see Dicky. Where's Dicky?"

"Now I know I shall never drink," Suzette said dryly. "If it affects the mind to the point that she would actually want to see that

120

blasted man, then I shall never touch a drop."

Christiana blinked in surprise. "I don't want to see Dicky."

"But you just said you did," Lisa protested as they reached the door to her bed chamber.

"Did I?" Christiana asked a bit befuddled as they urged her into the room. She then shook her head and explained, "Well, I don't want to see him."

"That's good," Suzette muttered as she closed the door.

"I just want to see his bottom," Christiana explained and frowned as *see* came out "shee."

"What?"

Christiana scowled at the screeched word, noting that the loudest screech of all came not from her sisters, but from Grace, who was pushing herself out of the chair by the fire where she'd apparently been awaiting her return.

"What what?" Christiana asked, perplexed by their upset as the maid rushed across the room to join them. It all made perfect sense to her. "I half to get Nicky naked," she explained and then frowned and corrected herself. "Dicky daked. No, that's not right either." She heaved a sigh and pulled free of

121

her sisters to weave her way across the room, waving one hand expansively as she added, "Well, you know what I mean."

"Not really," Suzette said dryly. "Why do you not explain it to us?"

Christiana turned back to her sisters, most distressed to find her earlier good cheer suddenly replaced with a deep depression, and then blurted mournfully, "Do you know I've never seen Dicky daked? A wife should see a naked Nicky."

"Or even a naked Dick," Suzette put in dryly.

"Suzie!" Lisa gasped, blushing furiously.

"What? It's his name," Suzette pointed out.

The words were innocent enough, but mirth was curving the corners of her sister's lips and Christiana was sure there was a joke there she was missing. However, she was rather consumed with the need to see Dicky's bare bottom, not to mention a bit distressed that the room would not stop swinging about her. It seemed to her that her room had never moved before and shouldn't be now. She'd heard that rooms on ships moved though, so perhaps they'd brought her to a ship rather than home, she reasoned as she sat on the edge of her bed. "I don't feel good. Can you make the boat stop pitching about?"

"Oh dear, are you going to be sick?" Lisa asked and Christiana noticed that she took a step or two back. Lisa never had been good with illness.

"She probably will," Suzette said dryly. "Just the thought of seeing Dicky naked makes me nauseous."

"Not all of Dicky, just his bottom," Christiana assured her earnestly. "I have to find the strawberry."

"I think you'd have more luck finding strawberries in the kitchen, Chrissy dear," Suzette said, laughing openly now.

"All right, now that's enough of this nonsense," Grace snapped with exasperation. Moving to stand before Christiana, she eyed her briefly with worry before glancing to her sisters to ask, "What on earth is the matter with her? Has she been drinking?"

"No," Lisa said at once, and then frowned and added, "Well, yes, but not on purpose. I'm afraid Langley gave her his whiskey by accident and she downed it without realizing what it was until it was too late, and then she had a glass of the Regent's punch as well, and apparently she'd already had another whiskey earlier so the combination . . ."

"I see," Grace said with a sigh, and then a smile tugged at her lips and she shook her head. "Well, a good night's rest will right what's wrong with her then. Come along, dear, let's get you out of this dress and ready for bed."

"But I have to find Dicky's strawberry," Christiana protested, trying ineffectually to stop Grace as she began to undo her lacings.

"Darling child, don't you worry about Dicky anymore. He's dead remember?"

"Actually, he's not," Lisa said unhappily and the words stopped Grace's cold where Christiana's efforts had failed.

"Of course he is. He's —"

"Alive and well and showed up at the ball," Suzette interrupted.

"No," Grace said with certainty and immediately strode across the room to the connecting door to the master chamber. She opened it, peered inside, and then slammed it quickly closed and whirled to them with horror on her face, "How?"

"A deal with the devil," Christiana answered morosely. "Now I have to get him naked. He should of stayed dead don't you think? The King should make a law, if you're dead, you stay dead. It's entirely too upsetting for dead husbands to show up at balls and spoil them like that . . . and then I wouldn't have to shee his bare bottom."

Grace stared at her blankly for a moment, and then shook her head and moved back to her side. "All right, you girls get yourselves to bed. I'll see my lady into bed."

"Oh, but I don't want to go to bed. I might fall asleep and miss Dicky's strawberry."

"Yes, yes," Grace interrupted soothingly, urging her to her feet and quickly finishing undoing her gown. "You want to see Dicky's bottom. But he's not here right now, is he? So we'll just get you ready for bed. You can see his bottom whether you're wearing a dress or nightgown, can't you?"

"I suppose," Christiana muttered.

"Go on, you two. I can handle this," Grace insisted, drawing Christiana's attention to the fact that her sisters were still there. Despite the maid's words, the two women seemed reluctant to leave and Christiana wondered if they wanted to stay and help her get a look at Dicky's bottom.

"I think they're gone," Richard whispered when silence reigned in the hall for several minutes. "We'd best move while we have the chance. Once they have Christiana in bed, the girls will no doubt seek their own

125

rooms and this could be one of them."

Daniel grunted agreement and eased the door open to check the hall. Apparently finding it empty, he stepped back and pulled the door wide for Richard to carry his burden out of the room. He didn't get far. Richard had barely stepped out the door when another one along the hall opened. He immediately whirled back to the room to return inside, but Daniel apparently hadn't heard the sound, wasn't aware of the threat of discovery, and blocked his way, still trying to exit the room.

More concerned about the body being seen than himself, Richard cursed and shoved George at Daniel, who had the wit to catch the blanket-wrapped body. He then pushed his friend back into the room with his burden. He pulled the door closed even as he whirled to face Christiana's sisters, who had appeared outside the door to the room he thought was Christiana's. The two women were looking back into the room, saying their good nights, and didn't turn his way until he'd taken a couple of steps toward them. Both women paused, their smiles fading.

"Ladies," he murmured, racking his brain for some way to delay the women from seeking their beds. Preferably something that would take them downstairs and give Daniel the chance to slip out of the house with George. The best he could come up with was, "Might I convince you both to join me in my office for a drink before you retire?"

"No, thank you," Lisa said stiffly as they approached. Suzette didn't even bother with a refusal, she merely snorted with disgust as she started past him, heading for the door to the room he'd just exited.

"I need to talk to you," he said desperately, catching at Suzette's arm to bring her to a halt. When she turned angry eyes his way and glared at the hand on her arm, he released her. "I realize I've been a bit of an ass to your sister —"

"A bit?" Suzette asked dryly.

"All right, a lot of an ass," Richard acknowledged and wished he knew exactly what George had done. "The point is, my brush with death tonight has awakened me to what is important in this life, and I would dearly like to make it up to Christiana and, if possible, mend our relationship. I was hoping you could advise me on how to do that."

He had thought it an inspired ruse, and one that wasn't entirely a ruse really. If he was going to step back into his life as it now was and keep Christiana for a wife, he needed to repair the damage George had done. Of course, there was still the small matter of who had poisoned George. If Christiana was the culprit, it was a matter that would have to be dealt with. However, his main concern at the moment was getting her sisters out of that hallway long enough for Daniel to escape.

"Are you sincere about this?" Lisa asked quietly.

"Of course he isn't," Suzette said with irritation. "A leopard does not change its spots."

"He changed his spots going from nice to nasty after marrying Christiana," Lisa pointed out. "Perhaps he can change again."

"That wasn't changing his spots," Suzette assured her. "Those spots were fake ones he'd painted on to get her to marry him so that he could get his hands on her dower. He just washed them off once he'd accomplished that and reverted to his true, nasty nature."

"I'm very wealthy, ladies," Richard said quietly. "I had no need to marry Christiana for money."

Suzette's eyes narrowed. "Then why did you marry her?"

That one stumped him. How could he answer that? He suspected George *had* married Christiana for her dower and he himself hadn't married her at all. Finally, he simply said, "I care about Christiana and her happiness." Which was true. He did care. He didn't want to see her suffering for his brother's actions. However, Suzette didn't look impressed, so he continued, "My behavior this last year is a direct result of what happened with my brother. I —"

"Oh," Lisa breathed, sudden understanding dawning on her face. "Of course."

"Of course what?" Suzette asked suspiciously.

"Don't you see, Suzette?" Lisa peered at Richard with pity and understanding. "No doubt in his heart of hearts he has always felt guilty for surviving the fire that killed his brother."

Richard managed not to grimace. He doubted George had felt a moment's guilt over hiring men to kill him.

"Meeting and falling in love with Chrissy must have been a balm to his wounded soul," Lisa continued in earnest tones. "But then they married and moved here, living just up the street from the charred remains of the townhouse where his poor brother died. It must be a daily reminder of his death. His guilt would have returned and trebled, because he was no longer experiencing just the guilt of surviving while his brother didn't, but now also for finding a love and happiness his poor dead brother would never have." She peered at Richard with big, wet eyes. "His soul tortured, his spirit wounded, he lashed out at Chrissy, the woman he loved, destroying her love and their relationship out of the guilt consuming him."

Richard stared at the young woman wide-eyed. So much dramatic drivel out of the simple comment that his behavior was a result of what had happened with his brother was just astonishing to him. The girl should write fiction, he thought, and then noticed that Suzette's expression had softened just a little, some of her suspicion easing away. Apparently, she wasn't as hard as she appeared to be and had something of a romantic streak as well.

"Is this true?" Suzette asked.

Richard cleared his throat, tried for what he hoped was a tragic expression, and murmured, "Guilt can lead a man to act like an ass and do the most foolish of things." Like breaking into his own house and stealing corpses, he thought grimly as it occurred to him that getting the body out of here would not be the end of their problems. What the devil were they going to do with it for the next few days? Richard hadn't thought of that when Daniel had made his ridiculous suggestion that started all of this. Apparently, Daniel hadn't either. But all they'd managed to do was create more problems. He hoped Christiana was worth all this trouble. He would be extremely annoyed if it turned out she was the murderer, or some waspish shrew.

"Please, Suzette," Lisa said quietly. "Can we not at least hear him out?"

A brief battle took place on her face, and then Suzette threw up her hands with exasperation and turned toward the stairs. "Very well, but only because Christiana is stuck with him now."

Lisa beamed and caught Richard's hand to drag him after her, saying, "I knew it could not have been all pretense when you were courting Christiana. You were so sweet and romantic, calling her Rosebud and showering her with gifts. She fell completely in love with you."

"Rosebud?" Richard muttered, glancing back at the door to Suzette's room and hoping Daniel would manage to get the body out without further problem.

"She loved that endearment most of all," Lisa assured him as she tugged him down the stairs. "Everyone could see the way she melted every time you called her that. She said you called her that because she was a fragile flower, beautiful and sweet smelling."

George had obviously had someone to coach him in wooing, Richard decided grimly. The man hadn't a romantic bone in his body and wouldn't have come up with such drivel on his own.

"Is drinking so early in the morning a result of your guilt as well?"

Richard blinked at those words from Suzette as Lisa led him into the room George had apparently used as his office. She was standing by the fire beside a small table with an empty glass and a decanter of amber liquid that he suspected was whiskey. He eyed the decanter, and then glanced back to Suzette, not having any idea what she was talking about. Finally he asked, "Drinking so early?"

Suzette clucked with annoyance and picked up the decanter. Removing the lid, she sniffed at it and wrinkled her nose. "When we found you this morning you'd obviously been drinking this stuff. And it was barely past the breakfast hour." She scowled at him for such debauched tendencies, before splashing some of the liquid into the empty glass. Setting down the decanter then, she raised the glass as if in a toast.

"Christiana said it was your best whiskey and you only drank it when celebrating. So what is there for us to celebrate?"

Her expression was challenging. Richard suspected she thought she knew exactly what he — or really George — had been celebrating. However, he didn't have a clue what that might have been. Instead, his mind had put together the smell of bitter almonds on George's breath with the knowledge that the amber liquid had been the last thing he'd consumed. Richard was suddenly quite positive that the whiskey Suzette was now holding aloft was how his brother had been poisoned.

"Come tell us what it was so we can all celebrate," Suzette suggested grimly. "We can use some good news about now."

"I wasn't celebrating anything," Richard said finally, starting across the room toward her. "I wasn't feeling well and my uncle used to always swear by a shot of whiskey every morning doing wonders for your health so I thought I would give it a try."

"Liar," she said sweetly, and then shrugged as if it were of no consequence and lifted the glass toward her lips. "Ah well, now we can celebrate you turning over a new leaf and making my sister happy for a change."

"No!" Richard sped the last few feet that

133

separated them, desperate to keep her from drinking what might be poison. He managed to knock the glass from her hand, sending it to the floor, but the contents spilled down her dress front as it went.

CHAPTER SIX

"Oh Suzette, your lovely dress!" Lisa cried rushing forward now.

"I apologize," Richard murmured, bending to pick up the glass. "I didn't mean to spill it all over you."

"No, you just meant to keep me from drinking your precious whiskey," Suzette snapped with disgust. "Christiana said you don't allow anyone else to drink it, but surely it was better in me than on the floor, don't you think?"

"I assure you, you are welcome to anything in my home," he said, straightening with dignity, and then added in a lie, "I just did not wish you to drink the whiskey out of anger. I'm quite sure you would never have consumed it under normal circumstances, and it's very strong. It would have gone right to your head."

Obviously not appeased by his explanation, she said dryly, "Yes, well now it's gone to my bosoms instead."

"Suzette!" Lisa gasped with shock.

"Well, it has," Suzette said unrepentantly, gesturing to her soaking bodice. She then clucked with annoyance and whirled toward the door. "Forgive me, but I no longer feel like talking tonight. I am going to bed."

"Perhaps it's best if we have this conversation tomorrow," Lisa said apologetically, following her sister to the door. Pausing there, she glanced back to offer him a crooked smile and added, "But I am very glad you have realized what guilt and loss were making you do and I shall do my best to help you repair the damage done to your relationship with Christiana. I promise."

"Thank you," Richard murmured, thinking that while Suzette was a virago, Lisa was really . . . well, she was incredibly young and sweet. If he stayed married to Christiana, and really took them on as sisters he would have to help protect the girl from her own romantic tendencies. Dear Lord, he still couldn't believe the tragic tale she'd come up with to explain George's nastiness, and all on the basis of one sentence. Shaking his head as the women left, Richard turned his attention to the glass in his hand and raised it to his nose to sniff it. He frowned when all he smelled was whiskey

136

without any hint of bitter almonds, then picked up the decanter and gave it a sniff too. No bitter almond scent. Unfortunately, he didn't know much about the poison and supposed the smell might not present itself until consumed. That or the whiskey wasn't the source of the poison.

Better safe than sorry, he decided and carried the decanter to the French doors leading into the yard. Opening them, he stepped outside and upended the bottle, emptying the contents on the grass.

Richard had just turned to head back into the office when a heavy thud to his left made him stop. Glancing in that direction, he stared blankly at the bundle that had suddenly appeared on the grass several feet away. Richard was slow to recognize his half unwrapped brother lying there, but once he understood what he was looking at, his gaze shot swiftly up to the second floor window above. He was just in time to see a man's leg appear over the ledge. Daniel. He'd forgotten all about the man. Obviously, his friend hadn't managed to get out before the women had returned upstairs and was now trying to escape via the window. Richard waited, ready to help if he could, but rather than his other leg appearing over the ledge, candlelight suddenly filled the room, framing Woodrow's dark shape in the window.

Cursing, Richard rushed back into his office. He deposited the empty decanter on his desk as he hurried past, and then rushed out into the hall only to nearly run down Haversham.

"My lord!" the butler cried, coming to an abrupt halt. "You're —"

"Yes, yes, I'm feeling better," Richard said with a forced smile, knowing the staff had been told he was ill. He was pleased to know the man still worked for the family and that George hadn't sacked the fellow, but really didn't have time for him at the moment. Moving around him, he added, "Excuse me. I have . . . er . . . something to handle above stairs."

Richard didn't wait for a response from Haversham, but left him gaping after him and headed upstairs at a run, desperate to save Daniel from the virago that was Suzette. He was sure he would arrive to find her beating Daniel viciously about the head with her candlestick and shrieking "intruder."

Instead, he arrived at her closed door, thrust it open and stopped dead. It seemed he needn't have worried about his friend, or the virago that was Suzette. The two were wrapped up in a most passionate embrace, so passionate in fact that neither appeared to have heard his arrival. At least she hadn't.

Richard was just wondering what he should do when Daniel removed one hand from Suzette's back to wave him away. He hesitated one moment, but then decided to obey the gesture. Daniel was an honorable man and wouldn't do anything to harm Suzette or her reputation. Besides, now that the panic had cleared, he suddenly recalled George's body lying out on the lawn.

Richard pulled the door gently closed and knew he'd made the right decision when he heard Daniel's voice muffled through the door, saying, "Suzette, we have to stop now. I should go. It's not proper for me to be in your room like this."

"Oh, but we have to discuss . . ."

Richard didn't hear the rest of Suzette's words, he'd started away from the door the moment Daniel spoke, secure in the knowledge that he would soon join him to take care of George's body.

Haversham was nowhere to be seen when Richard got back downstairs, but then he shouldn't have been the first time. The man had been with the family for forty years now, well before Richard and George had even been born. He was a mostly silent servant who went about his duties with the dignified reserve that all good butlers possessed, but, God in heaven, he was old. He should have been sleeping, not hanging about waiting for the house to go to their beds before he did. However, Richard knew that George wouldn't have cared about his age or frailty. His twin had probably ordered the poor old bastard to man his station until everyone else was abed, and to be up to see to them before he and Christiana arose.

Shaking his head at what else his brother might have done while he was gone, Richard hurried through the office and back onto the lawn. George was right where he'd left him, his head poking out one end of the unraveled blanket and the lower half of his legs hanging out the other. Richard took the time to roll him back up in the blanket, hefted him up into his arms with some difficulty and then paused.

Suzette's window looked out over the backyard and so that was where the body had landed. Richard would have preferred going around the house to Daniel's carriage with his burden, but that would mean traipsing through the stables, which would set the horses nickering and no doubt bring the stable master out of his room to see what was about. He would have to risk a quickstep through the house and out the

140

front door, he decided with a grimace.

Richard stepped back into the office, pulling the French doors closed as he went and then halted as a knock sounded at the hall door. He stared at it blankly, glanced back to the French doors, and then simply dumped his bundle on the floor between himself and the desk. He spared a quick glance to be sure nothing stuck out on either side of the desk and then called out, "Yes?"

The door opened and Haversham peered in with an expression that suggested he hadn't been sure what he'd find. It made Richard wonder what the hell the butler had caught his brother doing in here the last year. Surely George hadn't been crass enough to bring women into the same home where his wife slept?

"What is it, Haversham?" he asked quietly.

The man cleared his throat and straightened in the doorway. "I wondered if you would be wanting anything before you retire?"

"No. Thank you. You may seek out your bed," Richard said quietly, and then as the man began to back out of the door, he asked, "Are there any other servants still awake?"

Haversham paused and considered briefly,

before saying, "Not that I know of, my lord . . . except perhaps for Lady Christiana's maid, Grace. She is probably still about."

"Right," Richard muttered, and then waved him on. "Go ahead and go to bed. And in the future, Haversham, there's no need for you to stay up so late, but we will talk about that tomorrow."

"As you wish," Haversham murmured and pulled the door closed.

Richard waited a moment, giving the man time to get away from the door, and then bent to hoist the blanket-wrapped George up again. Sighing as he straightened with his burden, he crossed to the door Haversham had just closed, listened briefly, and then cracked it open. Once assured the hall was empty, Richard hurried out, and rushed straight to the front door.

The Woodrow carriage waited on the road where they'd left it. The driver was slumped on his perch, chin on chest, apparently asleep. Richard sped to the vehicle, opened the door and dumped George across one of the two bench seats, or tried to: stiff as he was, he rolled right off. He also stuck out the door.

Richard hesitated, but he couldn't leave him hanging out of the carriage. Cursing, he glanced nervously around and then began to massage and bend first his brother's neck and then his legs until he was able to bend him enough so that he could position him on his side on the bench seat. He then took a moment to make sure the blanket hadn't dislodged and that everything was covered before straightening and peering back at the house.

There was still no sign of Daniel. Where was the man? They had to sort out what they were going to do with George. Richard, himself, had no idea where they were going to keep the body for the next few days and since this was all Daniel's idea, he was hoping his friend had a thought or two in that regard.

After another couple moments passed with no sign of Daniel, Richard closed the carriage door and headed impatiently back into the house.

"Idiot man," Christiana muttered staring at the drapes over her bed and wishing they would stop swaying. "Dumb Dicky. Dumb Earl Dicky. Earl Dicky Dumb."

She made a face at the spinning drapes and sighed unhappily as she waited for him to return home so she could look at his bottom . . . which she didn't want to do, she assured herself and wouldn't *have* to do if he wasn't a big dumb Dicky. That was the conclusion Christiana had come to since Grace had left her alone, because frankly, she was a fine woman. She wasn't a raving beauty, but she wasn't ugly either, and she was smart enough and nice. Goodness, she never nagged the man or made demands: all she'd wanted was to love him. But he was a big dumb idiot who didn't seem to realize his good fortune. Or at least hadn't seemed to since their wedding. Before that while courting her he had . . . and to-night . . .

She closed her eyes and recalled their time on the dance floor. The man who had held her in his arms and showed such concern had been a far cry from the one who, with the two words *I do,* had suddenly decided she lacked all the intelligence and taste he'd complimented while courting her. The man who had announced that her kindness was a liability he needed *to guard her against,* and that no one would want her for a friend except social climbers.

Still, this evening, he had seemed a different man and had apologized for this last year, promising he would make it up to her, she recalled, and could almost feel his arms around her again.

Closing her eyes, Christiana shivered as she recalled his breath on her ear and the way he'd nipped at it. She then sighed as she recalled the feel of his hand sliding over her bottom and pressing her against him.

She'd wanted him to take her out on the balcony. She'd wanted to know what it would be like to be kissed properly by him, for other than the perfunctory peck on the lips during their wedding ceremony, he had never kissed her. It was not something Christiana had really missed . . . until he'd held her in his arms on the dance floor and stirred such warm sensations in her with his breath and touch.

Perhaps there was hope, she thought. Well, if he was Richard and not George, Christiana reminded herself with a grimace. She really needed to find out what her situation was and who exactly she was married to, she acknowledged, and glared toward the door between her room and his.

Where was the man? She knew from experience she would hear him banging about in there as he prepared for bed, but hadn't heard a peep yet, and he'd left the ball before them.

The sound of her bedroom door opening caught Christiana's attention then and she glanced over to see Lisa poking her head in.

"Oh good, you're awake," the younger woman said happily and slipped inside. "I couldn't sleep either. I was too happy and excited."

"About what?" Christiana asked curiously, managing with some effort to gain a sitting position in the bed. Really, things would be much easier if the room would just stop bobbling about.

"You and Dicky," Lisa announced as she settled on the edge of her bed.

It took Christiana a moment to realize that Lisa was answering the question of what she was happy and excited about. The realization made her grimace and snort with disgust. "*Dicky*. Ugh."

"Oh, Chrissy." Lisa sighed and took her hands. "I know that your marriage hasn't been all that you'd hoped for this last year, and that you're upset with him, but it's going to be all right. I promise."

"How?" Christiana asked with disbelief. "The blashted man's alive."

"Yes, and I know you were disappointed about that at first, but everything is going to improve now. You'll see, Chrissy. He loves you." Lisa squeezed her hands. "He does, Chrissy. He has just been tortured by the guilt and loss of his brother. That's why he's behaved so badly this last year."

"What?" she asked with disbelief.

"Don't you see?" she said earnestly. "Poor George died in a house fire in Dicky's home. One he survived himself. He must have been suffering horrible guilt over that afterward. And then he met you and that would have just made it worse, because he fell in love with you and married you and was enjoying a happiness his poor dead brother never would. He must have been racked with guilt, even tortured by it, poor man."

Christiana narrowed her eyes and spoke slowly in an effort not to slur. "Dicky is tortured?"

"Yes." Lisa nodded, looking pleased that she understood.

"So he tortured me?"

Lisa blinked. "Well, yes I suppose."

"That's not love. You don't take out your frustrations and guilt on someone you love." She shook her head. "He doesn't love me."

Lisa was frowning now. "But tortured, guilt ridden men always torture and hurt the ones they love. It happens all the time in the books I read. The hero is tortured and guilt ridden and is just horrible to the woman, but she is good and patient and her pure love is eventually rewarded when he discovers the error of his ways and mends them."

"Dear God," Christiana muttered with disgust. This was all her fault. She should have steered Lisa toward more elevated reading than the ridiculous, romantic and tragic stories she tended toward. Sighing, she said, "That is not a true hero, Lisa."

"But —"

"Would you treat Suzie or me horribly because you were sad?"

"I . . . well, I might be short and snap at you," she pointed out.

"But would you insult us and make ush feel unintelligent or useless? Tell us we had no taste, that no one would want to be our friend except for our title?"

"Well, no, of course not."

"Why?"

"Because I love you," she said and then blinked and breathed, "Oh. I see."

Christiana stared at Lisa silently, finding herself oddly disappointed that she'd won the argument rather than Lisa convincing her that Dicky might have changed. It would have meant her marriage might have a chance, that she might experience his kiss and see if it affected her as much as his mere proximity and touch had. Well, if he was Richard and not George, she reminded herself. She kept forgetting that little possibility. That and the fact that she could have the marriage annulled because it had never been consummated. Surely she didn't want to stay in this horrid marriage?

"But Christiana, can you not give him a chance to change? No one is perfect, and I truly believe he's sorry for what he's done. Besides you are rather stuck in this marriage now."

"That depends on what's on his bottom," she muttered, thinking that if she was married to Richard not George, and he was sorry, perhaps . . . But really, would the marriage change at all? One moment of kindness and holding her on the dance floor hardly meant the marriage might improve. Or did it? She was so confused and really wished she hadn't had those drinks at the ball.

"Not that again," Lisa said on a sigh.

"What?" Christiana asked uncertainly.

"This Dicky's bottom business," Lisa said with disgust.

"Seeing Dicky's naked bottom could fix everything," Christiana insisted, her mood lightening at the very thought. If there was no strawberry, she would know it was George, that he was a cold murderous bastard and that there was definitely no chance for their marriage whether he kissed her or not. Of course, if there was a birthmark, then things would get more complicated. She could still have the marriage annulled, or she could give it another chance and maybe experience his kisses, or she could experience his kisses and not give it a chance. Either way she could have the marriage annulled, she thought and then tried to remember why she had to see the strawberry at all. Oh, that was right. "If there is no strawberry, I'm married to George."

"George is dead," Lisa said patiently. "You cannot marry — Oh, Chrissy."

Christiana peered at the girl, wondering why she suddenly looked alarmed . . . and why there were two of her moving in circles in front of her eyes. Giving her head a shake to try to clear her vision, she asked, "What?"

"Please tell me you are not thinking of ending your own life," Lisa said worriedly.

"Of course not," she said at once, and Lisa began to relax until she added, "I'm ending Dicky's. Or George's." Certainly his life would be over if he was George and what he had done came out. Of course, that was only if Dicky was George and not Richard, she realized and added, "Well, maybe. It just depends on if there's a strawberry or not."

150

Lisa stared at her blankly for several minutes, her lips pursed, then cleared her throat and stood up. "I think perhaps we should talk about this in the morning when your thinking is clearer."

"Very well," Christiana said cheerfully and dropped back in her bed to contemplate how she might see Dicky's naked bottom. It suddenly seemed the most important thing in the world to accomplish it as soon as possible.

CHAPTER SEVEN

Richard pressed an ear to Suzette's door, trying to hear what was happening inside so he could decide how to proceed. He couldn't just knock on the door and ask for Daniel, the man wasn't supposed to be in there. But if anything scandalous was happening in that room, he bloody well would. Suzette wasn't legally his sister, but he felt a certain responsibility to the young woman. She was staying in what was ultimately his home, under his protection, and while he didn't think Daniel would do anything like debauch Christiana's sister, something was holding him up.

He'd barely made out the sound of soft murmurs when the opening of a door further up the hall made Richard straighten abruptly.

Instinct had him shifting quickly away from Suzie's door to prevent being caught loitering outside it and by the time Lisa stepped into the hall from Christiana's room, Richard was walking toward her as if merely heading for his own bed.

"Oh." Blushing at being caught in her nightgown and robe, Lisa managed a weak smile and murmured, "I just wanted to have a word with Chrissy."

"Of course," Richard said as they passed each other. He then continued to the door to his room. Once there, he glanced over his shoulder and — seeing Lisa by her own door, biting her lip as she watched him — he forced a smile and turned the knob . . . only the knob didn't turn.

"Oh! We forgot to unlock it," Lisa said softly and scurried up the hall toward him. She patted her pockets as she came as if the key might be in her robe. Halfway to him, she paused with dismay. "Suzie has the key."

She whirled back as if to rush to Suzette's door to get the key from her sister, but Richard forestalled her by saying, " 'Tis all right. Let her sleep. I will go through Christiana's room. We can unlock the door on the morrow."

Lisa paused and glanced back, then merely stood there looking uncertain. Afraid she might still go to Suzette and catch Daniel inside, he quickly moved to the door of Christiana's room. Richard paused there briefly, but finally murmured good night, opened the door and slipped into Christiana's room.

He had known she would be awake, of course. After all, Lisa had just left. Perhaps it was because of that he'd expected to find her still fully clothed and up, perhaps chatting with her maid. However, a quick glance around the room revealed no maid, and he wondered when the servant had left.

When a soft gasp sounded from his left, Richard turned to spot Christiana in the bed. She popped up into a sitting position at once, and gaped at him with a combination of horror and surprise similar to the expression she'd had on her face at the ball. It seemed obvious he was the last person she'd expect to see here in her room which seemed odd since she thought him her husband. Before he could consider that too deeply, his attention turned to the fact that her bed coverings had slipped to reveal the bodice of her nightgown, a lovely lacy, rose confection that made her slim figure seem fuller. All thought pretty much stopped right then and it wasn't until she grabbed the blanket and yanked it up to cover herself that his brain began to function again, although his thoughts were a little slow, as if moving through molasses.

Finding himself unable to turn away from the vision she made, he began to move sideways in the direction of the door to the master bedroom, murmuring a pained, "Ah."

When she raised her eyebrows, he realized a little more than "Ah" was required here, and managed, "Sorry, just passing through. My door is locked. The other one I mean, the one that leads to the hall. So I'm using this one."

"Oh." Christiana's eyes widened slightly, and then she began to push the linens and blankets aside. "Shuzie has the key to your door. I'll get it."

"No, no," Richard put his hands up in alarm and began to move a little more swiftly, sidling toward the door like a scrabbling crab as more and more of her in the really very attractive gown was revealed. "I'll just go this way. It's fine. You just —" Richard stopped protesting, and rushed forward to catch her as she started to get out of bed, tangled one foot in the bed covers and pitched forward. Fortunately, he reached her in time to prevent her tumbling to the floor, and caught her against his chest instead. He then moved back enough to ask, "Are you all right?"

Christiana stared silently up into his face,

a rather dazed look on her own and he found his attention focusing on her lips, noting that they were full and slightly parted as if awaiting a kiss. He had the sudden mad urge to do just that, press his lips over hers and slide his tongue out to explore her mouth. He may even have followed through on that urge had the strong odor of whiskey not reached his nose. It then struck him that she'd slurred her sister's name and he suddenly remembered the conversation he'd heard while hiding in the room up the hall with Daniel. The women had been talking about some drink or drinks Langley had given Christiana. Hard liquor. The woman was soused.

"Can I see your bottom now?"

Richard blinked at the bizarre request. "What?"

"Did I say that aloud?" she asked with a frown.

A surprised laugh slipped from Richard's lips, and he eased her gently away. "I believe it may be best if you got back in bed, my lady."

"I'll show you yours if you show me mine," she offered, and then tilted her head and muttered, "I think I said that wrong."

"Yes, well," Richard hesitated, an image rising up in his mind of her turning, and yanking her nightgown up. Oddly enough, it was a tempting offer. Giving his head a shake, he urged her toward the bed. "I managed to translate and while it is a most kind offer, I fear I am going to have to refuse it."

She gave a long sigh, "It always works with Lisa."

That brought him to a halt. His voice was choked when he asked, "You and your sister look at each other's bottoms?"

"No, our embroidery," she said with exasperation, "Why would I want to see her bottom?"

"I have no idea," he admitted weakly.

She muttered something under her breath that sounded like "Dumb Earl Dicky" and crawled onto the bed now of her own accord, her silk-covered bottom waving briefly in front of him before she twisted to sit on it. Peering at him then, she frowned. "Wasn't there something I was shupposed to do?"

Richard cleared his throat. "Sleep. You are to sleep, and I am to go to my own room now."

But he just stood there and stared at her sitting in the center of her bed, one strap of the nightgown half off her shoulder, so that the bodice sagged, revealing the top curve of one breast. Had he really thought her unattractive? He must have been stressed at the idea of confronting his brother and not thinking clearly. She seemed to grow more attractive every time he saw the damned woman.

"I'm sure there was something I was supposed to do."

Her fretful words stirred him from his contemplation of what he could and could not see of her bosom, and Richard forced himself to turn and head for the connecting door. "Nothing important, I am sure. Good night."

He stepped into the bedroom, pushed the door closed and then simply leaned weakly back against it.

"Can I see your bottom now?" he murmured her words with disbelief.

Good Lord, the woman was certainly full of surprises. From what he'd seen so far, life with her would never be boring. She'd packed her dead husband in ice and gone off to a ball for heaven's sake. Of course, that had been to help her sisters escape ruin. It wasn't as if the scandal would have troubled her much. Christiana had said tonight's ball was her first, and Daniel had verified it in the carriage on the way to the townhouse. It seemed George and Christiana had not been out in society at all this last year. No balls, teas, no soirees, dinners or plays. And Richard knew why: George had been avoiding society to avoid anyone's twigging to the possibility that he might not be Richard. He supposed the man had planned to avoid society for a year or two and then return after memories had had a chance to fade and the possibility of being caught out was lessened. Which meant Christiana had been forced into seclusion with him, relying on only George for her social outlet.

"Poor woman," he muttered stepping away from the door and then pausing as he realized he was neatly trapped in the locked master bedroom . . . and he'd done it to himself.

"Well hell." He glanced back to the door he'd just closed. Going that way was out. Christiana was wide awake and would just insist on getting the key for him and in so doing discover Daniel in Suzette's room. He didn't want his friend trapped into a marriage to save Suzette's reputation. One of them possibly being stuck in an unwanted marriage was enough.

Richard looked around the room for an alternate escape. He could try to pick the lock of the door to the hall, but suspected there wouldn't be anything in the room to accomplish the task.

His gaze finally turned to the window and he grimaced. It looked like if he wanted to meet up with Daniel and take care of George's body, he would be leaving the room the same way he'd first entered it on arriving here tonight, through the window.

Shaking his head at the tricks fate seemed to like to play, Richard walked quickly to the bedroom window. Someone had closed it since he and Daniel had snuck George's body out of the room. Richard now re-opened it and leaned out to peer about, then straightened abruptly at the sound of the connecting door opening behind him. The abrupt movement had him slamming his head into the window he'd just raised.

Cursing, Richard grabbed the back of his head and rubbed it to relieve some of the pain as he turned to see Christiana crossing the room toward him.

"I just remembered! Your valet is sick. I shall have to help you undress," she announced sounding very cheerful as she walked unsteadily toward him.

"My valet?" Richard asked with confusion.

"Is sick." She grinned widely as if the man's being ill were quite the most wonderful thing.

160

"Oh, yes, of course," he murmured as if just recalling it, and realized he had to be much more careful about such things. There would be much that had happened this last year that he knew nothing about. People he should know that he didn't, conversations he should recall but wouldn't. He would have to be very careful and — Richard's thoughts died abruptly as he felt a tugging at the back of his breeches. Christiana had continued forward until she was now behind him and appeared to be trying to pull down his tight knee breeches.

"What are you doing?" he asked with surprise, wheeling around to face her.

"Helping you undress." She tried to get around behind him again.

Richard turned with her. "There is no need for that. I can manage on my own."

"Do not be silly, Dicky. You died today. You shouldn't undress yourself." She continued to circle him like a bulldog looking for an opportunity to bite, and he just kept turning with her.

Growing dizzy, Richard finally grabbed her arm to stop her, and stated firmly, "Thank you, but I really can manage to —" The words died on an exasperated sigh. The woman wasn't listening. She had given up trying to get to the back of his pants,

161

however, and was now working to remove his dark, double-breasted blue coat. He had undone the buttons before trying to climb the tree earlier. All she had to do was push it off his shoulders, which she now did from the front, rising up on her tiptoes as she did. She wasn't very steady on her feet, however, and ended up leaning against him, her lace covered breasts pressing against his chest as she worked the material off his shoulders and down his arms.

"There." Smiling brightly, she tossed the expensive coat Daniel had bought him only that day to the side. She then set to work on the white, quilted, single-breasted Marseilles waistcoat he'd worn beneath. This time she had to undo the buttons, and Richard tried again to dissuade her from the duty.

"Truly, Christiana. There is no need to assist me. I —" Despite obviously being a little unsteady on her feet due to drink, she was surprisingly quick with the buttons and he paused as she now pushed that off his shoulders as well. This time she did not catch the item of clothing she'd just removed, but let it fall to the floor and simply stood staring wide-eyed. He was now bare from the waist up except for his cravat.

"Oh my," she breathed finally with something like surprised wonder. "What big shoulders you have."

"Er . . . aye, well . . ." Richard grimaced. She wouldn't have been saying that had she seen him six months ago. He'd been a pitiful shadow of a man after the illness he'd suffered. Fortunately, he'd filled out again since then and was probably more fit now than he had been before George had so disrupted his life and nearly ended it.

Richard shook these thoughts away and glanced sharply to Christiana when she suddenly slid her fingers into the front of his breeches. He thought she was going to try to tug them off from the front as she had tried to do earlier from the back, but then realized she had merely taken hold to steady herself as she dropped to her knees before him.

Even with the hold she had on his breeches, she lost her balance and fell forward, banging her head against his groin before steadying herself. Much to his relief she also then removed her hand from his pants. When she then reached for one of his feet and yanked it out from under him, Richard grunted in surprise and grabbed for the window ledge behind him, leaning heavily against it to stay upright as she lifted his foot between them.

"My, what big feet you have, Dicky."

Richard grimaced. He hated the name Dicky, and would have told her so, but instead grunted again and now held onto the ledge to keep from sliding forward and dropping to his butt as she raised his foot even higher and then rested it against her chest to free her hands so that she could work the buckle of his shoe. Richard simply stared then. His shod foot was nestled between her breasts like a lover's head and he had the sudden mad thought that he'd rather his face was there.

He was actually disappointed when his shoe slid off, until she resettled his now unshod foot against her chest again to set to work on his stockings. Richard stayed completely still, hardly breathing as he stared at the way the curves of her breasts cuddled his stockinged foot. He was hard-pressed not to wiggle his toes to feel the flesh surrounding them, but then his attention was drawn to his legs as she slid both his cotton under-stockings and the top silk ones down at the same time, her fingers gliding over his skin in an unintentional caress.

Richard sighed as she raised his foot to remove the stockings entirely, and then she let the foot drop back to the floor. In the next moment, she'd claimed his other foot, however, and rested it where the first had been. Christiana was equally quick about unbuckling and removing this shoe, and then he again suffered through the innocent caress of her breasts around his stockinged foot and the glide of her fingertips down his leg. It was over much too soon for his liking.

Sighing once she was done, Richard straightened, thinking surely Christiana would consider her duty done now, but apparently not. He was barely upright before she was reaching for the covered buttons on the front of his breeches.

"Christia—" Her name died on a choked gasp as her hands brushed against his groin through the cloth of his breeches as she worked and Richard simply stood there, feeling himself growing beneath this latest unintentional caress and incapable of doing a damned thing about it. Well, Richard supposed he could grab her hands and force her to stop, but frankly, he didn't want to.

Damn. How could such an innocent touch have such an enervating effect on him? He certainly wouldn't be growing were it a valet helping him undress. The thought died as she got his breeches undone and the proof of her effect on him sprang from his opening breeches to nearly slap her in the face.

"Oh my, Dicky, what a big —" Her words died on a startled gasp as Richard grabbed her by the upper arms and yanked her to her feet. The moment he could reach her mouth he covered it with his own.

CHAPTER EIGHT

Christiana gasped with surprise when her husband jerked her upright, and then gasped again when his mouth covered hers. This was definitely an unexpected turn of events. The very last thing she would have expected. Dicky hadn't kissed her since the wedding ceremony, not even on their wedding night during the supposed consummation. And he certainly hadn't kissed her like this. This was . . . her toes curled against the wooden floorboards and a small moan slid unbidden from her lips as his tongue slipped into her mouth and stirred up a wealth of sensation within her.

Who would have imagined a simple kiss could be so arousing? Why had no one told her this? And why the devil hadn't he kissed her like this before? Christiana was sure the last year would have been much less miserable had she had this to look forward to every night.

That was as much thinking as Christiana's poor passion-stunned mind could handle, and those thoughts drifted away to float in the far reaches of her mind as she was consumed by the different points of pleasure suddenly springing to life inside her. This was like their earlier dance times a hundred when it came to excitement level. Her lips were tingling where they met his, her breasts were tingling where they pressed against him, and there was a strange hunger that seemed to be yawning inside her, urging her to stretch and arch her back in his arms. She was so distracted by these things that she hardly noticed when his hands began to move over her. They were simply an extension of the kiss, shivering up and then down her arms. When he moved one hand to press against her bottom through the lace of her gown, urging her tighter against the hardness nestled between them, she went with it, pressing herself as close as she could get and moaning again at the well-spring of reaction it caused in her nether regions. The feeling was so intense that she nearly rubbed herself against the hardness prodding her, but then was distracted by his other hand traveling to and squeezing one of her breasts.

Christiana clutched at his bare shoulders

as Richard kneaded the tender flesh, a long drawn-out groan sliding from deep in her throat that ended in a gasp as he suddenly wrenched the fragile bodice of her night-gown aside to touch her without its encumbrance.

"Oh, Dicky," she cried when he suddenly broke their kiss, and was surprised at how breathless she was.

"Call me Richard," he muttered, dragging his mouth along her neck as he gently pinched the nipple he'd revealed.

"Oh Richard!" she cried dutifully, finger-nails digging into his shoulders. "Oh please."

"Yes," he muttered and suddenly his mouth was replacing his hand at her breast. His lips closed around the nipple, tongue swirling across it briefly before he began suckling, drawing on it and pulling little mewls of pleasure from her.

Christiana was vaguely aware of his hand moving on her bottom, squeezing it and us-ing his hold to rub her against his hardness as she'd wanted to do, but she was so overwhelmed with all the sensations attack-ing her that they were all melting into one raging storm of desire and a million wants. She wanted him to kiss her again, but didn't want him to stop the lovely things he was doing to her breast to do it, and she wanted him to do the same to her other breast at the same time, and she wanted free of her nightgown so that she could feel him against her more fully, and she wanted . . . she didn't know what, but she wanted something to end this sweet torture and yet didn't want it ever to end at the same time.

Desperate to ease one of the wants raging inside her, Christiana raised one leg, half wrapping it around his hip in an effort to get closer to the hardness rubbing so excitingly against her. She then groaned with pleasure at the increased pressure. He was rubbing against the very center of her now, the cloth of her nightgown the only barrier and it only added to the pleasant friction.

Richard groaned in response, the sound vibrating across the flesh of her breast. He then raised his mouth to claim her lips once more. Christiana closed her eyes and kissed him back the best she could, opening for him and then instinctively sucking on his tongue as it invaded her. She felt his hands shifting their position on her, but grunted in surprise when he suddenly grasped her by the waist and lifted her. She instinctively wrapped her other leg around him then, holding on by hooking her ankles together behind his back as the room suddenly spun around them, a whirl of color, light and shadow.

Christiana was vaguely aware that he was carrying her across the room, but this new position opened her to the caress of his hardness and had her hard-pressed to compose much in the way of thought. She was very disappointed when he paused after only two steps and set her carefully back on her feet.

"What — ?" she began uncertainly, but paused when Richard bent to untangle the knee breeches that she hadn't fully removed and had gathered about his ankles. Understanding struck her then, and her next thought was the strawberry. Leaning forward, she managed a quick peek before he shifted position and started to rise. Christiana straightened at once, but she was pretty sure she'd seen a red mark on his behind. She had married Richard Fairgrave, the Earl of Radnor, not his brother. He wasn't an imposter, which was a good thing since she was quite positive the marriage was about to be properly consummated. Now she just had to worry that it would be a bearable marriage bed she'd somehow made for herself in trying to spot the birthmark. Or she could flee the house right now, head to Robert to arrange for a doctor's exam and have the marriage annulled, Christiana reminded herself.

She was nibbling away at her lip, trying to decide what to do, when Richard finished with his task and straightened. A slow smile spread his lips when he saw what she was doing, and he suddenly cupped her face, his voice a husky growl as he said, "Every time I see you do that, it makes me want to nibble your lips too."

"It does?" she asked faintly.

"Mmm hmm," he murmured, proceeding to do just that.

Christiana's eyes drifted closed as he nipped and licked at the swollen flesh of her mouth, and then his lips moved to her ear and he nipped playfully at her lobe as he added, "Your lips and everything else."

"Everything?" she asked in a breathy voice.

"Everything," he assured her, one hand sliding down to press her nightgown between her thighs.

Christiana moaned and trembled as he found the core of her through the cloth. When his mouth suddenly covered hers again, she opened willingly to him, her kiss almost desperate as the tempo of his tongue thrusts matched the caress between her legs, both building an unbearable heat and pressure within her.

"I'll make this up to you," he gasped, suddenly breaking their kiss and removing his hand to lift her by the waist again. "I'll make everything up to you."

"Yes," Christiana breathed. Giving up any thought of annulling the marriage and giving up this heat and passion, she wrapped her legs around him again. Her eyes closed and she dug her nails into his shoulders as he walked forward again and his hardness took up where his fingers had left off.

"I'll be a good husband. I'll make you happy," he assured her, his mouth trailing over her cheek to her ear.

"Oh, yes please," Christiana sighed and it was almost a prayer that it would be so, that her marriage would no longer be the misery it had been, and then he was suddenly easing her onto her back and coming down on top of her. Richard's hips settled in the cradle of her thighs and then he ground himself against her again, this time with all his weight behind it as he rotated his hips, pressed forward and rotated them again, rubbing himself from side to side atop her.

When he suddenly broke their kiss, Christiana opened her eyes, recognizing her room and that it was her bed they lay on, and then Richard distracted her by suddenly latching on to one breast again. Her gown had somehow slid back into place as they'd moved from one room to the other, but he didn't seem to notice, or perhaps he didn't care because he was licking and suckling through the lace and then blowing on the damp cloth and flesh, making her shiver as wave after wave of pleasure slid through her.

"Richard," she moaned, her legs moving restlessly against his in a sort of frustration. While he was still lying on top of her, he was no longer grinding himself against the center of her and she wanted that building pressure again. But then Christiana felt a tickle along her knee and glanced down past his head to see that he had snaked one hand beneath the hem of her gown and was urging it up her legs, his fingers skating along her flesh as he went.

She shivered and wiggled beneath him as his fingers ran along the inside of her thigh, moving higher and higher in a teasing caress. When his hand stopped just short of the core of her, which seemed to her to be screaming for his touch, she dug her fingernails into his back and shifted with frustration, a low groan rumbling in her throat.

Richard nipped lightly at the nipple he was ministering to then, but finally allowed his hand to move again, the rough pads of his fingers gliding across her skin.

"Oh God!" Christiana cried out when he finally brushed lightly over the center of her.

"Not God, Richard," he said in a teasing voice from her breast, surprising a laugh from her that ended in a gasp as he touched the core of her again, this time more firmly. Her hips bucked instinctively in invitation and reaction, and then Christiana became aware of his other hand tugging at the bodice of her gown.

Eager to help, she pulled the gown off her shoulders and then shimmied a little to get the bodice off and push it down out of the way around her waist. Even as she did it, her hips were moving to a different rhythm, dancing under the caress of his fingers, but she stiffened in surprised confusion as she felt something pressing into her even as he continued to caress her.

"Richard?" she said uncertainly, not sure what he was doing.

His response was a soothing murmur as he raised his head to claim her lips once more and then his tongue was thrusting into her mouth in time with the invasion taking place below. The combination didn't so much soothe her worry as overwhelm it and she soon found herself responding to both caresses, kissing and sucking on his tongue as her heels dug into the bed and raised her hips into the other touch.

Under this onslaught it was only a matter of moments before Christiana was a trembling mass of need, her body demanding more as she strained toward something she couldn't quite define or understand. And then in the next heartbeat she understood as her world rocked under an explosion of pleasure so intense her whole body vibrated with it.

Tearing her mouth from his, Christiana cried out and then turned her face into Richard's shoulder and bit down, holding on to him with everything she had for fear he'd leave her to drown in this swell of sensation. However, Richard held her as she rode the waves, and only once the worst of her trembling passed, eased from her embrace.

Spent and lethargic, she opened her eyes to see what he was doing and then gasped in surprise when he reached for her nightgown and quickly tugged it gently from where it had pooled around her waist and hips, removing it from her completely.

Christiana felt herself blush, but raised her hips to allow the material to be removed. He tossed the material aside and then rejoined her in the bed, climbing between

176

her legs and urging them wider apart as he crawled up her body.

Richard stopped to press a kiss to the curve of one hip along the way and Christiana sighed as the gentle caress caused a tingling to erupt there and spread outward. He then moved further up, pausing to press a kiss to her belly that sent it jumping and rippling with growing excitement. He next took first one nipple into his mouth for a quick suckle and swirl with his tongue before turning his attention to the other to do the same.

By this time Christiana was breathing heavily again, the relaxed satiation of moments ago forgotten and she curled her fingers in his dark, silky hair and tugged lightly. As delightful as what he was doing was, she suddenly wanted Richard's mouth on hers again. He answered the silent demand, shifting further up her body until his hips rested between her thighs and he could reach her mouth with his.

She felt his hips shift and his hardness rub across her core as he claimed her lips in a kiss, and responded by groaning into his mouth and raising her knees again to tilt herself into the caress. Richard chuckled at her eager response, and then nipped her lower lip lightly as he rubbed against her again. Christiana sucked almost desperately at his tongue to keep him from withdrawing it again, however he did, easing it out, only to thrust it back in, this time plunging his manhood into her at the same time.

At least Christiana thought that was what he'd done. She was now full to bursting, her body straining around something much larger than what had invaded her earlier and the only thing she could think was that the very large appendage that had fallen out of his breeches when she'd opened them was now planted firmly inside her.

While Christiana had been ignorant of what exactly the consummation was, she was smart enough to figure out this was it. And she wasn't at all sure she liked it. However, while his tongue withdrew from her mouth, he stayed planted firmly inside her and merely lifted his head to get out in a choked gasp, "You're a virgin."

Christiana peered up at him blankly, wondering at his surprise since they definitely hadn't done this on their wedding night. But then she recalled that he'd had a good deal to drink at the wedding celebrations and it suddenly occurred to her that he might not even be aware that he had never properly consummated the marriage.

Clearing her throat, she pointed out

gently, "I *was* a virgin."

Richard groaned and dropped his face into her neck.

Thinking he was feeling unmanned by the news that he had not consummated the wedding as he'd apparently thought, she patted his back soothingly. "You were quite drunk on our wedding night. I am sure you would have consummated it otherwise."

"I'm sorry," he muttered into her throat. "Had I known I would have gone more slowly, taken more time to better prepare you."

Christiana wasn't sure what he meant by better prepare her, but didn't say so. She simply lay there and patted him again. However, now that the excitement that had possessed her for the past several minutes was fading, she was having second thoughts about what she'd done. And what she was doing. Dear God, she was soothing the man who had made her life so miserable for the last year. Worse than that, she'd actually consummated the marriage. It could not be annulled. What had she been thinking? Unfortunately, she suspected she hadn't really been thinking at all, at least not clearly. She wanted to blame it on the spirits she'd had to drink, but Christiana had felt pretty clearheaded when debating what to do while he was removing his breeches and suspected she hadn't been as affected by the drinks as she'd thought. She'd been more affected by his kisses and caresses. Of course, she hadn't known then that the end would be so disappointing. Really the first part had been lovely, but this last bit rather spoiled the rest.

Sighing, she stopped patting his back, and tried to decide what to do now. Surely it was over? Should he not get off her and leave her to sleep? If she was able to sleep, Christiana thought with a grimace. Rather than sleep she would probably lie here fretting about what she was to say to Robert when next she saw him. Perhaps she could just leave out the bit about the marriage no longer being annullable, and simply say she had decided to uphold her vow, and yes, he has the birthmark. She had seen it. Well, at least she'd managed a glimpse of a somewhat red spot on his behind anyway. It was probably the birthmark.

Christiana frowned, suddenly worried that it might not have been. It had been a brief glimpse and she couldn't say for sure it was a strawberry-shaped birthmark she'd seen. She supposed it could have been a red mark caused by his leaning on the windowsill as she'd disrobed him.

That thought made her frown and she raised her head to try to peer along his back to see if she could see his behind, but of course she couldn't. Her wiggling about in an effort to do so, however, roused Richard. It also had the rather startling effect of resurrecting some of her own passion that she'd thought gone.

Christiana was trying to ignore that, but Richard just made it worse by shifting slightly against her as he raised his head to peer down into her face.

"I am sorry," he said solemnly. "You deserved so much better than what you've had this last year."

Richard sounded incredibly sincere and Christiana looked into his eyes and did not see the cold emptiness she'd become used to. Instead, she again saw the warm concern and sympathy she'd seen in him at the ball. The combination brought the unexpected sting of tears to her eyes. She closed them quickly and turned her head away, swallowing a sudden lump in her throat as well, and then Richard pressed a gentle kiss to each of her closed eyes, the tip of her nose and then finally to her closed lips.

Christiana remained still for a moment under the caress, but then turned her face back and let her lips drift open, inviting him to deepen the kiss. She wanted to experience the passion again, she wanted to forget if only for tonight how miserable he had made her this last year and pretend for a few hours at least that she'd gained the happy ever after that she'd wanted.

Much to her relief, Richard did deepen the kiss, he also began to move, withdrawing from her and then easing back in. At first he was gentle, giving her body the chance to adjust, but then he slid a hand between them and began to caress her again, reinvigorating her already awakening passions until she was again the trembling mass of hunger she had been earlier. Once he'd achieved that, his gentleness gave way to a more vigorous tempo as they both strained for the release she'd just experienced moments ago. This time when Christiana found it, Richard joined her, and they shouted out their pleasure together.

Richard stared at the drapes over the bed, his mind replaying what had just happened. He had kissed Christiana, partially to silence her, and partially because he just couldn't resist doing it. He was only human after all and her unintentional caresses as she'd stripped off his clothes had been rather arousing. Once he'd kissed her, however, that hadn't been enough. He'd been like a house on fire, the flames raging through his body and ravaging his good sense. His only moment of clear thought had been when he'd set her on her feet and bent to finish removing the breeches she'd undone. He had almost put an end to things then and sent her back to her room. However, by then, Richard had wanted her with a passion he hadn't enjoyed even during his first experience as a callow youth. By the time he'd straightened, he'd concluded that if the only way to have her was to uphold the marriage George had initiated in his stead then so be it. It would protect all three women from scandal and he'd have a very passionate partner in his marriage bed. It was more than some men enjoyed.

Richard hadn't expected her to be a virgin, however. Bedding an experienced woman who thought she was your wife and whom you intended to allow to continue to believe that was one thing, slightly inebriated or not. But her virginity had put a whole new slant on things. It meant she'd had a choice. The marriage could have been annulled and probably with a minimum of scandal for her, since as the man he would be the one thought lacking for not bedding her this last year. But he'd taken that choice away with his actions.

Christiana murmured sleepily and shifted slightly where she lay snuggled half on his chest. It was where he'd put her after finding a cloth and water to clean them both after their exertions, an action that had seemed to embarrass and subdue her, which he found rather charming after what they'd just done.

Richard peered down at her with a little sigh. He may not have thought her attractive on first sight, but once she'd got that bug-eyed horrified look off her face she'd been attractive enough, still too thin for his taste, but passable. And when she'd smiled and laughed with Langley and the others as they danced, she'd been more than passable. But she'd been downright irresistible on her knees with his manhood waving in her face, he thought dryly and knew it was that very manhood that had thought so.

Still, looking at her now, her face softened in sleep, Richard acknowledged that Christiana was an attractive woman, adorable even, and he was briefly tempted to rouse her with soft caresses and kisses and take her again. However, there was the little matter of a dead George in the carriage outside his townhouse.

The thought made him grimace and ease

out from beneath the woman who would now definitely remain his wife.

Christiana stirred and murmured sleepily, her hand drifting down to his hip as Richard shifted, and then sliding across his groin in an unconscious caress as he slid out of the bed. The touch was enough to bring his manhood back to life and he had to grit his teeth against the temptation to simply crawl back into bed and forget about George. But that just wouldn't be a smart thing.

His clothes were still in the master bedroom and Richard made his way silently through the connecting door, grateful for the light cast by the dying fire to guide his way. He found the clothes by the window and started to draw them on, but paused as a glance out the window showed an empty street. Daniel's carriage was gone. Shifting his feet, Richard frowned, wondering why the man hadn't come in search of him, or at least waited for him to meet him by the carriage. He then worried over what Daniel would do with the body and briefly considered following in his own carriage to find out, but that would mean rousing the servants and waiting while a carriage was prepared, and really he had no idea where Daniel would take his brother. He wasn't likely to take him to his own townhouse, which meant he would go somewhere else and Richard had no idea where. He could head to Daniel's townhouse and wait to find out, but depending on where Woodrow took the body, he could be waiting for hours. It just seemed better to let the matter go until the morrow. He would go see Daniel first thing and find what he'd done with George, Richard decided.

Satisfied that this was definitely the smartest course of action and that a naked soft and warm woman in the bed in the next room had nothing to do with the decision, Richard dropped his clothes and slid back through the connecting door to Christiana's room. He moved to the side of the bed and peered down at her briefly, noting the way the fire cast light and shadow across her face in slumber, and then she sighed sleepily and rolled onto her back, the bed coverings sliding down off her breasts.

Richard stared at the pale globes briefly, unconsciously licking his lips, and then bent down to catch the edge of the bed coverings and draw them slowly down her body, revealing inch after pale inch of flesh. She *was* too thin and he would have to see about fattening her up, he decided, but she was still mouthwatering and he found himself climbing onto the bed intent on tasting to see if she was as delicious as she looked.

Christiana woke slowly, her body stretching and small mewling moans slipping from her lips before she was even conscious of what was causing them. All she was aware of at first was the pleasure coursing through her body, originating somewhere in her nether regions and sliding out to all points.

Groaning aloud now as she came fully awake, she found herself stretching again, her body arching on the bed and hands reaching blindly for Richard because surely he must be the source, for it was only with him she'd experienced this sweet torture before. It took her a moment to find him, however; the man was not directly atop her as expected and she had to open her eyes before she saw that he was further down her body. It took another moment for her mind to accept what he was doing. The man was not caressing her with his hands or his hardness as he had before, instead it was his head buried between her legs and while she wasn't quite sure what he was doing, it was delicious.

Still, it was also rather embarrassing. The man had his face buried between her legs as if searching for treasure. No one had ever even seen that part of her let alone at such close proximity and it just didn't seem lady-like to recline there while a man examined her quite so thoroughly. Biting her lip, she reached for him, intending to urge him away, but her hands never made it to his head. Instead, they stopped and grabbed for the bedsheets to hang on as something, his tongue she thought, rasped over the center of her excitement. The shock of it had her hips bucking off the bed and a small "ieeee" of startled pleasure slipping from her lips.

Richard chuckled softly at her reaction, the sound vibrating across her tender flesh and sending her scrabbling in an effort to escape the undignified and yet frighteningly exciting whatever it was he was doing. He didn't allow her escape however, but merely caught her thighs in his strong hands, urged them further apart and redoubled his efforts.

"No — Rich— Oh —" The words came out broken and gaspy as Christiana collapsed back on the bed and twisted her head, her fingers pulling at the sheets so violently she feared she would rip them. That fear wasn't enough to stop her tugging, however, as he did things to her Christiana had never even imagined.

Did all husbands do this? Was this what the marriage bed consisted of? Dear God, she'd been missing out on so much, Christiana thought dazedly, finding herself alternately grinding herself into his caress and still struggling to escape it. The depth of passion he was pulling from her was almost terrifying this time, perhaps because she didn't have him to hold on to in this position and as much as her body responded, her mind was looking for an anchor in the storm.

There was no anchor to be had, however, and when he slid a finger inside her to join his tongue's caresses, Christiana screeched and bucked like a wild thing, her body suddenly exploding as wave after hard wave of pleasure tried to pull her under.

Much to her relief, Richard moved up her body after that, crawling to cover her. Christiana immediately wrapped her arms around him, holding on for dear life as her body shivered and quaked beneath his. She groaned and held on even tighter when she felt him enter her, her legs instinctively wrapping around his hips, and her heels digging into his behind to urge him on as he began to build a new fire in her even before the last waves of the first had died. Spent as she was, all Christiana could manage at the start was to cling to him like seaweed, but as her excitement built anew, some of her energy returned and she began to move with him, shifting her hips to meet his thrusts, taking him as deep as she could manage.

While Christiana had been wholly uncertain she liked this part of the consummation when he'd entered her the first time, she now reveled in it, enjoying the way their bodies joined, how he filled her, how her body clung to him, trying to prevent his escape and then welcoming him back at each return. She thought they should do this all night and kept thinking that right up until they both found their release again, and even as she drifted off to sleep once more, satiated, spent and smiling.

CHAPTER NINE

Richard had been pacing Daniel's parlor for several minutes when the other man finally made his appearance. Before he could cry out the "Finally!" that was trembling on his lips, Woodrow rushed forward, saying, "What is it? What's happened? My valet said you told him it was an emergency and urgent that you speak with me."

Richard nodded. "Where is —" he paused to glance toward the still open door and then almost whispered, "— the *you know what?*"

Daniel came to a shuddering halt, his face going blank for a minute before he asked, "You mean —" he too paused to glance toward the door, and then whispered, "— the *you know who?*"

"Aye," Richard said impatiently.

"*That* is your emergency?" he asked with disbelief. "You had my valet roust me from a dead slumber to ask me *that?*"

"Well *you know who*'s whereabouts is rather important to me," Richard said stiffly, and then pointed out, "And I wouldn't have had to wake you from a dead slumber to find out where he is if you hadn't left without me last night."

Daniel dropped into the nearest seat with disgust. "Well what else was I to do? Sit about in my carriage while you gave *you know who*'s wife a tumble?"

Richard stiffened. "She is *my* wife, thank you very much."

"My, we've certainly changed our tune this morning," Daniel said dryly. "Last night you weren't sure you wanted to keep her."

"Yes, well, I changed my mind." He paused to scowl at the man. "How the devil did you know I tumbled her?"

Woodrow's eyebrows rose. "Was it supposed to be a secret? If so, you shouldn't have done it in the front window for anyone on the street to see."

Richard's eyes widened in horror as he realized they *had* been in front of the window at first. How much of Christiana had been on display? Good Lord, what had he been thinking? Richard knew the answer to that well enough. He hadn't been thinking at all, his manhood had been the one in charge last night, his presently very content, well spent manhood.

Richard had woken this morning thinking that marriage to Christiana might be a very fine thing indeed, and he'd been reaching for her again when he'd realized sunlight was peeking through the bedroom curtains. Then, suddenly his brain had managed to speak loudly enough to drown out his manhood and remind him of certain problems that needed dealing with. His brother's body, for instance.

Recalling his intent to hunt down Daniel this morning and find out what he'd done with George, Richard had leapt from the bed, found some clothes in the master bedroom that his twin had obviously purchased, and reluctantly donned them. George had always favored bright, flashy colors while Richard preferred more somber attire. He would have to see about a whole new wardrobe, he thought now.

"Well?"

Richard blinked his thoughts away and glanced to Daniel in question. "Well, what?"

"Are you really planning to keep her?"

"Yes, of course." He settled in a chair with a sigh, and then admitted, "She was a virgin until last night."

Daniel blew out a silent whistle. "That was very remiss of *you know who*."

Richard grunted, not bothering to mention that he'd heard a thing or two in the past that suggested it wasn't so much that George was being remiss in not consummating the marriage, but that he was incapable of it. He hadn't paid much attention to the gossip then, but now supposed it must be true.

"So after a year of misery with *you know who,* whom she thought was you, she just forgave all and fell into your arms last night?" Daniel asked quietly.

Richard heard the reprimand in his friend's voice and scrubbed his face guiltily. Daniel had been there listening at the door when the women had gone past. He too knew about the drink and how it had affected Christiana, so knew exactly what state she'd been in. And while it hadn't seemed that important last night when he'd thought her an experienced woman, now, in the bright light of day with his manhood finally quiet, it seemed rather shameful behavior.

Shaking his head, he muttered with self-disgust. "I took advantage of an inebriated virgin."

Woodrow did not let him off the hook, but left him to wallow in his guilt for several moments before finally clearing his throat and saying, "Well, at least you are going to do the right thing and stand by the marriage."

"Which isn't even a legal one," Richard muttered, and then his eyes widened suddenly. "What if she is pregnant from last night's tumblings? Technically, the child would be illegitimate."

"Well, one time isn't likely to bring about a child," Daniel said soothingly.

Richard grimaced. "True, but it wasn't one time."

"Well even two . . ." He paused as he noted his expression and then said, "Three?"

Richard merely stared back.

"Four?"

Richard remained silent.

"Oh," Daniel said, looking impressed. "Well, she must be very . . . er . . . inspiring. We must just hope she is not equally fertile." When Richard's shoulders slumped, he added, "Or you could marry her to ensure everything was legal."

"We are already supposed to be married," Richard pointed out dryly. "How the devil do I explain the need to marry again?"

Daniel opened his mouth, but then glanced to the door. In the next moment, he'd risen and crossed the room to close it.

As he returned to his seat they exchanged a grimace at having said so much before thinking to close it, and then Daniel suggested, "Rather than present it as a need, perhaps you could suggest to Christiana that you *want* to do it again, as a sort of fresh start to the marriage to make up for this last very bad year. She will think you are the most romantic bugger alive, and you will be assured that any heirs are legal."

Richard raised his eyebrows. "That is actually a good idea."

"I *have* been known to have a good idea or two on occasion," Daniel said dryly, no doubt a bit insulted by his surprised tone.

Richard merely grunted, his thoughts on what exactly he would say to Christiana and how he could convince her.

"And then you could travel to Gretna Green with Suzette and me when we head off to do the deed."

"Yes, we could leave —" Richard paused and blinked. "You and Suzette?"

Daniel cleared his throat. "Er . . . yes."

"You're marrying Suzette?" he asked, just to be certain he wasn't misunderstanding.

"I haven't quite made up my mind, though I am leaning that way," Daniel muttered, picking imaginary lint off his trousers.

Richard considered him silently, his eyes

narrowing as he recalled the passionate embrace he'd stumbled upon and the fact that the man hadn't rejoined him as he'd expected. Just how long had Daniel been in Suzette's room in the end? He tried to work it out, running through the events of the evening.

"I haven't tumbled her," Daniel snapped, apparently reading his thoughts, and then he sighed and admitted, "But it was damned close, and only *you know who's* presence prevented it in the end."

"*You know who* was in the carriage," Richard said at once.

"Yes, well, so were Suzette and I," Daniel muttered.

"You had Suzette in the carriage with *you know who?*" he asked with horror. "Did she know *you know who* was there?"

Daniel grimaced. "Can we not think of another name for him? This is getting annoying."

"Answer the damned question."

"Well, of course she didn't know. Hell, I didn't know until I got in. In fact it was my attempt to distract her from his presence that led to the 'damned close' bit." He sighed and added, "So it's ironic that it was also his presence that brought an end to it."

Richard almost asked how that could be,

197

but then decided he didn't really want to know. Running a hand through his hair, he asked, "If you haven't bedded her, why consider marrying her? It's rather sudden, isn't it? You hardly know the chit."

"Well, I know her as well as you know Christiana and you're marrying her."

"Christiana is a special woman and our situation is not a common one."

"Well Suzette is just as special and our situation is not common either," he shot back, and then sighed. "She proposed to me at the ball, and then when she found me in her room thought I had come to tell her yes. Rather than explain my real purpose in her room I let her believe it because I couldn't come up with an alternate explanation for my presence there. I am still trying to come up with one. But I am also considering her proposal seriously in the meantime."

"Why the devil would she propose to you?" Richard asked with surprise. "She wants a husband in need of money who will agree to her terms."

"Yes, well, I may have misled her as to my financial status," Daniel muttered.

Richard raised his eyebrows. "Why?"

"Because when she asked me about my income I assumed she was just another fortune seeking debutante and lied," he admitted wryly. "You can imagine my surprise when rather than scaring her off, it prompted a proposal."

No doubt he'd also been a little fascinated, Richard realized. They were both used to fortune seeking debutantes and their mothers chasing them about. Other than this last year and a half when he'd been absent, it had happened on a regular basis. A woman who wanted just the opposite would make an interesting change.

"So rather than just tell her that you have money —"

"I have no intention of telling her that, and you'd best not either," Daniel said grimly. "And don't even think about offering to pay off the father's gambling debts. I shall attend those myself whether I marry her or not."

More than a little fascinated, then, Richard thought with amusement, and asked, "Why should I not offer to pay them off? It would remove the pressure the women are under."

"Suzette is not enthralled with the idea of marrying after all she's learned about Christiana's experiences this last year. She may very well bury herself in the countryside and eschew marriage altogether should she learn it isn't a necessity, and I can hardly get to know her better if she is at Madison Manor and I am at Woodrow."

"Ah," Richard murmured, understanding more than his friend was telling. Whether he knew it or not, Daniel had already decided to marry the girl. At least that was his opinion, "Fine, I shall refrain from offering to pay . . . for now."

Daniel relaxed at once. "Thank you."

Richard waved his gratitude away and changed the subject. "The good news is that since I've decided to uphold the marriage to Christiana, we can simply dispose of *you know who.* I was considering our options on the way here —"

"That might not be the best idea," Daniel interrupted quietly. When Richard raised an eyebrow in question, he added, "I think perhaps it would be best not to dispose of him at all yet. At least not until we sort out this business of who killed him."

Richard sat back with a frown. "Why? It is not as if he can be a witness in his own murder."

"No, but we cannot prove murder without a body," Daniel pointed out and then added, "Whoever poisoned him will soon think they failed, if they don't already. They will try again."

"Then I shall have to be careful," Richard

said grimly. "But I see no need to keep *you know who* around until we catch his killer. We can charge whoever it is with attempted murder when they try to kill me."

Daniel frowned. "It just seems to me to be smarter to keep *you know who* around until we have it all sorted out."

"Very well," Richard said finally. "Have you hidden him somewhere safe?"

"Er . . . well, actually no," he admitted, looking uncomfortable. "I placed him in the pavilion in the back garden for the night."

"In the . . . ?"

"It was the only place I could think of. I needed somewhere cold but covered, and that was all I could come up with at the time. But he shall have to be moved before too much longer."

"Yes, he definitely needs to be moved," Richard agreed grimly.

"I had an idea about that too."

"Do tell," Richard requested dryly.

Daniel ignored his sarcasm. "I thought it might be best to put him back in the master bedroom."

"*What?* You —"

"Now hear me out before you protest," Daniel insisted, and then explained, "The girls have already seen that 'Dicky' is gone and so believe you are you . . . which of course you are. They also know the bed is now in ruins thanks to the ice they packed around who they thought was you. So, we dump him back in the bed, you keep the windows open to cool the room, and then lock off the doors and keep the keys. Then you say you have ordered a bed to replace the ruined one and that no one should bother entering the room until it arrives and the chamber can be set to rights." He sat back with satisfaction before adding, "That way he is close at hand if we need him for proof of anything, and yet out of the way of being found."

"I suppose that could work," Richard said thoughtfully.

"It will," Daniel assured him. "The only real problem I see is getting him out of here and back to your townhouse in broad daylight." When Richard raised his head at the suggestion, he said, "He has to be moved soon. One of the servants might decide to take a turn around the gardens and stumble upon him before the day is out."

"Damn." They had to move the body and quickly, but the question was how did one move a body about in broad daylight without anyone knowing it was a body? He lowered his head to consider the problem, his eyes staring blindly at his own feet briefly before they focused on the patterned rug under them. Smiling, he raised his head. "You don't happen to have an old rug you don't mind getting rid of?"

The sound of the door opening and closing stirred Christiana from sleep and she rolled over in bed to peer toward it, coming more awake when she saw Grace crossing the room toward her.

"Lord Langley is here and asking to see you," the maid said solemnly.

Christiana stiffened where she lay and then cast a quick glance to the other side of the bed to see that Richard was no longer there.

"He left nearly an hour ago," Grace announced as she gathered a fresh gown for her to wear.

"Oh," Christiana murmured, immediately assaulted by a variety of emotions. Not one of them good. Dawn was casting a harsh light on the situation at hand and forcing her to acknowledge that she had consummated the wedding with her husband, who may or may not be her husband, because she still was not sure if it was actually a birthmark on his behind that she'd glimpsed. Brilliant.

Worse than all of that, though, was that while she was now sober, lying alone in her bed with Grace there looking so grim, and the light of day shining through the windows and spotlighting her in her shame, had she woken naturally and alone with Richard, Christiana knew she might very well have merely rolled over, cuddled up close and begun to kiss and caress him awake to initiate another round of the consummation. It was how he'd woken her several times in the night and her body wanted it again even now. Just the thought of it was making her breasts tighten with desire. What they'd done had been that delicious, the excitement and pleasure he had shown her that addictive.

"Should I tell Langley you are unavailable?" Grace asked, setting a basin of water on the small table beside the bed.

Langley. Christiana grimaced, her shame increasing at the thought of talking to Robert. Here he had been trying to get her out of her miserable marriage and she had ensured that there was no way that she could. Dear God, she wished she'd never . . . well, she wasn't sure what she wished. Having tasted such pleasure, it was hard to wish she hadn't. God, her body ached in places she hadn't known it could, but she'd never

204

felt so physically replete. Christiana supposed the truth was she wished this was the first morning after her wedding and that the last year hadn't taken place, that she still had a chance of happiness, of enjoying the pleasure she'd experienced last night again and again and sharing a life full of laughter and joy with Richard . . . who would have to be Richard for certain, of course.

"I shall tell him you are still asleep," Grace decided for her and turned toward the door, but Christiana forced herself to sit up.

"No," she said on a sigh as she pushed the blankets away. There was no sense putting off this meeting. She may as well get the unpleasantness over with and out of the way and see what could be salvaged from it.

"Are you sure? I could —"

The way Grace's words died so abruptly as Christiana rose from the bed, made her glance toward her curiously. The maid was staring at the bed and the small splotches of blood that had been revealed when she'd pushed the bed covers aside to get up. The evidence of what had taken place last night, Christiana realized with a grimace and felt herself blush when Grace's sharp eyes turned her way.

"I knew he'd slept in here, his bed was ruined by the ice, but —" She paused, anger filling her face. "He took advantage of your inebriated state?"

Christiana grimaced and turned away, aware that she was blushing. Having no idea what to say, she moved to the basin of water and simply murmured, "He is my husband."

Grace snorted angrily and began to strip the bed. "This blood proves he has been less than a husband this last year. I suspected he had not visited your bed since the wedding, but I thought that night, at least, he'd done his duty. The devil!" she added with disgust. "Why could he not stay dead?"

Christiana bit her lip as she picked up the clean bit of linen, dipped it in the perfumed water and began to wash herself. She'd wondered the same thing many times last night. Well, at least she had before Richard had kissed her. She suspected she would have protested vociferously at his dying in the middle of their exploits, but she was certainly now thinking it would have made things much simpler.

"And look what he did to you!" Grace said with dismay, leaving the bed for now and hurrying to her side.

Christiana glanced around with confusion at that cry and then followed Grace's gaze over her body, her own eyebrows rose slightly as she saw that her body bore several dark red marks and even a faint bruise or two. She didn't recall how she'd got them and certainly hadn't felt any pain at the time. While Richard had been cruel and cold this last year, she didn't think he'd marked her deliberately last night, but the activities had got very vigorous at times and she knew she'd scored his back more than once during their more passionate moments.

" 'Tis all right." Christiana turned back to her washing. "They do not hurt."

Grace was silent for a moment and Christiana could almost hear the rant the maid wanted to let loose. Much to her relief, however, she didn't but returned to the bed, taking out her anger by almost ripping the bedsheets from it, no doubt imagining it was Richard and she was ripping his flesh off. Grace had been her mother's lady's maid before her and had become Christiana's on her mother's death. She had watched her grow up and had a great deal of affection for her, an affection that was returned. She also had something of a temper.

Both women were silent as Grace helped her dress. Confused and miserable herself, Christiana did nothing to end it, but was grateful to escape the room once she was dressed and ready. She wasn't exactly eager to have the conversation she knew was coming with Langley, however, so didn't rush downstairs. Unfortunately, despite dragging her feet, she did eventually arrive at the parlor, where Langley paced the floor as he waited. He stopped the moment she entered the room though and his first word was, "Well?"

Christiana felt her lips twitch into a grimace, and then turned back and closed the parlor door. It wasn't quite the done thing for a married woman to be in a room alone with a man who wasn't her husband and have the door closed. But it did seem smarter than leaving it open so that anyone passing might hear their conversation. Turning back to the room, she moved to sit primly in a chair and then just sat there, not sure what to say or how to start.

"Well?" Langley repeated, sitting on the corner of the couch. "Does he have the birthmark?"

Christiana felt her lips twist and lowered her head. After all that had happened last night she should be able to say yes or no, however she just wasn't sure. She wished she'd taken a closer look, or thought to try again later, but once passion had overcome her the last thing she'd cared about was getting a look at his bottom. Squeezing it with her hands to urge him on, and digging her heels into it as he drove his body into hers, yes, but look at it? It just hadn't been high on her list of priorities as he'd kissed and caressed, kneaded and touched, buried his face between her legs and drove her to, and then over the edge of madness before plunging his body into hers and driving her there again, and again, and —

"Christiana? Are you all right?" Langley asked with concern. "You are suddenly quite flushed."

Torn from her increasingly feverish recollections, she blinked and then glanced around and waved her hand in front of her face, asking, "Is it hot in here? I feel over warm."

"Er . . . I do not think so. It seems fine to me," Langley assured her and then asked a touch impatiently, "Did you get the chance to see if he has the birthmark?"

Christiana opened her mouth to say no, but then stopped, because that would be a lie. The truth was, of course, that she *had* had the chance, she'd just been too preoccupied with other things to take it. Finally, she said, "I am not sure if he has the strawberry or not."

Langley sat back with a sigh of disappointment, but then just as quickly sat forward again. "Well, we shall just have to think of another way to find out. I was worried sick last night about the three of you here in this house with him. I'll take you, Lisa and Suzie away today. You can stay at your father's townhouse while I arrange for an exam and an annulment."

"Er . . ." Christiana cleared her throat and then murmured, "I don't think there can be an annulment."

"Of course there can. The marriage hasn't been consummated."

"Well . . . yes, well, that's the thing," she muttered, "Last night I was trying to see the strawberry and — Well, I was trying to see it — I fear the alcohol had something of an effect on me, I — he — we definitely hadn't consummated it on the wedding night," she ended lamely.

"What are you trying to say, Christiana?" Langley asked slowly, looking like he already knew what she was saying but didn't want to believe it.

"We consummated last night," she blurted finally.

"Dear God," he groaned, closing his eyes, and then immediately opened them again and asked, "How could you?"

"Rather easily as it turned out," she muttered, and felt herself blushing.

Langley rubbed his forehead as if it were suddenly aching, and then sighed and sat up. "Okay. We shall have to force him into divorce then. We will pretend to be lovers, and flaunt the supposed relationship openly until he has no choice but to demand a divorce. There will be more of a scandal, but at least you will be safe. I —"

"Safe?" she interrupted sharply.

He frowned. "Well, surely you realize that if it is George, then it's possible Richard's death may not have been an accident."

Actually, she hadn't realized that, Christiana thought faintly. It simply hadn't occurred to her that George could envy Richard so much he might kill him to take his place. She'd just assumed that Robert was worried that George had taken advantage of what was an accident.

"Chrissy?"

"Just a minute, I must think," Christiana muttered.

Langley paused and waited, his expression questioning and she bowed her head, trying to gather her scattered thoughts. She was taken aback somewhat by his suggestion. It put a whole new slant on things. At least, it did for a moment, but as her mind raced over the events from the night before, her thoughts began to clear a little. While she might have believed the man she'd lived with this last year capable of such a thing, she just found it impossible to believe that the man who had been so considerate and kind at the ball, and then such a patient and giving lover last night, could have killed his own brother out of envy.

Christiana grimaced as she realized she was separating his good behavior from his bad behavior rather than considering it all as a whole, but that was how she was starting to think when it came to her husband. There was the Dicky she'd lived with this last year who she could believe would have done such a thing, and would be happy to find some way to escape. And then there was the sweet, considerate and passionate lover, Richard, from last night. The problem was she had no idea which man he was, and who she would be confronted with the next time they met. Would he be the Dicky who was so mean and cold to her, or the lover Richard? And if it was Dicky by day and Richard by night, was it worth spending her days in a sort of hell to enjoy nights of heaven?

She supposed that didn't really matter. The marriage was consummated, so unless it turned out Richard was really George, the marriage would stand firm. She would never allow Robert to sacrifice himself by pretending to be her lover to gain her a freedom she'd lost through her own wanton desires. Though she had to admit the very fact that he would even suggest it was touching. She didn't doubt that he'd carry it out if she agreed. She also knew without a doubt that he'd make the same offer to both Suzette and Lisa were they in similar situations. Truly, he was the best of friends, a brother in every way but blood . . . and she couldn't allow him to ruin himself for her.

"Chrissy?" Langley prompted again.

Christiana sighed and finally just said, "Why do we not just wait a bit? I am sure I can get to see his bottom tonight. I will make sure I do, and then we shall decide what is best from there."

"Christiana," he began sternly, but it was as far as he got, for the door opened just then and Lisa and Suzette entered.

"There you are," Lisa trilled brightly as she led Suzie to join them. "Haversham said Robert was here. Why was the door closed?"

Christiana blinked in surprise at the scowl Lisa cast on both her and Langley for such an impropriety. Lisa rarely scowled at anything or anyone. "I'm afraid I closed it

213

without thinking when I entered. Come sit down, I was just about to ask Langley if there are any balls we should attend tonight."

As the two girls took their seats, Christiana turned a warning glance to Langley. She didn't want the conversation to continue in front of her sisters. She really didn't want to discuss it anymore at all, at least, not unless Richard didn't have the strawberry birthmark. Then, she supposed there would be a lot of discussion going on.

Fortunately, Robert obeyed her silent plea and began to discuss balls.

"I hear voices."

Richard paused in the entry at Daniel's hissed words. After listening for a moment, he relaxed. "It is coming from the parlor. It sounds like the women are all in there, which means we won't run into them upstairs."

"Right, well that's something," Daniel grunted, shifting his hold on his end of the carpet-rolled George.

Nodding, Richard started forward again, moving quickly toward the stairs. George was a lot heavier with the added weight of the carpet around him and no doubt they would both be relieved to set him down. He just hoped they managed to do so without encountering anyone.

They made it up the stairs and were moving quickly up the hall with their burden, Richard thinking they might just manage the task undiscovered, when Haversham appeared from the master bedroom and started in their direction. Richard heard Daniel curse under his breath behind him and silently echoed the sentiment, but kept calm. It wasn't like they were carting a naked, dead George about for anyone to see. He was wrapped in the carpet after all. No one could tell he was in there, Richard assured himself. They would just carry the rug past as if nothing were amiss. That was the plan anyway, however, Haversham put an end to it by stopping in the middle of the hall directly in front of him, forcing Richard to a halt.

The elderly butler peered at the rolled up and slightly bulgy carpet, raised an eyebrow and then peered at Richard and asked, "Would you like me to send for a couple of footmen to help you with that, my lord?"

"Er . . . no," Richard forced a smile. "I — we are just — it's a bit chill in my room and Lord Woodrow offered this carpet to take away the worst of the chill."

"Hmm." Haversham nodded solemnly.

"The ladies had a similar problem just yesterday."

Richard frowned at his words, but before he could ask what the man meant by that, the butler continued.

"I would venture to suggest that closing the window of a night would help warm the room as well, my lord . . . which I just did. I noticed it was open as I was inspecting the bed. The upstairs maid feared it was quite ruined. I came to see what could be done, however it looks as if it somehow got quite soaked through."

"Oh . . . er . . . yes. It . . . er . . . I . . ." Grimacing, he simply said, "Don't worry about the bed, Haversham. I've ordered a new one and will just sleep with Lady Christiana until it arrives. I mean in her room, not — well, not that there is anything wrong with a husband sleeping with his wife, I just —"

"What his lordship means to say," Daniel interrupted Richard's bumbling. "Is that he will reside in Lady Christiana's room until his own bed is repaired. That being the case there is really no need for the maid to worry about his room at all for the time being. In fact, he will probably just lock the doors for now so she doesn't waste her time dusting an unoccupied room."

"Yes. Exactly. What he said," Richard muttered uncomfortably. Really, he tended to avoid lying because he wasn't very good at it. He supposed he didn't feel it was a very honorable ability anyway so had never practiced it.

"Ah." Haversham looked extremely solemn as he nodded. "Very good, my lord. I shall tell the staff to leave the room be until you say otherwise."

"Thank you." He smiled his relief and then steered around the man, eager to continue up the hall.

"Shall I tell Lady Christiana you are returned and will join the ladies and Lord Langley in the parlor soon?"

"Oh, no, that's all right. I — Lord Langley, you say?" he interrupted himself to ask as the name registered in his head. Pausing again, he frowned back at the butler.

"Yes, my lord. He arrived some time ago asking to speak to her ladyship and has been cloistered in the parlor with her and her sisters for some time now."

Richard felt his eyes narrow. "He has, has he? Well, yes, please tell her I shall join them shortly."

"Very good, my lord." The butler turned smartly and headed for the stairs, apparently to do just that.

Richard scowled after him, contemplating that Langley was here in his home, cloistered in the parlor with his wife and her sisters. And the man had asked for Christiana when he arrived. He'd also danced with her twice last night at the Landon ball, appearing very protective and caring of her as he did. Richard hadn't cared for it much at the time, but he liked it even less after spending the night with Christiana and deciding the marriage would continue. She was his now and he wasn't having Langley —

"For God's sake, Richard. Are we going to stand here all day? This *rug* is heavy."

"Oh, right," he muttered and began to move again. The sooner they had taken care of George, the sooner he could get down to the parlor and let Langley know Christiana was his.

CHAPTER TEN

Langley was answering about the hundredth question from Suzette on Lord Woodrow's character when Haversham cleared his throat, drawing their attention to his presence in the parlor doorway.

"Yes, Haversham?" Christiana asked as Langley paused in his answer.

"Lord Fairgrave has returned. He and Lord Woodrow shall be joining you here shortly, my lady."

"Daniel's here?" Suzette asked.

"Yes, my lady," Haversham said solemnly, and noting the way she was suddenly peering past him, added, "He is assisting his lordship in carrying something to the master bedroom."

"Oh." Suzette frowned, apparently not pleased with the news. Christiana noted that in an absentminded way, but her own thoughts were taken up with the announcement and what should be made of it. It was just so out of character for Dicky to have her informed of his return. He usually just appeared when he wished to, and disappeared just as abruptly without explaining anything. This was very thoughtful and completely unlike his behavior to date.

Realizing that the butler was waiting to be dismissed, Christiana murmured, "Thank you for relaying the message, Haversham."

"Of course, my lady." Haversham nodded solemnly and then turned to move away.

Christiana sighed and glanced back toward the others but her mind was in a bit of an uproar. Dicky was back. Richard, she reminded herself. He'd asked her last night to call him that and so she would.

"There!" Lisa said brightly. "Dicky's going to join us. That will be nice, won't it?"

Christiana glanced to her younger sister, noting the silent pleading on the girl's face, and sighed to herself. Lisa was silently asking her to give the man a chance to prove he'd realized the error of his ways and changed. And last night had certainly been like nothing she'd ever experienced in her marriage to date so he might very well have done so, but what was to stop him from changing again? Would it be Dicky, the nasty husband she'd lived with this last year who joined them, or last night's lover, Richard?

Aside from that, there was the whole "does he have a strawberry on his bottom" issue to worry about as well. The man might really be George, a murderer of his own sibling. Honestly, it was all enough to make a woman want to scream and pull her hair out. Surely, most wives did not have such issues with their husbands. How had she landed in such a tangled marriage?

"Chrissy?" Lisa asked and Christiana stood abruptly.

"I should have asked Haversham to have a tray prepared and brought to us. I shall do it now," she announced and hurried out of the room.

Christiana spotted Haversham about to enter the kitchen at the end of the hall when she stepped out of the parlor, and hurried to catch up to him to make her request. Once the task was done, however, she headed upstairs. Christiana simply could not stand to wait and worry about whether he had the birthmark or not, and what kind of mood he would be in when he arrived in the parlor. She wanted to find out both things at once and she wanted to do so in private rather than with witnesses.

Although, if she were to be completely

honest with herself, Christiana had already decided it must have been the birthmark she'd seen and that seeing it again would just be a formality. Because she simply couldn't believe the man who had held her in his arms and given her such pleasure could be a killer. That left her real worry being how Richard would treat her when next they met. This first meeting would tell her if she had made the biggest mistake of her life last night, or a smart decision.

Christiana didn't head straight for the master bedroom, but stopped in her own room to check her hair and make sure it was still in the nasty, tight bun Grace had automatically fixed it into that morning. Dicky — Richard, she reminded herself — would berate her if every hair was not in place and that was not a good way to start. She suddenly stopped dead as she realized what she was thinking.

Dear God, she was already falling back into the dutiful wife mold! Worrying about her hair being perfect so as not to upset Dicky — Richard? Well, she was done with that, Christiana reminded herself grimly. She'd experienced a few hours of freedom from her husband when she'd thought him dead, and that brief taste of freedom, along with the love and support of her sisters, had made her find her backbone once more.

Straightening her shoulders, she determinedly turned and strode purposefully across the room. She had paused at the door to the master bedroom and half-raised her hand to knock before she caught herself. She was supposed to see his bottom as soon as she could so if she entered without knocking and caught him changing or something of the like, it would actually be a good thing, Christiana told herself as she opened the door without knocking and walked in.

He wasn't half naked mid-change or anything of the like. Instead, he and Daniel were talking quietly as they crossed the room in her direction. Both men paused abruptly at her appearance, however, eyes widening with alarm as if they'd been caught doing something they shouldn't. Christiana felt her eyebrows crawl up her forehead at the strange reaction and glanced curiously from one man to the other.

"Ah." Daniel was the first to speak. His eyes moving to Richard he asked, "Should I . . . ?" He shifted his gaze over his shoulder in a silent question she didn't understand.

"No. That's all right. Go ahead," Richard said quietly. Apparently he understood the question.

Frowning, Christiana peered in the direction Daniel had glanced, but didn't see anything but the bed. It looked quite lumpy, but then Grace had said it had been ruined by the soaking from the melting ice. The other servants were apparently speculating on how the bed had come to be soaked as it was, but she doubted they'd ever come up with the truth. Christiana, her sisters and Grace themselves had gone out to fetch back the ice to avoid involving the other servants.

"Christiana?"

She blinked her thoughts away to realize that while she'd been wool gathering, Daniel had exited through the door she'd left open and Dicky — Richard — was now standing directly in front of her. His expression was questioning, but she couldn't help noticing that his eyes were locked on her mouth and darkening with a heat she recalled from the night before. It brought an answering heat to life inside her.

"You must be terribly uncomfortable with your hair pulled so tight," he murmured suddenly and reached up to begin removing hairpins.

"It's the way you insisted I wear it," Christiana reminded him, irritation slipping in to nudge aside a bit of the awakening heat.

224

"Then I was an idiot," he said simply as he finished freeing her hair and allowed the now loose strands to fall around her face. He smiled with approval. "Much better."

It felt much better too, she acknowledged with a sigh as the pressure was released from her scalp, but her eyes widened as he now caught her face between his hands and lifted it so their gazes met. They widened even further when he asked, "No kiss of greeting for your husband?"

Before she could respond, his mouth was on hers, coaxing that greeting from her. Christiana remained completely and utterly still at first, confusion rampant inside her head as memories from this last year of life with this man collided with the new reality. She wanted to push him away and demand some explanation for everything, for how he could have treated her as he had this last year, for how he could now treat her so differently. Unfortunately, her body had memories of its own from last night and didn't appear to care much about the worries her mind had. It urged her to just kiss the man. After all a good wife would, surely?

When his tongue traced a line across her closed lips and then tried to snake between them, Christiana gave in with a sigh and opened to him . . . and was lost. Suddenly, her body was on fire, her back arching, hips pressing forward to grind herself against his growing hardness, and her arms went up to allow her fingers to run through his hair.

When she then clutched at the strands to urge him to deepen the kiss even further, Richard's response was to release what sounded almost like a growl into her mouth. Christiana shivered in response and then moaned as his hands dropped away from her face to begin traveling over her body. One hand dropped to her bottom, urging her more tightly against him. The other slid to her breast, squeezing her through her gown and she gasped and twisted in his hold, pressing her breast more firmly into his touch and rubbing against his lower body with unfettered desire.

This was not the reaction she'd feared on meeting him, but it was still a damned good thing she'd met him in private, Christiana decided as the hand at her breast began to tug impatiently at the neckline of her gown to free her breast. Had they met in the parlor with everyone there, she wouldn't have been able to reach down between them and squeeze his now rock hard manhood through his trousers as she now did.

Richard's reaction to the touch was startling. Tearing his mouth from hers on a curse, he muttered, "I have to be inside you. Now."

Despite her confusion over the state of her marriage and identity of her husband, Christiana panted a breathless "Yes," and then gasped and clutched at him as he picked her up by the waist, carried her to the bed and tumbled them both onto it.

Richard was immediately kissing her again. Christiana kissed him back. However, it was now more of an automatic response without the earlier passion behind it, she was a bit distracted by whatever it was she'd landed on in the bed. It was hard and had hit right at the base of her spine so that her back was arched unpleasantly over it. She felt like she was lying across two small logs and it was really killing the passion that had so quickly stirred.

Turning her head to the side, she managed to tear her mouth from his and muttered, "Richard."

"Yes." The word was slightly muffled and distorted as his lips trailed down her neck.

"There's something — Oh," Christiana gasped with a start as he suddenly tugged her bodice down and latched onto the nipple he revealed. When he began to suckle and draw on it, she bit her lip and closed her eyes against the firestorm that set off inside her, but after the first shock of pleasure even that wasn't enough to fully distract her from her discomfort. Frowning, Christiana reached to feel what she lay on, hoping she might be able to tug it out from under herself, but whatever she lay on was under the covers and extended out to the side away from her.

Richard had apparently been drawing her skirts up as he worked at her breast. When he suddenly released her nipple to slide down her body and duck under the voluminous material, her attention was immediately reclaimed by what he was doing.

"Oh — er — Rich— oh —" Christiana gasped, clutching at the bedclothes as he kissed a trail up one thigh. This definitely managed to distract her from whatever she lay on, and she clenched her teeth against the tingles of excitement he was causing in her, preparing for the much stronger shock of pleasure she knew was coming as he neared the apex of her thighs. Even so, she cried out when his mouth finally found her center. It was the lightest of caresses, almost a teasing, but still had her half sitting up, her hands clawing at the bedclothes and drawing them away from both ends of the bed toward herself. The position immediately removed the discomfort at her back and Christiana felt a moment's relief until his mouth brushed over her again and she turned her head to the side, gasping for the breath that had seemed to rush out of her with the touch. The moment she'd drawn in enough breath, however, it whooshed right back out on a shriek as she found herself staring at Richard, now half uncovered in the bed, and definitely not looking very healthy.

The Richard under her skirt stilled and suddenly pulled out from under it, his expression surprised as he said, "Well, that was fast."

Christiana's response was to turn wide eyes his way and shriek again. She followed it up by planting her foot in his chest and shoving him away from her with a strength born of horror. Then she leapt off the bed and made a run for the door.

Richard landed on the hardwood floor with a startled curse and immediately sat up to peer toward his wife, only to find her scrambling off the bed . . . a bed where George lay half uncovered and most definitely dead. Cursing much more violently this time, Richard bounded to his feet and hurried after Christiana. Fortunately, she'd made a run for the door to the hall and it was locked. She was wrestling with it, trying desperately to get it open when he caught her arm.

"Christiana, wait, listen to me."

"Don't touch me," she cried, shaking off his hold. Giving up on the door, she backed quickly away from him, panic on her face as she glanced at him and to the bed and back.

"All right, I won't touch you," Richard said quietly, hoping that if he remained calm, she would calm down as well. " 'Tis all right. You are safe with me. All is well."

"All is well?" she echoed with disbelief, not sounding the least bit calmed by his voice. "Who are you?"

"I am Richard Fairgrave, the Earl of Radnor," he said solemnly.

"Then who is that?" she asked, pointing toward the bed.

Richard noted the way her hand was shaking, and sighed at her unnecessary upset. This was all his fault. He was the one who had fallen on her like a randy bull and then apparently lost all sense as the blood rushed to his manhood. That was the only explanation he could come up with for how he could have been stupid enough to try to tumble her on the bed where his dead brother lay. Good Lord, he'd completely forgotten all about the man's presence, able to think only of the nearest horizontal surface and getting her onto it and himself in her.

"That," he said wearily, "is my twin brother George."

Richard supposed it would have been too much to hope that Christiana would suddenly relax, and say, "Oh that's all right then, let's go to my room and finish what we started." But really, his still aching manhood would have been grateful for it. However, instead her eyes narrowed suspiciously and there was a sudden pinched look about her lips that assured him explanations were in order.

He ran a weary hand through his hair and said, "A little over a year ago I returned home to the sound of a muffled scream from the rooms above stairs. I rushed up to see what was about and found my valet struggling with four attackers. Unfortunately, I was too late to aid him. Even as I reached my room, one of them slit Robbie's throat and let him drop on the bed to die. I had grabbed up a bust from the entry on the way upstairs and brought it down on the skull of the man who had killed Robbie. I think it killed him instantly. Even so, there were still three men to my one and after a bit of a struggle they managed to subdue me.

231

"The only reason they didn't kill me outright was that George wanted me to know that he was the one who had hired them. He was staying with me at the time and my body was to be found, burned beyond recognition in his bed. It would be assumed that it was he who was dead and he could simply step into my place and become the Earl of Radnor. He would claim my name, the title, the lands and wealth that had been denied him simply because he was born three minutes after me. He wanted me to die knowing I had been killed by my own brother." Richard's mouth twisted bitterly as he recalled the sense of betrayal he'd felt that night. While the two of them hadn't been close for years, he'd still reeled under the news that his brother could hate him so much. Now he glanced toward the man in the bed and forced himself to continue. "That nasty streak in him is what saved my life. Not killing me outright gave me the chance to barter for my life. I had an iron chest hidden behind a false wall of the townhouse. No one knew about it but me and I offered it to them in exchange for my life."

His gaze slid back to Christiana to see that while she still looked wary, she was listening and that was something. "At first, I didn't think they would take the deal. The man I'd killed had been a friend to one of them and he wanted to just kill me . . . after beating the whereabouts of the chest out of me, of course. The second fellow was greedy, he wanted to let me live, keep me tied up somewhere until they could get the money George had agreed to pay them and then let me go and watch the chaos that followed when I came forward with the news that George had tried to have me killed . . . I gather he didn't like my brother much." He waited for her to nod or otherwise acknowledge what he'd said, but Christiana merely stared at him waiting, so he continued.

"The third fellow was the brightest of the bunch. He didn't think that even a beating would get them the location of the chest, especially since I knew they would just kill me afterward. But he also didn't want word getting out that they'd welsh on a deal as it might affect their getting future jobs. So, he suggested a compromise. They would let me live, and take me and the iron chest to the ship they worked on. It was setting sail for America the next day, where they would trade me to the Indians as a slave in exchange for some furs they could then sell off. They would more than treble the money they'd expected to get from George for just killing me.

"It took a bit of persuasion for the friend of the dead attacker, but in the end his greed won out and they all agreed to the plan. I wasn't too pleased about the being traded to the Indians part of the plan, but I would be alive and alive was better than dead so I told them where the false wall was, and how to open it, as well as the iron chest, and then they bound and gagged me. They dumped me in the back of a cart, set the townhouse on fire and drove to the prearranged meeting spot where George was to pay them." He glanced toward his brother again. "I heard it all. He wanted to know every moment of the night's events, wanted to know if I'd begged for my life, how crushed I'd been by my valet's death . . . He seemed to take delight in the idea that I'd suffered."

Richard shook his head with disgust. He'd never imagined his brother had hated him so much. "Once they had satisfied his morbid curiosity and gained their pay, the men took me to the docks and dumped me in the hold of a ship. I stayed there for what seemed like forever."

He closed his eyes at the memory of what had turned out to be one long, dark hellish journey for him. They'd kept him bound the entire trip and only removed the gag to give him food and water. Days had sometimes passed between feedings and the journey had seemed unending. By the time it did end, Richard had been half dead, weak and feverish, his wrists and ankles a mass of infected sores from the chafing of the ropes binding him. Uncaring of that, his three captors had dragged him from the hold, thrown him over the back of a horse and ridden out to try to trade him as a slave to Indians in exchange for furs. However, in the shape he was in, no one had been willing to trade anything for him. Finally his captors had simply pushed him off the horse, and then ridden off.

"They just left you there to die? After you'd given them your iron chest?" Christiana asked with outrage. "How did you survive?"

Richard blinked his eyes open, saw Christiana's upset expression and realized he'd been speaking the memories aloud as he'd recalled them. Clearing his throat, he shrugged. "I was fortunate enough that a farmer named Teddy McCormick found me. He put me in the back of his cart and took me to his farm. He and his wife, Hazel, both took care of me. They saved my life." He smiled at the memory of the couple.

"The moment I was well enough I wrote a letter to Daniel explaining all. I had no family except for George," he explained quietly. "And Daniel was my closest friend."

This time when he paused to look at her, Christiana nodded solemnly. She was aware of his lack of family, of course. She'd been married to his brother this last year. Well, sort of, Richard thought to himself, relieved to note that she was also looking much less suspicious and frightened. She believed him.

"I stayed with Teddy and Hazel and worked the farm with them to pay them back for their trouble in saving me, and waited what seemed like forever to receive a reply. It was almost a year to the day since the attack in my townhouse when who should ride up to the farm but Daniel."

Richard smiled at the memory, recalling his shock and joy on seeing him. "I'd expected him just to purchase me passage on a ship or send someone to fetch me, but he got on a ship and came after me himself. He brought clothes for me and had a ship waiting to bring us back to England."

"Us? The McCormicks too?" Christiana asked.

"What?" he asked with surprise. "Oh, no. They were happy on their farm, but I had Daniel leave some money with them for all

236

their trouble." He frowned now and added, "Which reminds me I have to pay him back. What with everything that's happened since our return I haven't got around to that yet."

"And exactly what is everything that's happened?" Christiana asked quietly. "How long have you been back in England?"

"Ah." Richard managed a crooked smile. "We arrived in port yesterday morning."

Christiana suddenly moved over to the bed to drop to sit on the edge of it. The action seemed to suggest her legs would no longer hold her up, but he couldn't tell what she was thinking from her expression.

"Daniel and I had decided that the best way to handle the situation was to confront George at the Landon ball. As the season opener, it would be attended by nearly everyone in the ton and the plan was to surprise a confession out of him."

"Except he was dead," she said quietly.

"Yes, and he was married to you, which put a wrinkle in our plans," Richard said quietly.

Christiana blinked at him in surprise. "Why did that put a wrinkle in them?"

"Because George had escaped justice by dying. It was only you and your sisters who would suffer in the scandal that would ensue if I revealed what he'd done, and the three of you are innocents."

Christiana was staring at him now as if he were some exotic creature she'd never encountered before. Uncomfortable under that steady, odd gaze, he added, "So when Daniel suggested that I simply step back into my life as if George had never stolen it from me . . . well, the truth is that I hesitated. I didn't wish to hurt you or your sisters, but on the other hand, I didn't know you and didn't wish to be punished further by his actions either. So we decided to remove George and hide him away for a couple of days while I saw if you and I would deal well together."

Christiana stood up abruptly, her face suddenly florid and Richard realized she'd taken what he'd said the entirely wrong way, thinking he'd meant whether they suited each other in bed. "Not *that* way," he assured her quickly. "Last night was wholly unexpected. In fact, if you'll recall I was trying to stop you from undressing me. It was you who was so determined to get my clothes off."

"I was trying to see your strawberry," she snapped and then narrowed her eyes. "Speaking of which, I should like to see it now."

"My strawberry?" he asked blankly and

peered down at his groin. It had been his pants she'd been so determined to remove last night as he recalled, but no one had ever called his manhood a strawberry before. In fact, he thought he might be insulted if that was what she was referring to.

"On your bottom," she said, her irritation of a moment ago seeming to transform into a mix of exasperation and embarrassment. "Richard Fairgrave is supposed to have a strawberry-shaped birthmark on his behind. I should like to see it, please."

"Oh." Richard relaxed and even grinned. "No one has ever said to me that it was strawberry-shaped."

She merely arched an eyebrow, apparently unwilling to be put off from seeing it. He supposed he couldn't blame her really. She'd been married to who she'd thought was Richard Fairgrave this last year and now he was telling her it had really been his brother George. He supposed it was reasonable for her to want proof of who was who. Sighing inwardly, he grimaced, turned his back to her, undid his trousers and dropped them.

Christiana simply stood there gaping at Richard for a moment, completely taken aback. She supposed she shouldn't be so surprised, she'd asked to see his bottom to check for the strawberry, but really she'd expected something of an argument perhaps, or a little modesty, but the way he'd simply dropped his drawers suggested there was very little modesty in the man.

"Well?" Richard asked impatiently.

Swallowing, Christiana took a tentative step closer to him and forced herself to focus on his bare derriere, but then frowned. The man was standing near the door about as far away from the light cast by the window as possible. He also happened to be standing in the bed's shadow. "I . . . erm . . . it's too dark. I can't see."

Richard clucked impatiently and turned around to make his way across the room. With his pants around his ankles it wasn't a fast maneuver and watching him duck march around the bed toward the window with his family jewels hanging out and swinging to and fro under his frock coat was really quite the most ridiculous thing she thought she'd ever seen.

"There. Is this better?" he asked, pausing beside the window and turning so that he was sideways to it.

Christiana cleared her throat to remove the laughter lodged there and made herself follow him across the room. She then bent

240

and peered at his behind.

"Oh! There it is," she said, reaching out to brush a finger over the mark. It was a pale red or dark pink-colored splotch on his left butt cheek as Langley had said. "It's not really a strawberry though, is it? It's more the shape of a rosebud. Langley said it was —"

"My lady? Your sisters are — Oh, dear Lord."

Christiana straightened abruptly and turned toward the connecting door that she'd left open and Daniel hadn't closed. Grace now stood in the entrance, eyes wide as she took in the portrait of the two of them by the window. A moment of silence passed as Christiana tried to think of something to say and then the maid started to withdraw, mumbling an apology that died abruptly as she spotted the body on the bed. Her gaze slid from the body in the bed to the man behind Christiana and back and she breathed, "Oh, dear Lord," again.

"I can explain everything," Christiana said at once, and hurried toward the woman. Hearing a resigned sigh and the rustle of clothing behind her, she glanced over her shoulder to see Richard looking exasperated as he pulled up his pants and did them up. She supposed between her discovering the

241

body, her demand to see his bottom and Grace's discovering the body, the man was having something of a difficult morning. Christiana could sympathize, she'd been having a difficult year and it didn't look as if things were going to get any easier in the near future.

CHAPTER ELEVEN

"So," Grace said the moment Christiana finished her explanations and fell silent. "Your marriage to Dicky-George wasn't legal, because it was Richard Fairgrave, Earl of Radnor on the marital contract and George was just impersonating Richard when he signed the papers?"

"I think that's probably true," Christiana admitted.

"But you've now consummated that illegal marriage to Dicky-George with Dicky-Richard . . . Does that make the marriage to Dicky-Richard legal now? Or . . ." Grace let the words trail off, but then she didn't have to say it, Christiana knew what she was asking. Was she now legally married to Richard or was she a fallen woman in a sham of a marriage with a dead man who hadn't been who he claimed to be?

Really, Christiana thought, she'd believed she had problems when Richard had come walking into the ball and she'd thought Dicky resurrected, but it just kept getting more and more complicated, the problems mounting up one atop the other. Clearing her throat, she said, "I do not think so, though Richard may let it stand. He wishes to see how well we deal together before he decides."

Grace snorted with disgust. "He apparently felt you dealt well enough together last night when he consummated the marriage his brother got him into."

"Yes, well, that may have been my fault," Christiana admitted, flushing hotly. "I was trying to see his strawberry and . . . er . . ."

"And fell on his pole?" Grace asked dryly.

"Grace!" Christiana cried with shock.

"Well, listen to yourself trying to take the blame," the maid said impatiently. "You were an untried girl ere last night, the blood on the sheets proves that. And you were inebriated as well. *And* you thought him your husband while *he* knew otherwise," she added grimly. "You are the innocent in this. It's those two in the next room at fault for all that has occurred."

"She's right."

Christiana swung around to see a grim-faced Richard in the connecting doorway to the master bedroom. He'd agreed to wait in the master bedroom while she explained the situation to Grace, but had apparently grown impatient. Christiana bit her lip as he now crossed the room toward them, worried that he might take Grace to task for what some would consider overstepping in even asking questions. However, Grace had been a member of her household all her life. While she was her maid, she was also like family to her. Christiana loved the older woman, and knew that love and caring was returned. It was the only reason the woman felt she could be so free with her tongue.

Fortunately, Richard seemed to understand that and gave Grace a nod of respect. "You are right. I am the one who decided last night that I would let the marriage stand." He turned to Christiana. "I had no idea you were still a virgin at the time, but I did know the marriage probably wasn't legal and that you were somewhat the worse for drink. I never should have allowed the situation to progress as it did."

Christiana stared at him wide-eyed. Dicky had never taken responsibility for his actions or faults. He had always blamed any mistake made or insult given on someone else, usually her. As far as she could tell he'd blamed her for everything from his stumbling over his own feet to the rain falling.

"Well, what are you going to do about it, my lord?" Grace asked abruptly when Christiana just continued to stare at the man.

"We shall have another ceremony to ensure it is legal," he announced solemnly. "We can tell everyone we wish to renew our vows to explain the need for it."

"Well, thank God for that." Grace stood abruptly and headed for the door. "I'd best go down and tell Langley and Lisa you are fine."

"Tell them she's fine?" Richard asked with a frown.

Grace nodded. "You've been up here a long time. Young Robert was worried, so I offered to check and be sure she was all right and report back."

Christiana saw a shaft of irritation flash across Richard's face, but he merely grunted and waited for the maid to leave. The moment the door closed behind her, he glanced to Christiana and gave a wry, apologetic smile. "I'm sorry. I didn't ask if you were willing to allow the marriage to stand. Are you willing? Will you marry me?"

She blinked in surprise, both at the apology and his comment. Christiana wasn't used to such consideration. Besides, it wasn't as if she had much choice in the matter. They had already consummated the marriage, legal or not.

Apparently taking her hesitation for reluctance, Richard knelt before her and took her hands in his. "I have heard enough to realize the last year with George has been hard. But I promise you I am not like him. I will be a good husband to you. I will —"

Christiana brought his words to an end by covering his mouth with her hand. When he frowned around her fingers and raised his eyebrows, she sighed and said, "Dicky made — I mean George. George made me many promises before we married about the wonderful husband he would be and the glorious life we would have together . . . and he broke every one. I would rather you not make promises, my lord. Lies are easily spoken. Actions are really more telling."

"Very well. No promises," Richard agreed when she let her hand drop away from his mouth. "But you haven't answered my question. Do you wish to let the marriage stand and hold the ceremony again?"

Christiana smiled wryly at the question. His first questions, *Are you willing?* And *Will you marry me?* would have been easier to answer. She had little choice really if she wished to avoid scandal. But his *Do you* wish *to let the marriage stand and hold the*

ceremony again? was much more complicated. Christiana was so confused at that
point she didn't know what she wished for.
Certainly Richard *seemed* much nicer than
George, but despite what they had done in
this room last night he was virtually a
stranger to her, and George had seemed
nice prior to the wedding as well. How was
she to know if Richard might not turn into
a controlling and critical monster the moment the vows were repeated as well? She
couldn't, and was afraid to trust that he
wouldn't and be hurt again as she had by
George, for truly that had been the worst
thing about the way he'd treated her, her
sense of betrayal and hurt that the man who
had claimed to love her had then treated
her so cruelly.

*At least she would have the nights to look
forward to this time,* some part of her mind
pointed out and Christiana glanced away
from Richard with a blush at the thought. It
was no small consolation. Her memories of
the pleasure they'd shared were vivid and
glorious. Christiana supposed she would
just have to hope that was not the only good
part of their marriage, that he was kinder
and showed her more respect and consideration than George had. Even a modicum of
either behavior would make it bearable if

she had those passionate nights too.

Clearing her throat, she forced herself to meet his gaze again and nodded solemnly. "Very well. The marriage will stand so long as we have another ceremony." She swallowed and then added quietly, "Thank you."

Richard shook his head. "Do not thank me. I do not want you to feel I have sacrificed myself and done you some great honor by standing behind the marriage. This does not just make things easier for you, but for me as well." He squeezed her hand and added, "And I have high hopes that we will deal well with each other and in time become good friends and partners."

Christiana peered at him silently. Aside from the fact that he was trying to ensure she did not feel beholden to him, which seemed very kind to her, Richard also wasn't making false claims of love and adoration or even like and attraction. He was being honest and stating exactly how the marriage would benefit him, and that he hoped for more in the future. Before she'd met George the very unflowery words would have upset her; now they made her relax and want to smile. She had learned her lesson well and would take truth over empty lies any day.

"All right?" he asked when she continued

to stare at him silently.

Christiana managed a small, sincere smile and nodded. "All right."

"Good." He smiled widely and stood, pulling her to her feet with him. "Now, come along. We should join your sisters and Langley before he comes charging up here to rescue you."

He said the words teasingly enough, but with a slight edge that made her wonder. However, it suddenly occurred to Christiana that she hadn't told him about Langley's suspicions.

"He thinks you are George," she blurted as he began to urge her out of the room.

Richard drew her to a halt, his gaze sharp as he asked, "He does?"

She nodded and quickly explained the conversation she'd had with Robert the night before. When she finished, they were both silent as Richard digested what he'd learned.

"I see," he said finally as he took her arm to walk her along the hall. "That explains a lot of his behavior, and I suppose I should have wondered how you knew about my birthmark. It's not common knowledge." He was silent as they descended the stairs, but at the bottom he paused, and turned her to face him. "Do you trust Robert?"

Her eyebrows flew up at the question. It seemed to suggest he would trust her judgment in this very serious matter, which definitely made a nice change from George, who hadn't even trusted her judgment in the day to day running of the house or the choosing of clothes.

"Yes," she said simply. "He is like family."

Richard nodded. "Then I shall take him aside and explain matters to him."

Christiana felt something unclench the slightest bit around her heart. She also felt the sting of tears in her eyes and turned away from Richard before he could see them. She didn't know where they were coming from anyway. It was foolish to want to cry with gratitude just because he was being both kind and apparently respecting her opinion. Ridiculous. Pathetic, really, she decided with self-disgust.

"There you are! I thought I heard voices out here."

Christiana glanced around to see Robert Maitland standing several feet away, in the parlor door. Grateful for the distraction he offered, she beamed a smile on the man, but her smile dimmed when she noted Lisa behind him. The displeasure on her youngest sister's face had her eyebrows rising, but then she glanced back to Robert as he spoke again.

"The tea is growing cold. You should really come join us," he said firmly.

"Actually, Langley, if you don't mind, I need to have a word with you first," Richard said, taking Christiana's arm and urging her up the hall toward the other man.

"Oh?" Langley narrowed his eyes and then glanced to Christiana.

Reading the silent question as to her well-being in his eyes, she smiled gently and said, "He has the strawberry. Though, it's really more of a rosebud if you ask me, Robert."

Langley didn't comment, in fact he didn't look any happier to know Richard was Richard and Christiana supposed it was because he worried she was now stuck in this marriage to a man who had been horrible to her the last year. Sighing, she reached out to squeeze his arm in passing and said, " 'Tis all right. He's not the man we thought he was. He'll explain everything."

Christiana then continued on into the parlor, leaving Richard to sort out Robert. She didn't get far into the room, however; Lisa blocked her way and didn't appear eager to move.

"Shall we sit and pour the tea while we wait for the men?" Christiana suggested uncertainly. When Lisa didn't respond at once, but merely glared after Robert as he moved off with Richard, she asked, "Is something amiss?"

Lisa let her breath out on a small impatient, huff. "He's just so . . . annoying."

"Robert?" Christiana asked with surprise.

"Yes, him." Lisa turned abruptly and stomped back to drop into a chair by the tea tray. "He wouldn't stop worrying about you. From the minute you left he was watching the door like a hawk and then started asking where you were and even sent Grace to check on you. Good Lord, he was acting like Richard was some murderous fiend. He's your husband. What did Robert think was going to happen to you?"

"Ah." Christiana sat down on the sofa across from Lisa, unsure what to say. Part of her wanted to babble out all that had happened. However, she'd rather explain it to both sisters at the same time than have to do it twice, so merely said, "Robert is aware that things have not been ideal between Richard and myself this last year and is just worried."

"Well, he worries too much about you," she grumbled, unappeased.

Christiana's eyebrows rose. Lisa actually sounded jealous and it made her wonder if the girl's feelings for Langley weren't more than just the sisterly type affections Christiana and Suzette felt for the man, but merely said, "He worries about all of us: you, me and Suzette. Speaking of Suzette," she added with a frown. "Where is she?"

"Oh, she muttered something about changing her slippers and left shortly after you did," Lisa said on a sigh.

"Oh." Christiana glanced toward the door, wondering where the girl was . . . and where Daniel was as well. Lord Woodrow had left her and Richard upstairs some time ago and, she'd thought, joined everyone in the parlor, but it seemed not.

"We may as well drink the tea before it grows stone cold," Lisa decided and began to pour.

Christiana murmured a thank-you as the younger girl handed her a cup.

"I knew he wasn't you," Langley muttered, peering over George's face when Richard pulled back the blanket for him. "Not at first, or I would have warned Christiana away from him. But then I saw little of him at first. It wasn't until they were married and living here in London that I began to suspect something was amiss. Christiana was so tense the first time I came to visit, her smile strained, her eyes constantly dancing to him as if afraid she may have said or done something to upset him. Then the next time he had the butler turn me away. The second time that happened I knew something was wrong and waited until I saw Grace come out. I made her tell me what was going on and when she told me how he was treating her . . ." Langley's mouth tightened and then he sighed and said, "The bastard has treated Christiana like dirt this last year, and from what I recalled of you from school, you just didn't seem the type. George, on the other hand . . ."

Richard pulled the blanket back up to again cover George's face. His brother looked worse every time he looked at him and it was becoming obvious they couldn't keep him around much longer. While the open window was keeping the room cool, he would soon start to smell. They had to resolve the matter of who had poisoned George swiftly so they could lay the man and the matter to rest and get on with life.

"Will you be moving him to the family vault on the way to Gretna Green then?" Langley asked, heading for the bedroom door, apparently eager to escape the room.

"Daniel seems to think we should keep the body here until the situation is resolved, just in case," Richard admitted as they left the bedroom.

"Well you aren't going to be able to keep him here much longer," Langley said dryly as he watched Richard lock the door. "Surely he would be fine in the family vault? At least you needn't worry a servant or someone else will come across him there."

"True," Richard murmured and liked the idea of moving his brother to the family vault. Really it was starting to get a bit disturbing having him here, and it was becoming obvious that their efforts to keep him chilled weren't working all that well. "I think perhaps you're right. I will talk to Daniel and see if he can come up with any faults in the plan."

"Faults in what plan?"

Both men turned to peer at Daniel as he strode toward them. Richard couldn't help noticing that the man was already halfway up the hall to them and yet the hall had been empty just seconds ago when they'd stepped into it. That realization made his eyes shift instinctively to Suzette's bedroom door, which was just steps behind Daniel now.

"Where did you come from, Woodrow?" Langley asked abruptly, apparently having noted the same things Richard had. Or perhaps it was the fact that Daniel's hair was a bit mussed, his jacket was wrinkled, and his cravat missing that put the displeased suspicion in Langley's eyes, he thought with amusement as he waited for Daniel to explain himself.

"Oh . . . I . . . er . . ." He waved vaguely back the way he'd come, and then paused abruptly as Suzette's door suddenly opened and she hurried out, headed for the stairs, hissing, "Daniel! Daniel, you forgot your cravat."

Richard bit his lip to hold back a laugh, and glanced to Daniel to see him rolling his eyes. It was Robert, however, who snapped, "Suzette!"

Coming to a shuddering halt, she glanced back, her already wide eyes growing even wider as she spotted the three men in the hall.

"Oh." Straightening, she turned to face them, and gestured toward the stairs, but stopped as she noted the cravat waving about, and quickly jerked the hand behind her back as if she hoped they hadn't noticed it. "I was just going downstairs."

Richard coughed into his hand to hide the laugh that would not be held back and Suzette scowled at him, and then sighed with exasperation and moved up the hall toward them. She shoved the cravat at Daniel without another word and then simply turned to march silently away up the hall. Daniel put his cravat back on as he watched her go, his eyes locked on her behind, Richard noted. When he'd finished, he turned back, took in Langley's narrow-eyed gaze and said stiffly, "We are getting married."

"You've decided for certain have you?" Richard asked with amusement.

"I am not certain that is the correct phrasing for it," he said wryly. "It would be more fitting to say I have bowed to the inevitable. The woman is a force of nature."

"That she is," Langley agreed, his tone dry and attitude relaxing now that he knew Suzette's reputation and future were safe. "So, when is the trip to Gretna Green to occur? I should like to accompany you."

"The sooner the better," Daniel said grimly. "If Suzette jumps out and drags me into one more room I cannot guarantee she will reach Gretna as pure as she is now, and she is already less pure today than she was yesterday."

Richard burst out laughing.

Even Langley smiled, apparently not minding the frankness now that Daniel had assured him he was marrying the girl, but he also raised an eyebrow in Richard's direction and asked, "What are you laughing about? From what Christiana said to me earlier she is definitely not pure anymore."

"She told you that?" Richard asked with amazement.

"I was assuring her that we could get the marriage annulled and she had to explain that that wasn't the case anymore," he said dryly, and then shrugged. "Since last night at the ball was when we realized it *could* be annulled, I'm guessing last night *after* the ball was when that situation changed."

"Erm . . . yes, well —" Richard paused and raised his eyebrows as he noted Christiana's maid, Grace, striding up the hall leading two maids. All three women carried a collection of bedding, blankets and pillows. As she drew abreast of them, he frowned and asked, "What's all this?"

"I asked Milly and Sally to help me make up a room for you," Grace said calmly as she opened the door to the guest room across from the master bedroom.

"A room for me?" he asked with surprise as she ushered the younger girls inside.

"Yes. You cannot sleep in the master bedroom until the bed is repaired," she said sensibly.

"No, but there is no need to go to this trouble, I will just sleep —"

"In the spare room until a certain situation is made legal," Grace said firmly. She gave him a hard smile and added, "Lady Christiana asked me to see to it, and so I am."

Richard gaped after the woman as she slipped into the bedroom and closed the door.

"Hmm. I suppose we shouldn't be surprised," Daniel said, not hiding his amusement. Langley was no better, chuckling openly without even bothering to try to cover it behind a cough.

Richard scowled at them both. "I think we should head for Gretna Green this afternoon. There is really no need to wait."

"Er . . ." Daniel glanced to Langley and then urged Richard a few feet away to say quietly, "What about the business with George's murder? Do you not think we should try to sort out who killed him before we do anything else?"

"Langley knows everything, Daniel," Richard said quietly. "You can speak in front of him."

"He does?"

"I do," Langley assured him closing the distance between them.

"Oh, well," he frowned and then repeated, "As I was saying, do you not think we should resolve that matter before we —"

"No," Richard interrupted firmly. "You are the one who pointed out that the killer would now think he'd failed and may try again. I think the most important thing is to ensure Christiana is legally wed to me in case a second attempt is successful."

"You may be right," Daniel murmured.

Richard relaxed a little, glad he didn't have an argument on his hands, and then added, "Langley suggested stopping off at the family vault on the way and dropping off George there. I think that may be a good idea."

"I suppose it's better than leaving him here unguarded for days," Daniel said dryly.

Richard nodded.

"Well then, all we have to do is convince the girls to go," Langley said dryly.

"Oh, I'm sure that will not be a problem," Richard assured him, quite certain the women would be as eager to get to Gretna Green and get married as he and Daniel were.

Langley snorted at the suggestion and started toward the stairs commenting, "You have a lot to learn about women, my friend."

Richard frowned after him and then glanced to Daniel, who shrugged.

"Suzette is definitely eager to be wed, I do

not think she will be a problem. However, Christiana may fuss a bit."

"Nay." Richard shook his head. Christiana had been like wildfire in his arms last night, she too would be eager to be wedded and bedded. At least he hoped she was. It hadn't even occurred to him that she might frown on the idea of sleeping together again before they ensured their marriage was all legal and proper. But if that was the case, he wanted it done with quickly so that he could have her in his arms again. Surely she would feel the same way?

"Are you two coming?" Langley asked, pausing at the top of the stairs to glance back at them.

Richard and Daniel started forth at once, Richard marshaling his arguments in his head as he went. They needed to ensure their marriage was legal in case anything happened to him. She could be pregnant after all. The other reason for the rush was that they needed to then get back and look into who could have poisoned George. Of course, he hadn't yet told her that George had been poisoned, Richard realized and didn't suppose now was the time to do it. Suzette and Lisa weren't even aware that the Dicky of the last year had been his brother George who was now dead, and that he himself was the true Richard Fairgrave, newly returned from America.

"Good luck."

The words, accompanied by a pat on the back from Langley, drew Richard's attention to the fact that they'd arrived at the parlor door. Glancing to the man, he noted the pitying look he was giving him and frowned, but merely led the way inside the parlor, where Christiana, Suzette and Lisa were all chattering cheerfully away.

Approaching the sofa and chairs around the tea tray, he cleared his throat and started. "Ladies, I —"

"Oh, Richard, Suzette was just telling us that Daniel has agreed to her proposal. They are going to Gretna Green." Christiana beamed as she made the announcement.

"Yes." Richard smiled back. "In fact, I thought we might accompany them and —" his gaze slid to Suzette and Lisa before he continued, "— renew our own vows. It could be a fresh start for us."

"Oh, how romantic," Lisa breathed and grabbed for Christiana's hands to squeeze them excitedly. "Isn't that wonderful, Chrissy? That's so wonderful," she hugged her and then pulled back to ask, "When do we leave?"

"Now. This afternoon, as soon as I have —"

"No." It wasn't Christiana that said it, but all three sisters together, reacting with the same horror they'd had to his arrival at the ball last night.

"Er . . ." Richard glanced toward Daniel and Langley, but they were both apparently content to stay out of this.

"We cannot possibly pack and prepare for a journey that quickly," Christiana said reasonably, drawing his attention back to the girls. "Why, we shall be lucky to manage it by morning. It will have to be tomorrow, and then only if we start right away."

Suzette and Lisa nodded agreement and rose, apparently ready to rush off at once. Richard stopped them by raising a hand.

"Now, wait. There is no need to panic. We can manage it today. You needn't pack much, just one change of clothes, we —"

"One change of clothes?" Christiana echoed with dismay. "Richard, it is at least a two day ride from here to York by carriage and Gretna Green must be another day or day and a half after that. We cannot manage with one change of clothes."

"We can make Gretna Green in two days if we ride straight through only stopping to change horses," he assured her gently. "And since we will not be stopping either way there is no need to don fresh clothes except when we can actually stop and bathe at an inn in Gretna Green. Besides, I want to take only the one carriage. There would be no room for wardrobes for the six of us and —"

"The six of us?" Lisa squawked. "What about our maids?"

"Lisa is right. We need our maids. I intend to look nice at my wedding and my maid Georgina is the only one who knows how I like to wear my hair. No, your plans just will not do," Suzette said firmly.

"Christiana and Lisa could help you with your hair," Richard pointed out desperately.

Christiana clucked her tongue impatiently. "Even if we agreed to forgo taking our maids, you cannot expect us to ride for two straight days and nights there and then two more back, the six of us crammed into one tiny carriage. How do you expect us to sleep jostling about in a tiny, cramped carriage with you three large men? No, we shall have to stop each night to rest."

Lisa and Suzette nodded, and then Lisa added, "We shall need at least two carriages, preferably three if we are taking the maids. And we definitely need more than one change of clothes. Let me see, if we stop

265

each night the journey shall likely take four days and three nights there and the same back . . . We need at least eight outfits each, and then there are night clothes and shoes and — Oh, we really need to get started if we want to get any sleep at all tonight."

"You are right." Christiana stood and headed for the door. "You two go on up and start choosing what you wish to take. I shall find our maids and join you directly."

Richard stared after Christiana and her sisters as they hurried from the room chattering away. He really had thought she'd be as eager to get to Gretna Green and legalize their marriage as he was. He was sure she'd enjoyed last night as much as he and would be eager to be able to do it again. It seemed, however, that he hadn't a clue when it came to Christiana. It also looked as if he would be sleeping in the guest bedroom tonight . . . alone.

"I did warn you," Langley said dryly once it was just the three of them. "You should have listened. I *have* known them all my life, after all."

"Yes, you have," Richard agreed, turning on him. "And while the women are packing, you can tell us everything you've learned about them in that time."

CHAPTER TWELVE

"I do not know how you can do that with the carriage bouncing about as it is."

Christiana glanced up from her embroidery at Richard's words and smiled wryly. The truth was she was poking her fingers more than the cloth and the stitches she had managed would have to be ripped out and done over again anyway, they were such a mess, but it helped pass the time and distracted her from the fact that she was shut up all alone in a carriage with Richard.

In the end, the men had agreed to take three carriages for this trip to Gretna Green. Each man had contributed one. The maids rode in Langley's carriage at the back of their little procession, she and Richard rode in the Radnor carriage at the front and Suzette, Lisa, Langley and Daniel all rode in the Woodrow carriage in the middle. It seemed an unfair distribution of their party to Christiana and she would have preferred at least one more person in the carriage with her and Richard to act as a buffer, but when Daniel had suggested he and Suzette needed a chaperone in their own carriage for the journey, Langley had volunteered and Lisa had insisted on joining them. Apparently, none of them considered that Christiana and Richard were not yet properly wed and should also have a chaperone.

Of course, her sisters still had no idea Richard was Richard and Dicky had actually been George and she wasn't legally either man's wife. But the men knew it. Obviously, they weren't as concerned for her reputation as she was. But then Christiana supposed she had little reputation to save after the night she had spent with Richard when she'd still thought him her husband. Despite that, she was determined to behave as she'd been raised to and not make the mistake of sleeping with Richard again until they were legally wed. The problem was, she really wanted to. Temptation was an awful thing, she decided.

"It helps me pass the time," she said finally in answer to his comment.

"Hmm." Richard peered out the window at the passing scenery. "It *is* a long journey."

"Made longer by our insistence on three carriages and stopping at night," she sug-

268

gested gently. "I am sorry about that."

"No." He smiled wryly. "Now that we are on the road I am grateful you ladies insisted on it. I am already looking forward to getting out and stretching my legs. And sleeping tonight in something that isn't bouncing up and down will be nice."

Christiana murmured agreement and struggled on with her efforts at embroidery.

"Have you been to Radnor?" he asked suddenly. "Has George taken you there since you married?"

Christiana lowered her embroidery to her lap and smiled wryly. "We stopped there for a night on the way to London after the wedding, but it was only a brief stop. We arrived after dark and left at first light so I didn't get to see much."

"The wedding was at your father's home?" he asked.

Christiana nodded.

Richard peered at her silently for a moment and then said, "I was surprised neither yourself nor your sisters suggested collecting your father on the way. I would have thought you'd want him to attend your weddings."

Christiana sighed and stabbed her needle into the cloth, set it down and admitted, "I considered it, but Suzette was so angry at

269

Father for gambling again and forcing her to marry so abruptly that . . ." She shook her head unhappily. "I just thought it better not to even bring up the subject."

"And you? Are you angry too? If not for the first round of gambling you would never have had to marry George."

"I didn't have to marry him," Christiana said quietly. "Had I seen through him and refused his troth Father would have supported me in my decision. Marrying Dicky was my choice. He wooed me, I believed his lies sincere and made the wrong choice."

"What other choice was there?" he asked.

"What Suzette is doing now, I suppose," she said with a shrug. "Find myself a man in need of money and strike a deal with him."

He frowned slightly and then commented, "Christiana, you have a tendency to take responsibility in every situation . . . even when it is not yours to take." When she started to protest, he pointed out, "You understand why Suzette is angry, but don't claim that anger for yourself for being forced to marry Dicky when if the gambling hadn't happened the first time you never would have been forced to make the decision at all."

"But —"

"And then while talking to Grace, you tried to take responsibility for our night together when it was wholly my fault."

"I was a party to it," she said blushing and lowering her head with embarrassment. It was the first time they'd spoken of that passionate night. "I am the one who started stripping you and set the whole thing in motion."

"And you thought I was your legal husband while I knew we weren't legally wed," he pointed out quietly. "That night was my fault. As a gentleman I should have brought a halt to things."

"Yes, well . . ." She sighed, terribly uncomfortable with the conversation and not sure what to say.

"I bet you have spent a good deal of this last year trying to figure out what was wrong with you or what you had done to make George treat you the way he did," Richard murmured.

Christiana turned to peer unhappily out the window. She *had* spent the last year trying to work that out and trying to figure a way to fix things and bring back the sweet, complimentary man who had courted her.

"I hope you realize now it wasn't you," he said gently. "George would have treated you poorly no matter who you were. He treated everyone that way."

"I suppose," she murmured, peering down at her embroidery again.

Richard sighed, a sound that struck her as slightly exasperated, but he let that subject go and instead said, "While I understand why you and Suzette would be angry with your father, I think it may be undeserved."

She raised her eyebrows in question. "Oh?"

"Do you know how the first losses happened?" he asked.

Christiana shook her head. "All I know is Father went to town to meet with his solicitor about estate business and came back several days late, terribly upset. It took some effort to get him to tell us what was wrong, and then he finally confessed he'd somehow wound up at a gaming hell and gambled us into debt and that the owner of the gaming hell was demanding payment and while he'd managed to pay some of it, he just didn't have the money to pay the rest. We were all upset and trying to work out a way to get the money when Dicky showed up to save the day."

"How did he know to save the day?"

Christiana blinked at the question. "What?"

"You said Dicky showed up to save the

272

day," Richard pointed out. "How did he know the day needed saving?"

"Oh." She frowned. "Well, I didn't mean that he knew about it when he arrived. It was just a grand coincidence, or at least I think it was. I'm not sure about anything now, but at the time it seemed coincidence, and I just assumed that Father told him of his troubles while they talked and Dicky offered to pay his remaining debt to sweeten his offer of marriage."

"Hmm," Richard's mouth thinned out, and then he said, "Well, Daniel and I suspect Dicky had something to do with getting your father to the gaming hell in the first place that time too."

"You do?" she asked with surprise. "Why?"

"Because there are rumors in town that the Earl of Radnor has become friendly with a certain owner of a gaming hell where it's suspected the players are drugged and fleeced. I believe it's the same gaming hell where your father lost his money. And it wouldn't surprise me to learn that George had taken your father there both times." He frowned and added, "I shall ask your father about that on our return. If I'd been thinking clearly I would have done it yesterday."

Christiana stared at Richard blankly, and

then blurted, "But why? Why would he do such a thing?"

"Well, if he did it the first time, it was probably to force an opportunity to marry you and get his hands on your dower," he said apologetically.

"But no one knows about it."

"Langley does," he pointed out.

"He's like family. Robert wouldn't tell anyone," she assured him firmly.

"While I knew him as a child, I don't know him as a man yet, so I will trust your judgment on that," he said and then asked, "Who else knows?"

She frowned. "No one. Robert only knows because we were playing in the attic when the lawyers visited and there is a spot where you can hear what is said in Father's office."

Richard was silent for a moment and then asked, "Who is your father's lawyer?"

"An older gentleman with a funny moustache . . . I believe his name is Buttersworth," she said after a moment's thought.

"Ah." Richard, said with understanding and sat back in his seat. "John Buttersworth Junior has been a friend of George's since school."

"You think his father told him about my grandfather's will?"

"He wouldn't have to. John Junior works with his father now. The plan is for him to take over his father's clients when the time comes."

Christiana scowled at this news. "So you think that John Junior told Dicky about our dowers and that he deliberately took Father to the gaming hell both times to be drugged so that he'd gamble when he wouldn't normally?"

"Your father isn't a gambler?" Richard asked.

She shook her head. "He'd never gambled before in his life until that one time last year. And then he didn't gamble again until now. Father is more a stay-at-home type. He works the estate and spends the evenings dining with friends in the area or reading by the fire. Even when he had to travel into the city to see his lawyer or manage other business, he was more likely to stay in than go out, and then it was only to stop at the club for a drink and catch up with old friends. That's why it was so shocking and upsetting when we learned he'd gambled and so deeply."

"And this time? Was it as much?" Richard asked.

Christiana shook her head. "No. I gather it's about half what it was the first time. But

Father drained the estate to pay his debt the first time. Dicky only paid off what was still outstanding after he'd squeezed all the money out that he could. The estate would recover slowly, but there is little actual money to hand, so even the smaller amount this time would force the sale of the estate."

"Unless Suzette married," Richard said thoughtfully.

"Yes." Christiana frowned. "I suppose it makes sense that Dicky took Father to the gaming hell the first time to force my marrying him, but why would he do it this second time?" That had been troubling her even before she'd heard Richard's suspicions that Dicky had been the one to take her father to the gaming hell the first time. Why had Dicky taken him there when he'd known what had happened the first time?

"I don't know," Richard admitted on a sigh. "He wouldn't have profited from it this time."

Christiana clucked impatiently and stabbed her needle into the cloth, wishing it was Dicky. She wished the stupid man would come back to life long enough to answer these questions, and then kindly drop dead again. However, that simply wasn't going to happen. She'd seen Dicky when the men had taken him from the bed and folded him into the chest presently resting on top of the carriage she and Richard rode in. The man was definitely dead, and they were removing him from the house none too soon. It was time he was buried. And good riddance to him, she thought unhappily.

Of course, it just meant she would be married to the real Richard Fairgrave, Earl of Radnor instead, but even after the last two short days it was becoming obvious that he was nothing like his brother. He hadn't once tried to control her, not even raising an argument against having to sleep in the guest bedroom though she'd expected he would. He also hadn't criticized her even once yet, but instead had given her a handful of compliments, which was a handful more than she'd received from Dicky during their marriage. Many of those compliments had been during their night of passion, which might not be that reliable. But one had been at the ball the night they'd met, and he'd greeted her that morning with another, saying she looked lovely with her hair in the much softer style Grace had arranged it in. More importantly though, he seemed to respect her opinion, trusting Langley on her say-so twice now, and that was very important to her. She had always considered herself a relatively intelligent and sensible young woman, but George had made her feel stupid and clumsy. Richard didn't make her feel that way.

"I am surprised you do embroidery," Richard said suddenly. "From all Langley has told me it sounded as if you were more into horseback riding and other physical pursuits while growing up."

"Yes." She smiled faintly at the thought of her childhood, and explained, "Robert was often at our home while we were growing up, and we were always running, jumping, riding and whatnot. I fear my sisters and I were never really interested in the more ladylike pursuits such as" — she glanced down at the cloth in her hand and grimaced — "needlework."

"And yet you do it now," he pointed out.

"Dicky — I mean George —"

"You can call him Dicky if you like," he interrupted gently. "I don't mind so long as you never call me Dicky again. That was George's nickname for me and I always hated it."

Christiana nodded, but simply said, "He insisted I learn embroidery and other more ladylike pursuits. He said I was far too unruly and needed to learn discipline and needlework would teach it to me."

"Controlling idiot," Richard snorted with

278

disgust, and suddenly leaned across the small space and snatched the cloth from her.

"Richard!" she cried with surprise, and then half rose from her seat to try grab it back. "Give me that back."

He merely held the cloth behind his head and asked, "Do you enjoy it or do you only do it because he said you should and it has become a habit?"

"I — well . . ." She frowned and muttered, "It would not hurt me to learn to be a proper lady. Mother died shortly after Lisa was born and I fear Father let us run a bit wild. We didn't learn what most girls do."

"That does not answer my question. Do you enjoy it?" he repeated, grabbing her arm to steady her as they hit a rut in the road.

"No," she admitted on a sigh. "I do not like it at all."

"Just as I thought," he said dryly. Richard opened the window and tossed the embroidery out.

Christiana gaped after the fluttering bit of cloth, and then turned to peer at him in amazement. "I cannot believe you just did that."

"Believe it," Richard said solemnly. "You do not need to do embroidery if you do not like it. I will not try to change you. You can be yourself with me."

She stared into his face for a moment and then swallowed a sudden lump in her throat and shook her head. "You do not know me. What if you do not like me once you do? Dicky said I was —"

"My brother was an idiot," he assured her solemnly. "He was selfish and self-absorbed and lacked the capacity to care about anyone but himself. In truth, I suspect all those efforts to try to control and change you were based in envy."

"Envy?" Christiana asked with surprise.

Richard nodded. "You have something he never possessed and never could. You appear to have a basic optimism and joy in life. I've seen it. Oh, I'm sure you worry when trouble strikes and can have a sad day like anyone else, but you can also just as quickly shed your fears and worries and smile and enjoy life once those worries pass. I do not think George enjoyed a single day in his life. I do not think he ever felt hope, or happiness. Perhaps he was afraid that if he did find happiness it would be snatched away, but whatever the case, he just did not have it in him. I suspect that is why he liked to take it from others." Richard peered at her solemnly. "From what I can tell he spent the last year trying to browbeat that happiness out of you."

"And he tried to steal it from you by having you killed and taking your name and position in society," she said quietly. "And yet as you say, he wasn't happy."

"No, he wasn't," Richard agreed, but his voice was distracted this time, his gaze suddenly fixed.

Christiana raised her eyebrows at the change in both his expression and the sudden tightening of his fingers on her arm, and then glanced down and saw what had caught his attention. She still stood in the half-bent position she'd taken when she'd tried to grab back her embroidery. It left her slightly bent at the waist, and her chest directly before his eyes with the neckline gaping to reveal a good deal of her bosom. Blushing furiously she forgot she was in a carriage and started to straighten, managing to bang her head on the roof, and then they hit a rut in the road and she stumbled forward.

Richard reached to steady her even as she caught at his shoulders and between the two of them she came to a halt with her bosom just a hair's breadth from his mouth.

"I should really sit down before I fall down," she said breathlessly, the moment she could find her voice.

"Yes," Richard agreed, but rather than

release her, his hands shifted to the back of her legs and with a little pressure and guidance she was suddenly straddling him on the bench seat.

"Oh, I don't think —"

The rest of her very lame protest was lost when his mouth suddenly covered hers. Christiana didn't even try to pretend she wanted to protest further, but opened to him at once and let her arms creep around his neck with a little sigh. She did so like his kisses. Christiana had been able to think of little else since their night of passion, the memories of what they'd done and how he'd made her feel had interfered with her every thought since then.

When he deepened the kiss, driving his tongue into her mouth, she gave a little moan and tilted her head for him, her fingers tightening on the strands of his hair and then scraping across his scalp as the familiar heat began to build in her lower belly. His hands had settled on her hips once he had her on his lap, but began to move now, riding up her sides and then around until he could cup her breasts in his hands through the cloth of her gown. Christiana arched into the caress, groaning as he began to knead the eager flesh through the soft material. As nice as it was, she found herself wishing her gown away so she could feel his flesh against her own. She knew from experience how much nicer it was when his hands, work roughened from his time on the farm, were unimpeded by material.

Christiana had barely had the thought when Richard gave up caressing her and began to tug at her gown, trying to pull it off her shoulders. Releasing her hold on his head, she reached to help and then gave a little sigh and shiver as the cloth slid down her arms, freeing her bosom. Richard broke their kiss then to allow her to lean back and remove her arms from the sleeves. The material soon dropped away, leaving her completely, brazenly bare from the waist up.

Christiana would have pressed herself shyly against him then and kissed him once more to help ease the embarrassment suddenly claiming her, but Richard held her back, determined to look his fill. His eyes traveled hungrily over what she'd revealed, and then he said, "You're beautiful. Absolutely perfect."

His voice was rough with a need that called out to the hunger she was experiencing and then his hands rose to cover both naked globes and she sighed with a combination of relief and pleasure as he began to caress her. Covering his hands with her own, Christiana squeezed as well, urging him on and then moaned and tipped her head back, eyes closing as he caught her nipples between thumbs and forefingers and toyed with them. The heat in her belly was now a wildfire, spreading outward and making her very core ache in a way she'd never experienced before Richard.

Gasping with want, she squeezed his hands harder and then raised her head and kissed him with all the hunger he was causing in her. It wasn't enough. Even when he drove his tongue between her lips, and she writhed into his hands, her hips pressing down into his lap, it still wasn't enough. She wanted more. When he slid one hand out from under hers, it left her own covering the abandoned orb and Christiana instinctively squeezed it herself and then stiffened with a gasp as she felt the roughened fingers of his hand touch her knee beneath her skirt and begin to glide up her inner thigh. When it reached the apex of her thighs and brushed over the damp, swollen flesh there, her hips rose up with a jolt, but his caress followed and she broke their kiss to groan his name desperately. And then to squeal it with shock as the carriage suddenly shuddered to a halt and she went flying backward.

Fortunately, Christiana landed on the bench seat across from Richard, though she arrived there in something of a muddle, her skirts flying up to cover her face and chest.

"Are you all right?" Richard was there at once trying to right her and brushing her skirts down so that he could see her face.

"Yes," Christiana assured him, pulling her gown up to cover her chest and peering about uncertainly. "What happened? Why have we stopped?"

"I'm not sure," Richard admitted and turned to peer out the window. While he was distracted, Christiana quickly slid her arms back into her sleeves and pulled the top of her gown back into place. She was feeling her hair, trying to tell if it was all right or needed fixing when he muttered, "It would appear we've reached Stevanage. I told them to stop there for lunch."

"Oh," she murmured and let her hands drop as he turned back to her. His eyebrows rose when he saw what she'd done.

"That was fast, and you look as perfect as you did this morning. Well done," he praised and then pressed a quick kiss to the tip of her nose before turning back to open the carriage door.

Christiana stared after him with amazement as he got out of the carriage. The compliment was nice, but the kiss on the nose had seemed . . . well, it had been the affectionate sort of thing her father would have done when she was younger. Not that she thought Richard's feelings toward her were in any way fatherly, but the action seemed to speak of affection.

"Are you coming, Christiana?"

She blinked and stared at the hand Richard was holding out to her, but then took it and descended from the carriage, noting that there appeared to be something in his expression that could have been affection as well. Or perhaps she was just imagining that because she wanted to believe it was there, Christiana acknowledged on a small sigh.

"Is something wrong?" Richard asked, apparently having heard the sigh.

Christiana shook her head at once. "No, no. Everything is fine," she assured him glancing around to see the other two carriages had drawn to a halt behind them and everyone was disembarking.

"Come, let's get you inside and find you something to eat," Richard said, taking her arm to lead her toward the inn.

"What about the others?" she asked, glancing over her shoulder.

"They'll follow. I'm more concerned with you. You skipped breakfast this morning in favor of packing and I suspect you didn't eat much of the tray I had sent up to your room last night when you didn't join us at the table."

"I was helping Grace pick out what we should bring," she explained.

"I know, and I understand, but you're looking a bit pale now and a good meal will probably set you to rights."

Christiana fell silent and merely allowed him to lead her inside, but her thoughts were not silent. George had always been nagging at her about eating, using it as an opportunity to force her to eat unpleasant things she didn't care for when he was annoyed with her. She didn't deliberately skip eating. The problem was she'd been so miserable this last year she hadn't really felt like doing anything, even eating. That wasn't what had happened last night and this morning, though. Her forgetting to eat then had just been because she was so busy.

But Richard wasn't nagging at her and using it as an opportunity to berate and insult her as George had always done. Instead he was being sweet and understanding and even concerned. It made her feel . . . cared for.

"Here we are." He settled her at a large table where everyone could join them and then glanced toward the innkeeper and back before asking, "Is there anything you don't like?"

Christiana felt her eyes narrow. "Why?"

"So I don't accidentally order you something you don't care for," he said with a laugh as if that should be obvious, and she supposed it should have been. Richard was not George.

Smiling, she said, "As long as it is not kippers, kidney, or liver, I should like it."

Richard nodded and headed off to speak with the innkeeper. Christiana watched him go, thinking that her life had definitely changed for the better. If he continued to treat her as he had since their meeting at the ball, she thought she could have a nice life, perhaps even a very nice, happy life.

Or not, Christiana thought on a sigh, because between the pleasure he gave her, the respect he showed her, and the kindness with which he dealt with her, she could easily fall in love with this man, truly in love, not the infatuation she'd decided she'd had for George. And that would be awful if he didn't love her back.

"Men!"

Christiana glanced around with surprise

as Lisa suddenly dropped into the seat beside her, her face disgruntled and eyes glaring as she watched Langley walk over to join Richard by the innkeeper.

"Don't mind her," Suzette said, taking up the seat on Christiana's other side as Daniel went to join the men. "She's just annoyed with Robert."

"Why?" Christiana asked, glancing from one to the other.

"Because if he is not ignoring me, he is treating me like a child and I am heartily sick of it." Lisa said grimly. "I think I shall ride with you and Dicky for the rest of the journey."

"Richard," Christiana corrected, and felt a moment's regret that she would not be alone with him again. It was quickly followed by the more sensible side of her mind deciding that might be a good thing. She had no doubt that had the carriage not stopped, by now she and Richard would be doing things a girl wasn't supposed to do until she was married. And while she'd thought she was married this last year, she wasn't, so shouldn't be doing them . . . which was really a shame because she liked it very much. But in a couple days they would reach Gretna Green and be married and could do it all they liked, Christiana reminded herself . . . unless Richard was like George and suddenly changed the moment the "I dos" were said. That thought had her frowning and glancing to the man worriedly.

"You can't leave me alone with the men, Lisa," Suzette protested. "Who will I talk to?"

"The men?" Christiana suggested, forcing her attention back to the conversation.

Suzette snorted at the idea. "They don't talk. Not when they're together. Daniel talks to me when we're alone, but with Langley in the carriage I couldn't get him to talk about anything."

"When have you been alone with Daniel?" Christiana asked with a frown.

"Oh . . . erm . . ." Suzette shrugged. "Just for a minute or two here and there the last day or so."

"Hmm." Christiana eyed her suspiciously, able to tell when Suzette was lying, but not sure she wanted to know the truth in this instance.

"Well, you can come ride with Chrissy and Dicky and me too," Lisa said unrepentantly.

"Richard," Christiana corrected again. Dicky was the hateful imposter she'd been married to. Richard was the true man she wasn't married to . . . yet. Unfortunately, what with the rush to pack and set out, she hadn't got the chance to explain things to her sisters yet.

"Here we are."

Christiana glanced up and murmured a thank-you as a glass of some beverage was set before her. It smelled like cider and she smiled appreciatively at Richard as he settled across the table from her.

"The innkeeper's wife has a pot of beef stew bubbling in the back. It smells delicious so I ordered us both that. But I didn't think to ask you what you'd like to drink, so I asked Langley what you like and he said cider. Fortunately, they had some."

"Thank you," Christiana murmured again. "Beef stew sounds delicious and I do like cider."

"Married a year and you had to ask Langley what she likes," Suzette muttered with disgust.

Christiana kicked her under the table and glared when Suzette glanced to her in surprise.

"Well, at least he asked," she said grimly. "Dicky wouldn't have bothered."

It was only when Suzette peered at her with confusion that Christiana realized what she'd said. Before she could explain, Lisa, who apparently hadn't caught the slip, said,

"Dicky, it's all right if Suzette and I ride with you and Christiana the rest of the way, isn't it?"

"Richard," Christiana and Richard corrected as one, and then shared a wry smile.

"If the girls are going to ride in your carriage, you're welcome to join Robert and me in mine," Daniel offered, setting a glass of lemonade in front of Suzette as he sat down next to Richard.

"Oh." Richard glanced her way, but then sighed in defeat and nodded. "Yes. Fine. Thanks."

Christiana picked up her glass and took a sip to hide her expression. She could tell he wasn't pleased with this turn of events and had probably hoped to continue what they'd started before the carriage had stopped, but events were conspiring against him.

CHAPTER THIRTEEN

"I don't know how she can sleep."

Christiana smiled faintly at Suzette's dry comment, her gaze shifting to Lisa, who had chattered away nonstop for the first several hours after leaving the inn, but had slowed down and finally nodded off with her head on Suzette's shoulder. "She always used to fall asleep on carriage rides when we were children."

"Hmm." Suzette twisted her head to try to look at Lisa's face, but then glanced to Christiana and asked, "So would you care to explain what you meant back at the inn?"

Christiana glanced to her with confusion. "Explain what?"

Suzette narrowed her eyes, but before she could say anything else, Lisa's bag slipped from her lax hands and dropped to the carriage floor with a small thunk. Christiana immediately leaned forward to pick it up. The bag carried a small notebook, quill and a sealed pot of ink. Lisa tended to carry it with her whenever she thought she might find something interesting to write about. She had aspirations to someday be a writer of those horrid adventure novels she was always reading.

"You missed something," Suzette said as Christiana straightened, and she glanced down to see that there was an envelope on the floor. Bending again, she picked that up as well, but straightened much more slowly this time. There was nothing on the outside of the envelope to indicate who it was to, and it had been closed with a blob of dark wax without any seal impression pressed into it, which for some reason sent a shiver of apprehension through Christiana.

"Oh, I forgot about that," Lisa murmured sleepily.

Christiana glanced to the younger girl to see that she was yawning but awake. "What is it?"

"A letter for Dicky," Lisa answered sitting up.

"You mean a letter for Richard," Suzette corrected dryly.

Christiana ignored her and asked, "Who is it from?"

"I don't know. I didn't open it," Lisa said indignantly.

"No, I can see that," she said with exasperation. "But why was it in your bag?"

"Oh." Lisa shrugged and took the bag from her. "It was this morning when Daniel and Robert were helping Dicky bring out his chest."

"Richard," Christiana murmured as Lisa paused and frowned, no doubt because the men had loaded it themselves rather than let the servants do it. Christiana was the only one of the three of them who knew that the men had loaded it themselves because George was in it and they hadn't wanted to risk it being dropped and its contents spilling out.

"Anyway," Lisa continued. "The cutest little boy came running up. He asked which of the men was the Earl and I pointed out Dicky —"

"Richard," Christiana corrected.

"— he started to go toward the men," Lisa continued without stopping. "But I suggested he give the letter to me rather than trouble them when they were busy. I meant to give it to Dic— Richard once they were done with the chest, but then Grace came out of the house, tripped on the step and fell and I shoved the letter in my bag and went to help her up, and . . ." She shrugged. "I forgot all about it till now."

Christiana peered down at the letter. Something about the blank face and black blob of wax gave her a very bad feeling. Besides, it must be for George, not Richard. Richard was only newly returned from over a year in America, and the only person who knew that was Daniel. Daniel would hardly send Richard a note when he had been at the house almost every waking moment since their return.

She turned the letter over in her hands and stared at the blob of wax, and then began to open it.

"What are you doing, Chrissy? That's Dicky's!" Lisa tried to snatch the letter from her.

"Dicky's dead," Christiana snapped, shifting sideways on her seat and ripping the letter open.

"What?" Lisa gasped.

Ignoring her, Christiana held the letter to the window to read it. It was growing late in the day, the sun was setting and there wasn't much light to read from, but she managed and cursed as she did.

"What is it?" Suzette asked and snatched the letter from her.

Christiana didn't bother to try to stop her, but waited silently as she read it. She had meant to tell them at some point. Suzette's reading the letter was as good a way to bring up the subject as any.

"I knew it!" Suzette exclaimed suddenly.

"You knew what?" Lisa asked curiously.

"I knew there was something going on," Suzette explained, her tone distracted as she continued to read.

"Why? What's going on?" Lisa asked, turning narrowed eyes on Christiana.

"Dicky's dead," Suzette announced. "I knew he was. The man was cold as stone when we left for the ball."

Lisa blinked in dismay. "Whatever are you talking about? Dicky's fine. He's in the carriage with Daniel and Robert."

"That's Richard," Suzette muttered, continuing to read.

"What? I don't understand." Her gaze slid to Christiana. "What is she talking about, Chrissy?"

"The man I married —"

"Murder!" Suzette squawked suddenly. "Dicky wasn't murdered."

"Of course he wasn't," Lisa said with exasperation. "He's alive and fine."

Suzette ignored their younger sister and waved the letter with disgust. "I wouldn't even bother to show this to Richard. It's all just claptrap. Threatening to tell everyone Richard murdered George to get his title and name back. What nonsense."

"Yes, I know, but the other business is true enough, and even that would cause a scandal if what George did got out," Christiana said unhappily as Suzette continued reading. "I need to tell Richard about this and the sooner the better. Suzie, bang on the wall and tell the driver to stop."

Suzette lowered the letter and raised an eyebrow. "Don't you think it's better if we wait until we reach Radnor? We must be almost there by now and if that chest the men insisted on loading themselves holds what I think it does, we definitely need to leave it at Radnor and not take it back to town."

"What does the chest hold?" Lisa asked at once.

"George," Christiana answered, verifying Suzette's thoughts.

"Who's George?" Lisa asked with a frown.

"Dicky," Suzette answered.

"*What?*" Lisa squawked, and bounced on her seat impatiently. "You aren't making any sense! I demand someone explain what's going on this instant."

Christiana and Suzette exchanged a glance and then Christiana sighed and sat back. Suzette was right, they probably were almost at Radnor. Richard had said they should arrive before dark and that was almost upon them. And they did need to get George there and leave him. She certainly didn't want him back in the master bedroom in town. It was a bit disturbing to sleep in the room next to your dead, not quite legally wed, husband.

"Is someone going to explain?" Lisa asked grimly.

"Ask her," Suzette said dryly. "I have an idea of what's happened, but am not sure of all the specifics."

When Lisa and Suzette both turned to her, Christiana grimaced and said, "I was going to tell you this yesterday, but wanted you both together to explain, and then with the sudden need to pack and the trip and everything, there never seemed a good time to —"

"Yes, yes, you were going to tell us," Suzette interrupted impatiently. "Just get to it."

Christiana took a breath and then said abruptly, "The man I married was an imposter. It was Richard's twin brother George."

"But he's dead," Lisa protested.

"He is now," Christiana said grimly, and then sighed and said, "Just listen and let me explain."

When Lisa and Suzette both nodded, Christiana quickly explained things as clearly and concisely as she could. She then sat back and waited expectantly.

Lisa was the first to speak. Releasing a deep sigh, she said, "It's just like one of those books I read." Turning on Suzette she added, "And you said they were all nonsense and wouldn't happen in real life."

Christiana blinked. "It is not like one of your novels."

"It is," Lisa insisted. "George was the evil villain, you are the beautiful heroine, and Richard is the brave hero who loves and rescues you."

"There is no love," Christiana said firmly.

"Of course there is. Why else would he marry you?"

"Because he's a good man who doesn't wish to see us pay for his brother's sins."

"Oh, he's so good," Lisa gasped. "You have to love him, Chrissy."

"For heaven's sake, Lisa," Suzette said with exasperation. "He is saving himself from scandal too."

"Men do not really suffer from scandal," Lisa said grimly. "It is only the female who does. Why, when word got out that Lord Mortis had assaulted and deflowered Penelope Pureheart, the scandal barely touched him. He was still welcomed into the finest homes and free to go to his club. It was Penelope who was banished to the wilds of —"

"Lisa, that is fiction," Suzette interrupted impatiently.

"If I were to tell someone the tale Christiana just told me they would probably think it fiction too. I — Oh!" she interrupted herself, eyes going wide. "I could write it!"

"No," Christiana and Suzette said as one, both equally horrified. It was Suzette who pointed out, "Someone might realize it is about Christiana and Richard and —"

"Oh, I would change the names," she said with irritation. "Never fear. It will be fine."

Christiana opened her mouth to protest further, but paused as the carriage slowed. A glance out the window showed that they were winding up a driveway toward a large house. She recognized it at once as Radnor.

"We are here," Suzette murmured, peering out the window on the opposite side of the carriage.

"Thank God," Christiana muttered, and then turned to Lisa. "You are not to write a word of this ever. Do you understand?"

"Oh, very well," Lisa said resentfully. "But it would have made a wonderful love story."

"It is not a love story," she insisted.

"It will be," Lisa assured her solemnly. "Trust me Chrissy. He is your hero, you will love him."

Christiana rolled her eyes and opened the carriage door, leaping out before it had even come to a complete halt. The last thing she needed was Lisa's drivel about her falling in love with Richard. She had no desire to have her heart broken all over again. She'd been through that with Dicky-George already and it hadn't been pleasant. But she feared it would be a thousand times worse if she were foolish enough to fall in love with Richard, and the most depressing thing about that was she feared she was already halfway there.

"Christiana! What the devil are you doing leaping out of the carriage before it's stopped?" Richard demanded, doing the same thing himself from Daniel's carriage to stride forward and berate her. "You could have been hurt."

"I wasn't though," she said quickly, and then held out the letter and added, "Besides, this is important."

Richard scowled at her for another moment, but then took the letter and peered at the broken seal.

"A young boy gave it to Lisa this morning saying it was for the Earl. She got distracted and forgot to give it to you and I opened it in the carriage just a few minutes ago. I thought it was probably for George, but it's for you."

Eyebrows rising, he opened the letter and began to read.

"What is it?" Daniel asked as he reached them.

"Blackmail," Suzette answered, stepping down from the carriage and moving to his side. "Someone knows what George did and that he's dead. They actually think Richard killed him to get back his name and position and is threatening to reveal all if he isn't paid a good sum of money."

"I see. Then Christiana explained — ?" Daniel began, but Suzette cut him off grimly.

"Yes, she explained everything. Something that you, as my soon-to-be-husband, surely should have done before this, don't you think, Woodrow? Husbands and wives really shouldn't have such secrets, should they?"

Christiana bit her lip at Suzette's tone and the use of Daniel's last name. It was a good indicator that Suzette wasn't pleased. Daniel seemed to realize that, but merely shrugged and said solemnly, "It wasn't my secret to tell."

Suzette hrrumphed and glanced to Richard as he closed the letter again.

"We need to get back to the city at once," he announced.

"But —" Christiana said, and then gasped in surprise as he caught her elbow to urge her toward the Radnor carriage.

"I only have until the day after tomorrow to get the money together and will receive another message telling me where to leave it then," he said. "We have to go."

"No, wait," Christiana said breathlessly, forced to run to keep up with him.

"Surely you aren't going to pay the blackmail?" Daniel asked, falling into step on her other side.

"I hope not. That's why I want to get back at once. We need to try to sort out who it could be. But if we don't figure it out, I will pay rather than risk the scandal damaging the girls."

"But —" Christiana tried again, only to gasp in surprise as they reached the carriage and he caught her by the waist and lifted her in. Once on her feet on the floor of the carriage, however, she whirled and blocked his entrance. "Dammit, husband, listen to me."

Richard stopped at once, eyes wide and mouth round with surprise. Daniel too was rather agape. However, Suzette and Lisa were both biting their lips to keep from smiling and Robert was grinning like an idiot.

"There she is," he said with a grin. "That's the take-no-nonsense Chrissy I grew up with." Expression turning solemn, he added, "You disappeared after marrying Dicky, and that worried me more than anything else."

"Me too," Suzette announced. "I couldn't believe it when you let Dicky treat you as he did. If one of us had tried it with you, you would have slapped us silly."

Christiana sighed and merely shook her head. Now was not the time to explain that she hadn't lost this side of herself right away on marriage, that George had beat it out of her with insults and criticisms until she'd no longer had the confidence to stand up for herself. Instead, she turned her attention back to Richard. "We need to see to your brother before we head back," she said reasonably. "It seems silly to have come all this way and not at least do that. Besides, we really can't keep him any longer. All the ice in London is not going to keep his presence hidden much longer."

Richard glanced toward the carriage roof and the chest there, and then sighed and nodded. "Yes, of course. We should . . . er . . ." He hesitated, and then called the driver over. The man had moved around to the front of the horses to examine the beasts, but came at once and Richard ordered him to drive the carriage around the house to the family chapel. When he then started into the carriage, Christiana backed out of the way to allow it. She settled on a bench seat, squeezing up into the corner to make room as Richard sat beside her. The others climbed in after to join them.

It was rather cramped with the six of them in the cab, but no one complained and the carriage set off the moment Langley pulled the door closed. It was a quick ride around the house, thank goodness, and the moment the carriage stopped they all piled out.

The men lifted down the chest and then Richard paused to order the driver to take the carriage to the stables and change the horses for another journey. When the carriage started away, Daniel and Richard each lifted one end of the chest and carried it around behind the chapel. Christiana and the others followed, walking silently until they reached the family vault, a small, low stone building. Robert then rushed ahead to open the door, revealing steps descending down into darkness.

"We should have thought to bring a

torch," Daniel muttered, peering down the steps.

"We won't go far from the door," Richard decided as they started down the steps. "I'll have him moved to a proper casket later."

Christiana followed Robert down the steps, aware that Suzette and Lisa were on her heels. Her nose wrinkled as she glanced around the dark interior once they reached the bottom step. The weak early evening light cast a pale square on the floor, but it didn't light up much more than that. Judging by the smells assaulting her, Christiana suspected that might be a good thing. Her imagination was supplying gruesome enough images of rotten, collapsing coffins and ravaged corpses. She didn't need to see the real thing.

"We'll put him here," Richard said directing Daniel to the very edge of the square of light coming through the doors. The two men set the chest down and immediately turned to head back out, but paused on seeing the others.

"Shouldn't we say something before we go?" Christiana asked uncertainly.

Richard paused and glanced uncertainly back toward the chest.

"It just feels wrong to simply dump him and hurry away," she said uncomfortably when everyone was silent.

"Oh, come on then," Suzette said and slid past her to move to the chest.

Christiana followed and took up position beside her and then waited as everyone else came to form a half circle around the chest.

Suzette then clasped her hands together, closed her eyes and lowered her head.

Biting her lip, Christiana did the same, aware that the others were following suit.

She heard Suzette clear her throat, and then her sister intoned solemnly, "Here lies George Cainan Fairgrave . . . Thank God he's dead. Amen."

Christiana blinked her eyes open and gaped at her sister.

"That works for me," Daniel said with amusement. "Short, sweet and honest."

Christiana sighed, sure something more should have been said, but at the same time knowing Daniel was right. It was certainly honest. There wasn't a person there who wasn't glad the man was dead.

She started to turn toward the steps leading back out of the vault, but paused at the sight of a man standing there, a silhouette against the lighter backdrop of early evening outside.

"Reverend Bertrand," Richard said with surprise.

"I arrived as your driver was bringing the carriage around the house. He said you'd come to the vault and I presumed it was to visit your brother," the man said quietly. "Imagine my surprise when I realized it was to lay him to rest here."

Christiana heard Richard curse and bit her lip as he moved quickly past her to mount the steps.

"If you'll come with me to my office, I will explain," he said quietly as he urged the pastor out of the vault.

Christiana and the rest of their group followed, more than eager to escape the musty atmosphere with its pall of death. Richard had started to lead the reverend away, but paused and glanced back to suggest, "Christiana, perhaps you could greet the staff and arrange for a basket of food to be packed for the trip back to London?"

"Yes, of course," she said at once.

"Thank you," he said and then continued forward with the pastor.

"Do you think we should go with him to back him up on the story?" Robert asked with a frown.

Daniel considered the question, but shook his head. "He'll send for us if he needs assistance."

They were all silent as they watched Rich-

309

ard lead the pastor not around to the front of the house, but in through a pair of French doors Christiana thought must lead to the office here.

"Well," Daniel said as the two men disappeared. "Shall we?"

Christiana nodded and started forward, leading the way around the house to the front door. The servants were all lined up on either side of the hall when she opened the door and led the way inside. Some time was spent explaining that Lord Radnor had been detained and would be along shortly. Fortunately, the butler recognized Christiana from her one visit and made introductions to the rest of the staff. There was a good number of them, however, and it took longer than she would have liked to meet everyone, but she didn't feel she could be rude and refuse so smiled and shook hands and nodded to everyone from the housekeeper to the lowliest maid. They had just finished with the last introduction and Christiana was about to ask to have a word with Cook when one of the hall doors opened and Richard peered out.

"Christiana, can you come here please?" he asked and then peered back into the room to listen to something the reverend was saying. He then turned back to say,

"Actually, if everyone would come in here, that would be good."

He then left the door open and moved out of sight. Richard was standing talking to the pastor next to a large, dark wood desk by the French doors when Christiana entered. She moved immediately to his side, catching the pastor's last words as he said, "absolutely legal."

"What is?" she asked, pausing beside Richard.

He glanced down at her and smiled. "The wedding Reverend Bertrand has agreed to perform for us."

Christiana's eyes widened and she glanced to the holy man in question.

"My lady," the pastor said, taking her hand and smiling at her kindly. "I am sorry to hear of all the troubles you and his lordship have suffered this last year. George always did seem to have the devil in him. Still, I am a little surprised and saddened to hear just how much devil." He patted her hand. "We'll set this right today, though, and make it all legal. And I don't see any reason anyone else need know about it. George did enough damage without us adding to it, and it seems God meted out his own punishment."

"Thank you," Christiana murmured.

311

"If we're ready then?" Reverend Bertrand asked glancing to Richard.

He nodded and turned toward Daniel, but then paused with surprise. Seeing his expression, Christiana glanced about the room, her own eyes widening. It wasn't just Daniel, Robert, Suzette and Lisa who had followed them into the room. Apparently the servants had thought Richard had meant them too when he'd said everyone and every last one of them, including Grace and Christiana's sisters' maids, were now crammed into the room as well.

Clearing his throat, Richard said apologetically, "I didn't mean —"

"It's all right," Reverend Bertrand interrupted and then stepped to Richard's side and smiled at everyone. "The Earl and Countess would like to renew their vows and be married again to each other and you are all going to be witnesses."

A buzz went around the servants and Suzette immediately moved to Christiana's side to whisper worriedly, "Will it be legal now?"

"I think so," Christiana whispered back.

Both women gave a start as the pastor turned and whispered, "Yes, my dear lady, it will. The banns were read, and the license issued for the original wedding between

312

Richard Fairgrave and Christiana Madison . . . and handily the license was right here in the office. Apparently, it was left here for safekeeping when you stopped on the way to London. We will carry out the ceremony in the church here at Radnor in front of several witnesses. Once the ceremony is over and we, as well as witnesses, sign the marriage register in the church, it will most definitely be legal."

Christiana smiled uncertainly at the man and then gave a start as Richard took her arm. "Shall we?"

"Yes, of course," Christiana murmured, but felt some trepidation as he urged her to follow the pastor, who was making his way through the now parting people in the room. She was going to be married . . . Again. It hadn't been that long since Christiana had vowed to herself that she would never marry again and yet here she was doing it, and while she knew they had to for several very good reasons, not least of which was that she might even now be carrying Richard's child, she couldn't help worrying that it would be her first marriage all over again. That the moment the ceremony was over, Richard, like George before him, would suddenly find her wanting and turn from the considerate kind man he'd proven to be, to a critical, cold stranger. The thought was a depressing one and she felt more like she was being led to the gallows than to a wedding as they followed Reverend Bertrand out of the house and to the chapel with her sisters, Daniel, Robert and every last Radnor servant following.

Richard, on the other hand, didn't appear to be suffering the same misgivings, Christiana noted, glancing at him from under her lashes. He was rushing along, nearly treading on the pastor's heels in his eagerness to get to the church. Weren't men supposed to be the reluctant ones when it came to weddings?

"Here we are." Reverend Bertrand led them to the altar in the small church and busied himself positioning Christiana and Richard where he wanted them, then took a moment to arrange everyone else before rushing off to collect his bible. He was back almost before Christiana could take a breath.

The service was a blur for Christiana and she gave her responses automatically without really taking in what she was saying. Her mind was on the worry of what would happen once it was done. In that state, she was taken rather by surprise when it ended, even giving a start when Richard kissed her.

Before she could gather herself enough to kiss him back, he was straightening and urging her to follow the pastor to sign the marriage register.

Christiana signed first, her hand shaking as she did, and then she stepped back to make room for Richard to sign and found herself surrounded by her sisters and the servants, all offering congratulations. She managed to smile and nod in response, but was distracted by the panic that wanted to claim her. She noticed that Daniel and Robert signed as witnesses, then the three men put their heads together with the pastor. She wondered what they were talking about when he suddenly nodded and then Richard turned to make his way to her as the pastor clapped his hands to get everyone's attention.

"We shall go back to the house now and eat the fine meal Cook prepared for the arrival of the Earl and Countess and their guests. Come along. Let us head back to the house."

Richard took her arm as the servants all began to leave. "Did you and your sisters wish to freshen up before the meal?"

"I thought we were going to head straight back to London?" she said with surprise.

"The men convinced me to alter the plans

315

slightly," he said quietly, urging her to follow the servants outside. "I'm sure you and your sisters would like to wash and change after the long journey today, and a meal would be nice too."

"I suppose," Christiana murmured as they started toward the house. It would be pleasant to have a quick wash and change of clothes, then a meal before setting out again. "But Richard, I have been thinking. You can't pay this blackmailer."

"I don't want to," he admitted, "And we will do what we can to catch the blackmailer rather than pay, but I also won't risk it getting out that George tried to kill me and married you in my name. The scandal would destroy you and ruin any chance of your sisters marrying well."

Christiana stared. His concern was for her and her sisters. He hadn't suddenly changed . . . yet. Clearing her throat, she said, "That is very thoughtful, but I suspect if you pay him once, the blackmailer will continue to demand money. And it just isn't right that you should have to pay when all of this is George's fault to begin with, especially since you didn't kill him."

"And you and your sisters shouldn't have to pay by suffering the scandal either," he pointed out quietly, glancing around to be sure no one was close enough to overhear their conversation. "George was my brother. If anyone is going to pay, it should be me."

Christiana frowned. She didn't want a scandal any more than he did. Her sisters would suffer horribly from it, but . . . She wasn't foolish enough to think if they paid once, it would be done. The blackmailer would no doubt ask for more later, and then again, and this would hang over all their heads until they were all dead and buried. Frowning, she asked, "Can we not take the body to the authorities, claim George didn't die in the fire after all as we had all assumed, but that he was the one away in America this last year? That he left a letter to that effect when he departed, but it apparently burned up in the fire. We can say he returned because he was feeling unwell and that we found him dead in his bed this morning. The authorities can examine him, will find he died of natural causes and all will be well." She smiled widely, sure she'd found the answer. "That way there would be no scandal, and no way the blackmailer could blackmail us."

"Ah, well . . ." Richard grimaced, and then sighed and admitted, "Actually, Daniel and I suspect George *was* murdered."

"What?" she asked with shock and

stopped walking.

"We smelled bitter almond around his mouth when we went to move him the first night," Richard explained, urging her to walk again.

Christiana stared at him blankly. "I don't understand."

"We think he was poisoned." Richard glanced around as they reached the house and urged her to follow the others inside. "Don't worry. We have a plan to catch the blackmailer."

"What is this plan?" she asked worriedly as he started to lead her upstairs.

"I'll explain later," Richard said rather than answer the question. He also started to move more quickly, urging her upstairs and along the hall to the master bedroom. "You just go on inside and refresh yourself before the meal. All will be well. I'll have Grace and your chest brought up. Would you like a bath?"

Christiana frowned. "No, that would take too long and I know you want to head back to London. A basin of water to wash with will do."

"Right. I'll see it's brought up," he assured her opening the bedroom door.

She started to automatically walk into the room, but he caught her back, drawing her around to face him and then suddenly kissed her. It was no quick pressing of lips like the one in the church, but a hard, demanding kiss that quickly had her sinking against him with a sigh and wrapping her arms around his shoulders.

"To tide me over until we can consummate the marriage," he said with a sigh as he ended the kiss a moment later, and then he smiled crookedly and added, "You are now most definitely, and legally, my wife."

Christiana managed a smile despite her reservations, and he urged her into the room. "I shall send up Grace and your chest. Take your time. I'm sure Cook will need a bit of time to get the meal on the table."

He then pulled the door closed, leaving her alone in the master bedroom. Christiana sighed and glanced around as she moved further into the room. She had never been in it before. When she and George had stopped on the way into London she'd been given the connecting room next door and never stepped foot in the room. She'd also cried herself to sleep wondering why George had been so short with her that day and why he hadn't come to her that night. She'd cried herself to sleep many nights during the first six months of their marriage wondering the same thing.

Shaking those memories away, she walked around the room, looking over everything curiously as she waited for Grace. It seemed to take forever for the woman to arrive with two footmen in tow carrying Christiana's chest. Despite Richard's telling her to take her time, she was quick about her ablutions and change of clothes. Even so, Suzette was stepping out of her room when Christiana left the master bedroom to head downstairs.

"I feel better," Suzette commented as the two of them started toward the stairs.

"As do I," Christiana murmured.

"I'm not looking forward to the ride back to town though."

"I'm sorry about this, Suzie," Christiana said. "I know you cannot welcome this delay. Perhaps you and Daniel should continue on to Gretna Green and leave us to deal with this other business."

"As if we would," Suzette said dryly and shook her head as they started down the stairs. "No, this is more urgent. We have some time yet. If things drag on and it's necessary, Daniel and I can travel through the night, stopping only to change horses. We could make the journey to Gretna in a couple days that way and be back just as quickly. So as long as we do not delay much more than a week we should be able to make the two-week deadline Father was given."

"Thank you," Christiana murmured and wondered if Suzette's marrying Daniel was even necessary anymore. Richard had said he'd make up for what his brother had done. Did that include paying off the gambling debt? He hadn't said so specifically, and he also hadn't said anything to suggest Suzette and Daniel needn't marry to gain the dower and pay the debt, but things had been a bit chaotic and confusing since the night of the ball. Perhaps he just hadn't had the chance to say anything. Or even think about it really. She would have to broach the subject with him the first chance she got just to be sure, Christiana decided. She didn't wish to see Suzette forced into marriage, even if on her own terms, if there was no need.

"Wait for me!" Lisa cried out, suddenly appearing at the top of the stairs behind them. "I don't know where the dining room is."

Suzette and Christiana paused, smiling at their younger sister as she rushed down to join them and then the trio headed up the hall to the dining room.

Christiana had expected Richard and the

other men to be there, entertaining the pastor when they arrived, so was a bit surprised to find Reverend Bertrand standing all by himself, peering out a window when they entered.

"Sorry we took so long," Christiana murmured as she glanced back up the empty hall in search of her husband.

"Not at all," the pastor said at once, beaming at them as he turned from the window. "You are all three well worth the wait." Moving toward the table, he began to pull out a chair and suggested, "Shall we sit down? I believe the meal is ready and the servants were merely waiting for your arrival to serve."

Christiana felt her eyes narrow at the words. "What about the men?"

"Ah." Reverend Bertrand, pulled out a second chair and moved on to do the same with a third before saying, "They wished me to explain that they felt they could travel more swiftly with just the one carriage and thought you might be more comfortable waiting here with your maids while they dealt with matters in town."

"They left?" Suzette snapped with disbelief.

"Er . . . yes," he admitted, looking uncomfortable.

Christiana turned on her heel and started out of the room at once.

"Really, my lady, I think you would do better to simply wait here as they wish. They left some time ago, directly after seeing you ladies upstairs. You will never catch up to them," the man argued, hurrying after them when Suzette and Lisa followed her.

All three women ignored him.

CHAPTER FOURTEEN

"They're going to be very, very angry."

Richard grimaced at Robert's prediction, knowing the man was right. But really, leaving the women behind was the best choice. Christiana and her sisters could now relax and enjoy themselves together at Radnor and be out of harm's way while he, Daniel and Robert hunted down their blackmailer. Besides, it seemed ridiculous to drag the maids, the chests, and all three carriages back to London when they would just have to make the return journey in a couple of days' time for Suzette and Daniel to marry. And they could travel much more swiftly with just the one carriage.

They had taken Woodrow's carriage because it was the fastest. They were making good time. They'd stopped at three different inns along the way to change horses, but were still more than three quarters of the way back to London and Richard was sure it wasn't yet midnight.

"They will get over their anger," Daniel said now, not sounding at all worried about Suzette's reaction to their defection.

Robert just shook his head. "Trust me. I have known the Madison sisters all my life. You will not get off easily for this. Either of you." He let that sink in and then glanced to Richard. "I was glad to see Christiana stand up for herself and make you listen back at the house. It was a good sign."

"How so?" Richard asked curiously, recalling his surprise when he'd placed her in the carriage and she'd suddenly snapped at him.

"She is being herself with you. It shows she isn't afraid of you as I think she was with Dicky . . . er . . . George," he corrected himself. "The one time I saw them together after the wedding she was as jumpy as a cat. I feared he was taking his fists to her, but she assured me he wasn't."

"Did you believe her?" Richard asked, frowning at the possibility that George may have beaten Christiana on top of everything else.

"Yes. Christiana is a terrible liar and I'm sure she was telling the truth, but she was still afraid of the man." He shook his head. "Perhaps she just feared what would happen if he did lose his temper."

Richard scowled. No one should have to live in fear. A body should feel safe in their own home.

"That doesn't matter now though," Robert said after a moment. "The good news is she doesn't appear to fear you the same way. I think the two of you will make a fine match."

"Thank you," Richard said dryly, but was secretly quite pleased with Robert's words. Christiana was proving to be intelligent, passionate and capable. He liked the woman, and suspected he could more than like her with a little time.

"Does Christiana like —" Richard began, and then grabbed for something to hold on to as a loud crack preceded the carriage suddenly pitching to the side. The next moments were a chaos of shouts, and whinnies as the three men were tossed about. The carriage seemed to roll and crash end over end, and then everything suddenly went still and silent.

For one moment, Richard was too dazed to be quite sure what had happened and where he was, but then he heard a groan beneath him and realized the lumpy something he was lying on was either Daniel or Robert. He also became aware that something heavy lay on top of him, making it hard to breathe. Grimacing, he lifted a hand to touch whatever it was and was rewarded with another groan and a heel or elbow — he wasn't sure which in the darkness — dug into his groin as whoever was on top of him began to struggle to get off.

"Lord Woodrow?"

The darkness surrounding them was suddenly relieved when the carriage door was yanked open above them and the driver peered in with a lit lantern in hand. It was then Richard realized the carriage had come to a halt on its side. He grunted as the man on top of him unintentionally jabbed him in the side as he struggled to sit up. The fellow then reached up for the opening and began to pull himself out, but it wasn't until he was halfway through the opening, his face lit up by the driver's lantern that Richard knew it was Robert.

"Damn, Richard, get off me, I can't breathe," Daniel gasped beneath him, apparently recognizing Robert as well.

Richard immediately began to move, doing his best not to elbow or otherwise poke his friend as he did. Of course, that was impossible and he muttered several apologies as he shifted his weight to the side. Kneeling in the overturned carriage, he then turned back to ask, "Are you all right?"

"Battered and bruised, but otherwise fine I think," Daniel said grimly, sitting up beside him. "You?"

"The same," Richard said on a sigh and then glanced up to the opening and the still waiting driver. Robert was now also peering back in at them.

"What happened?" Daniel asked his driver as he stood and began to pull himself through the opening.

"I'm not sure, my lord," the driver said unhappily. "We were riding along fine and then I heard a crack, and the carriage pitched and began to roll. Fortunately, the carriage body snapped just behind the boot and the horses weren't dragged with it or they would have died for certain."

"And you weren't hurt?" Richard heard Daniel ask the man as he followed him out of the carriage.

"I was tossed, but landed on a bush. I'm all right," the man muttered, and then added with disgust, "But the coach is a wreck. I don't think it can even be fixed."

"As long as everyone is all right," Daniel said and raised an eyebrow in question at Robert.

"Fine," the other man assured him, easing to the edge of the carriage to leap down. "I got an elbow in the face during one of the rolls and will probably have a black eye, but otherwise am fine."

Daniel grunted at this news and moved to inspect the two wheels on the upraised side of the carriage. Richard shifted to the edge of the carriage to look them over as well, but both seemed fine so they followed Robert to the ground and moved to peer at the broken wheel.

"That's a rather straight break," Daniel muttered suspiciously as they peered at the spokes.

"You think they were cut?" Richard asked peering at what remained attached to the carriage.

"Those three spokes certainly look like they could have been," Daniel pointed out. "The rest are more splintered and natural-looking breaks. They probably snapped under the pressure when those three gave way."

Richard frowned at the suggestion and straightened to glance around. "I agree. The question is if it was deliberate, who did it and why? And when?"

"The why is easy," Daniel said quietly. "As far as George's killer knows, the poison didn't work. As for when . . ." He peered back at the broken wheel. "It couldn't have been done in town. There were four of us in the carriage this morning on the way to Radnor. The wheel would have given out under that kind of weight before we left London. Besides, you weren't even in my carriage on the way out of town."

"So it was done at Radnor or one of the three stops since we left," Richard reasoned and glanced around again. He didn't doubt for a minute he was the target, but he was more concerned with the possibility that someone may have followed them from London and might yet be following them.

"Is that a carriage I hear?" he asked suddenly.

"Yes, and it's moving quickly. We'd best get off the road." Daniel called to his driver to warn him and the man immediately urged the horses onto the grassy verge. He then moved back to the edge of the road with his lantern and lifted it in the air to swing it back and forth to get the attention of the approaching vehicle.

"A coach and six," Robert muttered as the vehicle careened around the bend and into view on the moonlit lane.

The oncoming coachmen spotted Daniel's driver and swerved to miss him. He didn't slow, however, but raced right past them.

"Wasn't that — ?" Robert began.

"Yes," Richard said grimly, having recognized the Radnor coach with Christiana, Suzette and Lisa all gaping out the window at them.

"I did tell you they would not take our leaving sitting down," Robert said with amusement.

"You didn't say they would follow," Daniel pointed out.

"Why spoil the surprise?" Robert laughed.

Richard rolled his eyes and then watched the Radnor coach return from the direction it had gone. He wasn't surprised to see it returning. However, he *was* surprised when it pulled to a halt next to them and the women did not immediately pile out exclaiming with concern over their well-being after their accident. Instead, it sat silent and still, the driver glancing uncertainly from the men to the still closed coach door and back.

"Time to face the music," Robert said dryly, heading for the door.

Daniel grunted and then glanced to his own driver and ordered him to tie the leads of their horses to the back of the Radnor carriage and then join the driver on the front. They would stop at the next inn to leave the horses. Daniel's driver would stop there as well to arrange for someone to collect the broken carriage and see if it could be fixed.

"Hello ladies," Robert said cheerfully as he opened the carriage door and got inside.

There was a polite chorus of hellos and then silence, Richard noted as he approached the open door. Glancing in, he saw that Robert had settled next to Christiana on one bench seat, leaving Suzette and Lisa on the other. His gaze moved over the women's sour expressions as they peered back at him and he sighed, but said, "Hello ladies," as he entered as well. This time, however, there was no response and thick silence reigned as he squeezed onto the bench seat between Robert and Christiana. There was also no response when Daniel entered with the same greeting. It was obvious the women were holding him and Daniel responsible for leaving without them, and despite being with them, Robert was not being held accountable.

At least not by Christiana and Suzette, Richard thought as he tried to find a comfortable position on the seat. Lisa alone was glaring at Langley.

The carriage started forward then, and Richard found himself jolted and then tossed against Christiana as they turned to head toward London. He quickly tried to ease back to give her more room, but found himself pressing uncomfortably against Robert to do so. Muttering with irritation, he gave up trying to force more space on the narrow seat and simply lifted Christiana onto his lap and slid over into her spot.

"Put me down," Christiana cried at once.

"This is more comfortable," Richard said.

"Perhaps for you," she snapped.

"For you too," he said confidently, relaxing and wrapping his arms around her waist. "You are just too angry at me to admit it."

She twisted sideways across his lap to scowl at him and asked, "Why ever would I be angry at you? Just because the three of you snuck out like a trio of cowards leaving the poor pastor to explain you'd headed back to London without us?"

"We thought we were doing you a favor at the time," Richard said quietly. "You would have been much more comfortable waiting at Radnor with your maids."

"The maids are following in Robert's carriage," she announced, and then added grimly, "And if you'd thought you were doing us a favor, you would have told us yourselves you were leaving."

"I didn't say I thought *you* would believe

it a favor," he said calmly. "Just that we knew it was."

Christiana snorted and turned away, folding her arms angrily across her chest. "Oh, aye, we would have been terribly comfortable waiting at Radnor not knowing what was happening and worrying ourselves silly. My, I can't think why we followed you with so much to look forward to."

"Well, I'm glad you did. Thank you. We could have been stuck out there on the road all night," he said solemnly.

Christiana stilled, and then turned to peer at him suspiciously in the light cast by the lantern outside the window. After a moment, she relaxed enough to ask, "What happened?"

"It looks like three spokes in the front left wheel may have been cut. The whole wheel collapsed under the stress when they gave," he answered promptly, deciding there was no sense keeping the information from the women. It was better if they were prepared and had an eye out for trouble too.

Christiana turned sharply to peer at him. "Cut? Are you certain?"

Richard hesitated. "Not completely, but the breaks on three spokes side by side were almost straight across while the others were jagged and splintered."

"George's poisoner?" she asked unhappily.

"That would be my guess," he acknowledged.

"What? George was poisoned?" Suzette asked at once, and Richard glanced over to see that Daniel had drawn the young woman onto his own lap to make room on their side of the carriage. Suzette was sitting, arms crossed and expression grim like her sister, apparently not really happy to be there either.

"It seems George may have been poisoned," Christiana explained. "Daniel and Richard smelled bitter almonds by his mouth."

"Almonds aren't poisonous," Suzette said at once.

"Bitter almonds are used to make cyanide," Lisa explained solemnly, drawing every eye her way. Shrugging, she said, "I read a lot."

"She does," Suzette said dryly and then turned to Christiana. "What else don't we know?"

"You know everything I know now," she assured her. "And I only found out about the poison after the wedding. I just hadn't yet had a chance to tell you."

Suzette nodded and then turned to spear

Daniel with a look. "What else?"

"That's it," he assured her.

"And why didn't you tell me yourself before this?" Suzette asked.

"It wasn't my secret to tell," he said simply.

"Where have I heard that before?" she asked dryly, turning back to face forward again, apparently not appeased.

"So we have a murderer as well as a blackmailer," Lisa murmured thoughtfully. "Or do we think they are the same person?"

Richard and Daniel exchanged glances.

"They don't know," Suzette said for them when neither man spoke.

"Well . . ." Lisa frowned. "Surely it wouldn't be easy for someone to get poison inside the townhouse without being discovered?"

Richard almost piped up to say that they had got George out without discovery, but then realized that wasn't true. Daniel had been caught in Suzette's room by Suzette, and he would have been caught there too had he not thrust the body at the man and rushed out to lead the women downstairs. He hardly could have done that were he a stranger to the house. Had he been a stranger, they both would have been caught in Suzette's room. Perhaps it wouldn't have been easy for an outsider to get the poison in undiscovered.

"So it is probably someone in the town-house who did it," Christiana followed her reasoning.

"Someone could have paid one of the servants to do it," Suzette suggested.

There was silence as everyone contemplated that. It seemed the most likely scenario, but no one was eager to embrace it. Members of the ton depended on the steadfast loyalty of their servants. Without it the number of scandals made public would probably treble. Of course, it happened on occasion that a servant wasn't as loyal as one would hope, but it was never something anyone wished to consider.

"I shall have to question the servants when we arrive back in London," Richard said with a sigh, acknowledging that a betrayal by one of the staff was most likely what had happened.

"That leaves the blackmailer . . . if it isn't the same person who paid someone on staff to administer the poison," Lisa said.

"It is someone who knew what George did last year and that he took Richard's place," Christiana said, her expression thoughtful. "There can't be many who know that. I hardly think he would trust that information to many people."

"No," Richard agreed, and asked, "Who among his friends do you think he would have trusted with the information?"

Christiana snorted at the question. "You are asking me? I daresay you would know that better than I. I haven't even an idea who his friends were. No one ever came to call, and he certainly didn't deign to tell me where he was going or with whom when he went out."

"Do you have any idea, Daniel?" Richard asked, glancing to his friend.

He shook his head. "I have been stuck at Woodrow since Uncle Henry died last year, trying to bring the estate back up to scratch. I only left because I received your letter from America. I didn't even know you — or George pretending to be you — had married. I have no idea what he's been up to this last year or with whom."

"It shouldn't be too difficult to find out," Robert put in. "There's nothing the ton loves more than a good gossip. A question here or there should tell us who George considered a trusted friend."

"So we need to question the staff, as well as nose out any gossip we can about what George was up to this last year and with whom . . . and I need to make arrangements

338

for the money." Richard paused and glanced around the shadowed faces in the carriage. "Can anyone think of anything else we might do to solve matters?"

Silence was his answer as everyone looked at each other and then Daniel said, "I guess we shall have to start with that and hope we uncover some useful information."

Richard nodded, and then glanced to Christiana as she suddenly shifted on his lap. He thought she was trying to get off him and grabbed her hips to hold her in place, but found himself staring at her derriere as she leaned down to collect something from under the seat. He quite enjoyed the view and was rather disappointed when she straightened, bringing a large basket with her.

"What's that?" Robert asked curiously from beside him as she began to dig through its contents.

"We had Cook pack some food for the journey while we waited for the carriage to be readied," Christiana answered.

"Food?" Richard asked hopefully, his attention immediately shifting to the basket as his stomach growled hungrily. He hadn't eaten since the stop at Stevanage for lunch.

"Yes." She turned to peer down her nose at him. "Did you three not think to have a basket prepared before sneaking off like thieves?"

She was still annoyed with him then, Richard acknowledged with a sigh as he shook his head. That being the case, he was sure the women would refuse to share with them as punishment.

He was proven wrong when Suzette suddenly leaned down and dragged out a second basket under the opposite bench seat as Christiana said, "Then 'tis fortunate we brought enough for everyone."

A kiss on her forehead and Richard's whispered, "Wake up, sleeping beauty. We are almost home," are what woke Christiana. Blinking her eyes open, she peered about the dark interior of the carriage noting that Daniel was waking Suzette much the same way, while Robert had leaned forward to shake Lisa's leg to wake her.

Forcing herself to straighten, she glanced out the window to see that while the sky was lightening, dawn was still a good distance off. They'd made good time, she realized, her gaze moving over the dark buildings lining the road they were traversing. She's just recognized it as their street when the carriage stopped in front of the townhouse.

Robert was the first to alight. He then offered Lisa a hand to help her disembark.

After the long hours in the carriage, Christiana found her legs stiff and shaky under her when she moved to follow and was grateful for Robert's hand when he held it out. Even with it, she stumbled a bit, and then gasped with surprise as Richard stepped down and quickly swept her up in his arms.

"I can walk, husband," she whispered with embarrassment as he carried her up the path to the front door of the townhouse.

"But I like carrying you," Richard whispered back, amusement in his voice.

Christiana peered at his face in the darkness to see that he was smiling, and then glanced over his shoulder as Suzette stumbled sleepily out of the carriage next. It made her feel better to know she wasn't the only one unsteady on her feet after a day and night of travel.

"Can you get the door?" Richard asked, drawing her attention again.

Christiana glanced to the door in front of them and reached down to open it for him, giving it a push to send it swinging open. Richard immediately carried her across the threshold. He didn't set her down then as she'd expected, but simply started up the stairs with her still in his arms.

"Should we not wait for everyone else?" she asked, glancing back toward the still open door.

"They will be fine," Richard assured her. "We discussed it as you slept and rather than wake the servants to prepare another room, Daniel and Robert are going to share the guest room Grace made up for me the night before we left. We will all get a couple of hours' sleep and then start into our investigations and plans for the day."

"Oh," Christiana murmured, hardly hearing the last part of what he'd said. She was contemplating that with Daniel and Robert sharing the guest room, Richard would be sharing her bed . . . which was perfectly appropriate now that they were married, of course, but Christiana found herself suddenly nervous at the prospect.

She would have to undress in front of him. Richard would disrobe in front of her too. And which side of the bed would he prefer? Should she let him undress and get in bed first so he could pick his side? But then he would be free to just lie there and watch as she disrobed, Christiana realized. Besides, why did he have more right to first choice of which side of the bed to sleep in? It was her bed, she reminded herself.

Christiana was still fretting over the matter when Richard said, "Can you get the door again, please?"

When she pushed the bedroom door open, he carried her in and straight to the bed. Richard set her down beside it and then immediately went back to close the door. Christiana shifted nervously, her hands fluttering to her gown and away as she realized she could not reach the fastenings at the back on her own. She glanced to Richard, considering how to ask for his help, but in the next moment the question slipped from her mind and her jaw dropped. He was coming toward her, removing and discarding his clothes along the way. The dark coat went first, the vest and cravat followed and he was dressed only in his trousers and hessians as he moved to sit on the bed. Christiana watched blankly as he removed his boots, then he straightened and his trousers joined them on the floor so that he stood before her completely nude.

She was busy staring at all that had been revealed when Richard suddenly caught her by the shoulders and turned her. Christiana felt his hands moving down her back as he undid the fastenings of her gown and murmured a thank-you as she felt the material gape to allow cool air to caress the skin of her back. She then sucked in a startled breath when his hands suddenly slid inside the material and glided around her sides to the front under it until he found and cupped her breasts. Richard used that hold to pull her back against his chest and Christiana let her breath out on a whoosh as he began nibbling at her neck while caressing her.

For one minute, Christiana was so startled at the suddenness of it all, including the desire that was sent rushing through her, that she simply stood there, unsure what to do. And then she realized that there was little she could do in this position. His arms inside her dress made it impossible for her to reach back and touch him, and his mouth was traveling up her neck, urging her head slightly to the side, but was out of her reach to kiss him.

"We're married," he whispered by her ear, before nipping at it lightly.

"Yes," Christiana breathed as he sucked the lobe into his mouth.

"We haven't consummated it yet though," he added, startling her by swirling his tongue in her ear.

"I — No, I suppose we — ah!" She gasped with surprise as one hand suddenly left her breast to ride down over her stomach and then slide between her legs. The action forced the gown off one shoulder and down her arm to allow room for the maneuver. Christiana immediately slid her arm out to let the material drop away. She then tugged the material off her other shoulder and removed that arm from its sleeve as well, leaving the gown to pool at her waist. She was now as bare as he from the waist up, and found it oddly erotic to see his tanned hand cupping her one breast while his other disappeared under the material of her dress. And then he pressed the heel of his hand against her pelvic bone, urging her back more snugly against his growing hardness as his fingers glided over her most sensitive spot.

"I — Oh," Christiana moaned, now grinding her bottom against him herself. She covered the hand at her breast with one of her own and then used the other to reach back over her shoulder for his head. Christiana managed to catch him by a handful of hair and tugged gently as she turned her head, desperate for him to kiss her. Richard responded at once, covering her mouth with his own as his hands continued to move over her.

It wasn't enough and Christiana was sure it would drive her mad if she weren't able to touch him as well, so managed to slip her arm beneath his and reached back between them to find the hardness pressing so insistently against her. Richard reacted as if she'd burned him, his body stiffening, fingers tightening almost painfully around her breast. Then he suddenly released her and turned her to face him so that he could tug her gown over her hips. The moment the material hit the floor he urged her back against the bed.

Christiana dropped to sit on the edge of it, one hand instinctively reaching out to grab the erection waving before her as he stepped up to the bed. Richard stilled at once and she glanced up to see that his jaw was clenched, his eyes squinted almost closed and his throat moving as he swallowed. She watched him and let her hand drift lightly over his erection, noting that his eyes immediately closed all the way and his head tipped back as he sucked in a long breath. Encouraged, Christiana leaned forward and down to run her tongue over the tip, trying to emulate what he did to her. She stilled briefly as he suddenly caught her head in his hands and said her name in a tight voice, but when he didn't force her head away, she rasped her tongue over him again and then took him in her mouth so that her tongue could reached further down the shaft. That's when he did force her head away. He also urged her to lie back on the bed.

"Was that wrong?" she asked uncertainly as she fell back.

"No," he assured her sounding grim. "It was too right. Much more and I would be useless."

"But you do it to me, and I want to —" Her protest ended on a gasp when he caught her beneath the knees, and pulled her bottom to the edge of the bed. She started to sit up again then, but fell back with another gasp as he suddenly spread her legs wide, stepped between them and drove himself into her. He paused briefly then and Christiana blinked her eyes open, aware only then that she'd closed them. She immediately wished she hadn't. He stood, peering down at her and she was completely revealed in this position. Before she could cover her nakedness he lifted one of her legs to press against his chest and leaned against it as he reached with one hand to caress her breast. The other then moved between her legs, caressing her again as he began to move inside her and Christiana quickly forgot her self-consciousness and everything else as he pounded vigorously into her, his

actions and caresses taking them both to
the precipice and over.

CHAPTER FIFTEEN

The murmur of voices stirred Christiana from sleep, and had her rolling onto her back in bed. Opening her eyes, she found the room awash with sunlight and Richard up, dressed, and at the door talking to someone in the hall. He closed the door now and turned back into the room, a smile curving his lips as his eyes landed on her.

"Ah, you're awake." Richard approached the bed, pausing to collect a dressing gown off the back of a chair as he came. "Your bath is ready, and everyone else is gathering downstairs. Cook is making breakfast, which should be ready soon, and then we need to start moving on our plans for the day. You're still willing to take care of interviewing the staff today while Daniel and I go see about the money, aren't you?"

"Of course." Christiana sat up, taking the robe from him and managing to pull it onto first one arm and then the other while still holding up the bedclothes to cover her nakedness. Before she'd nodded off in the carriage on the journey back to London, the group had discussed and decided who would handle what tasks today after they'd rested. Daniel was going to accompany Richard to arrange for the blackmail money, Lisa and Robert were to visit the park and various other areas in search of gossip to see if they could not find out who George had seemed most friendly with this last year in the hopes of sorting out who the blackmailer could be, and Suzette and Christiana were to question the staff and see if they couldn't figure out who might have been paid to poison George's drink.

Christiana had been rather surprised he'd trust her with the responsibility when Richard had asked if she'd be willing to handle the interviews. George wouldn't have.

"Good." He smiled, and offered a hand as she pulled the robe around herself and pushed the blankets away.

Holding the robe closed with one hand, Christiana clasped his fingers with the other and got out of bed, ducking her head and blushing as she realized that — despite her best effort — she'd flashed quite a bit of leg. She kept her head bowed, fussing nervously as she tied the sash, and then stiffened with surprise when Richard suddenly caught her under the chin and tipped her face up to his.

"Good morning." The words were a soft whisper as his mouth descended to hers.

Christiana remained still and self-conscious under the gentle caress, unsure how to respond. She wanted to throw her arms around his neck, press her body to his and open her mouth to him in a most wanton fashion. However, it was the middle of the morning. She wasn't sure he would welcome such a brazen display in the light of day, so she merely stood still and waited to see if he would deepen the kiss. Much to her disappointment, he didn't, but ended it with a little sigh and straightened.

"I suppose I should let you start your day. I'll be downstairs waiting with the others."

Christiana watched him go with confusion. He seemed somehow disappointed and she wasn't sure why.

"Come take your bath before it gets cold."

Christiana glanced around with surprise to see Grace standing next to the steaming tub. She hadn't noticed the woman's presence on first waking, and now smiled in greeting as she crossed the room. "Your carriage made it back all right then?"

"I gather we didn't arrive long after your

carriage did." Grace moved to collect a cloth and soap as Christiana removed the robe she'd just donned and stepped into the tub. She then returned to the tub and knelt to wash her back for her, commenting, "His lordship seems a good man."

"Aye," Christiana murmured noncommittally.

"He has proven himself thoughtful, arranging the bath to be brought up for you, and letting you sleep as late as he could while it was prepared."

Christiana nodded, and accepted the cloth to wash the rest of herself when Grace finished and straightened.

"And he's trusting you to interview the servants as well." Grace moved to collect a gown for her to wear once she'd finished. "Dicky-George didn't trust you to buckle your own shoes."

"No, he didn't," she agreed with a grimace. The man had thought her useless. At least, that was how he'd made her feel this last year.

"And though they were born brothers and twins, Richard is obviously nothing like George was."

Christiana remained silent. Everything Grace said was true. So far, Richard seemed to be a good man. He hadn't yet criticized her or treated her coldly, and he had been in her bed twice now, even before the ceremony at Radnor, which was definitely different from George. But George had seemed to be wonderful and caring when he was courting her, and yet had proven to be nothing like that once they were married.

"He'll make you happy," Grace added firmly when Christiana remained silent. "If you let him."

She glanced to the maid with surprise. "What do you mean, if I let him?"

Grace set aside the clothes she'd gathered and moved back to the tub. "Child, I know George hurt you. You thought you loved him and he betrayed you by turning into the cold, critical man who has tormented you this last year. But Richard isn't George."

"I know that," Christiana muttered, turning her face away and continuing to wash herself as she admitted, "And I know now that I didn't really love George. I loved the romantic hero he pretended to be, but that man didn't exist and the real man . . ." She shrugged wearily and dipped the cloth in the water with a sigh.

"Richard isn't George," Grace repeated solemnly.

"But what if he too isn't the man he appears to be now? How do I know he will not turn just as George did?" Christiana asked almost plaintively. Tears glazed her eyes and she shook her head on a sigh, confusion rife within her. She wasn't sure why she wanted to cry, and then she was and admitted, "I'm afraid."

"George turned the moment the 'I dos' were said, or very nearly," Grace pointed out. "He also didn't even consummate the marriage. Richard hasn't yet started to treat you differently. I haven't heard anything even remotely resembling a criticism of you from him, and he trusts your judgment where George didn't. As for consummating the marriage, the man did that before the two of you were even married."

Grace sighed. "Child, you have a choice here. You can trust that he is the man he is presenting now and treat him accordingly, or you can keep him at arm's length lest he hurt you as you have been doing."

Christiana frowned. "I haven't been keeping him at arm's length."

"Oh?" she asked dryly. "Well, you haven't been yourself around him either. I have known you all your life and you have always been a bit of a hoyden. You may fool others, but I know you are not the prim proper lady who embroiders on a journey in a bouncing carriage."

She glanced at her sharply. "How did you know —"

"I saw it in your hand as you got in the carriage," Grace said dryly, moving to kneel beside the tub again. "I also saw it go flying out the window before we stopped for lunch."

"Richard threw it out. He asked if I liked doing it and when I said no, he snatched it away and threw it out the window. He said with him I didn't need to do things I didn't care to do."

"Then listen to him," Grace said firmly, urging her to lean back and dip her head in the water to soak her hair. Once she was upright again, Grace began to soap the long strands and said, "You have not been yourself since marrying George and that was understandable the way he picked and chewed away at your self-respect. You are better now than while he lived, but —"

"He has only been dead for a couple days," Christiana pointed out in her own defense.

"I know that," she assured her solemnly. "But his death freed you from a cage of sorts. You should be fluttering about like mad, happy to be loose. Instead you are still trying to be the proper little lady he insisted you should be. There is no sparkle in your eye, no bubbly chatter, no running about barefoot under your gown as you used to." She used her hold on Christiana's hair to tilt her head to meet her gaze, "And you stood there wooden as a doll when Lord Radnor kissed you before leaving this morning. Tell me you didn't want to kiss him back. I could tell you did. Your hands balled up into fists to avoid the temptation and you swayed, and then caught yourself. You wanted to kiss him, didn't you?"

Christiana blushed. "Yes, but it is daytime and I was not sure a proper lady would —"

"No man wants a proper lady in his bedroom, or in his house for that matter," Grace assured her dryly. "Certainly, be proper when out in society, but you need not be so proper at home around him. Do you think your mother was always the proper lady? No, she wasn't. Where do you think you learned to run about barefoot in the first place?"

Christiana's eyebrows rose. She had only been five when her mother died and didn't recall much of her. She hadn't realized her mother had run about the estate barefoot.

"If you want marriage with a man who loves you, then you have to be the true you, not some proper lady you think he wants.

That is the game Di— George played to convince you to marry him. Do not play that game with Richard. Be yourself," she said firmly.

"What if he does not like the real me?" Christiana asked unhappily.

"Then we shall pray he drops dead like George did and find you a man who will," Grace said stoutly.

"Grace!" Christiana cried with shock.

"Oh, you know I am teasing," Grace muttered, urging her to lean back so she could rinse her hair. "Do not worry about his not liking the real you. That won't happen, my lady. Take it from me, you are easy to love."

Christiana opened her eyes and met Grace's gaze. She would have hugged the woman for the kind words if she weren't reclining in the tub as the woman poured water over her hair to rinse away the soap. The best she could do was reach up and squeeze her arm affectionately. She then quickly closed her eyes as the soapy water splashed toward them and murmured, "I love you too, Grace."

The maid "hrrumphed" at the words and continued rinsing her hair.

Christiana remained silent for a moment, her thoughts on how she had behaved this last year, and more importantly, the last few

357

days with Richard. She wasn't as miserable as she had been with George, in fact, she hadn't felt a moment's misery since the man had died, but she had still felt slightly restricted and tried to temper her behavior. Well, except for when she'd grown impatient back at Radnor when Richard had been hustling her back to the carriage and not listening to her. Biting her lip at the recollection, Christiana blurted, "I yelled at him at Radnor."

"I know. I saw." Grace sounded amused. "He was startled but didn't get angry."

"No, he didn't," she agreed. "Dicky — George would have been furious."

"Hmm." Grace finished with her hair and released her. "I think I would be happy never to have to hear either of those two names again."

Christiana nodded in agreement and sat up in the tub again.

"You'd best get out now. We have to get you dressed and downstairs. They are holding breakfast for you."

Christiana nodded and stood up to wring out her hair. She dried off and dressed quickly, and then waited patiently as Grace brushed out her hair to dry it further. She expected her to pin it up on top of her head then, but Grace set the brush aside.

"You are not planning to go out, why do you not leave it down today and see what he says?" she suggested gently. When Christiana just stared at her uncertainly, Grace added, "And perhaps not bother with shoes today, just this once to see what he says."

Christiana bit her lip. She was tempted, her feet always seemed to be hot and uncomfortable in shoes, and it really was more comfortable to have her hair down.

"Just this once to see if he reacts like his brother did," Grace said quietly. "Do you not think it is better to know now than wait in an agony of worry?"

Christiana gave in with a sigh and headed for the door. It was better to know, she supposed. And really, it was more comfortable she thought, smiling slightly at the feel of the cool wood underfoot. By the time she was halfway up the hall, she was beginning to feel a little more like her old self.

"Oh, good."

Christiana glanced over her shoulder as she reached the top of the stairs, eyebrows rising slightly when she saw Lisa coming out of the room she was occupying.

"I was worried I would be the last one downstairs this morning," her youngest sister admitted, hurrying toward her.

"You will be," Christiana assured her with

a grin and started down the stairs. She heard Lisa squeal and the patter of her feet as she ran after her, and promptly snatched up the skirts of her gown and broke into a run as well, charging down the stairs with more speed than care. She jumped the last two steps, landed on the hardwood and whirled to hurry up the hall toward the breakfast room, her feet slipping on the polished floor. Christiana kept her balance and hurried forward, not slowing until she neared the door, but then her worries flowed back to crowd her mind and she skidded to a halt just short of the breakfast room, and took a breath to calm her heavy breathing before stepping inside.

Daniel, Suzette, Robert and Richard were all seated around the table talking over cups of tea, but every eye turned Christiana's way as she stepped inside. So everyone was watching when Lisa burst into the room and crashed into her back.

"Phooey," Lisa gasped, grabbing at Christiana's arms to steady herself. "You win."

Christiana bit her lip, and reached back to steady Lisa, but she was watching Richard warily as she did. Her heart sank when he rose from the table and came around toward her, sure he was about to admonish her for racing about the house in so unruly a manner. However, he paused before her, and bent to kiss her cheek, whispering, "Your hair looks nice this morning." Straightening, he asked, "Ready for breakfast?"

Christiana nodded wide-eyed and allowed him to lead her to the sideboard.

Where George had insisted on a variety of foods available to him in the morning, it seemed Richard had requested a much more conservative selection. This morning the sideboard held breakfast items she was more used to, plum cake, baked eggs, sausages, and hot rolls. Smiling she picked up a plate and quickly made her choices, bypassing the baked eggs but taking one of everything else.

"No eggs?" Richard asked as she reached for a slice of plum cake, having to rise up on tiptoe to reach over the rest of the food to the plate on the back of the sideboard.

Christiana tensed and sank back on her feet, but said, "I don't care for baked eggs. Our cook used to boil them for me."

"Sorry, I didn't realize. I prefer them baked myself, but I'll tell Cook to make both in future."

Christiana relaxed and smiled at him, then turned back and rose up on her tiptoes again to get a slice of the plum cake.

"Er . . . Christiana, I think you forgot

something."

She glanced toward him in question, and then down toward her feet as she saw where he was looking. Realizing that her position revealed her bare feet, she released the cake and dropped self-consciously back to her heels again.

"I doubt she forgot," Robert said with a laugh, piling sausages onto his plate next to Richard. "She was forever running around barefoot at Madison."

Recalling Grace's words, when Richard glanced at her with surprise, Christiana straightened her shoulders and said, "My feet get hot. I'm more comfortable barefoot and most of the time see no reason to don shoes unless I'm leaving the house or have company."

Richard nodded. "I see. That's fine. I just thought in your rush that you had forgot them. If you're more comfortable without, then don't wear them."

"Really?" she asked doubtfully. "You don't mind?"

"Why would I mind?" he asked with surprise.

"Well, George said —"

Richard silenced her by catching her by the chin and urging her to meet his gaze, and then said solemnly, "I am not George."

362

She met his gaze, and then nodded equally solemnly. "No, you aren't."

Smiling, he turned back to the sideboard and Christiana watched him for a moment, and then let her breath out and turned away to head to the table, thinking that maybe Grace was right. Maybe she could be herself with this man. Maybe he wouldn't hate her for it as George had.

"Christiana?"

She paused and turned back, and then glanced down with surprise when he set a piece of plum cake on her plate. "I *know* you forgot this. You tried to grab it twice before being distracted."

Christiana smiled wryly and murmured, "Thank you."

There was little conversation as they ate. Christiana supposed no one wished to discuss either the blackmailer or the murder of George when they suspected a member of the household staff might be involved. They were also apparently eager to get on with their individual tasks for the day and were soon finished and excusing themselves from the table.

"Shall we head out?" Daniel asked Richard as the group left the dining room.

Christiana noted the distaste on her husband's face as he glanced to the wrinkled dark coat he wore and wasn't surprised when he said, "I need to change my clothes first. I should have sought out a change of clothes on awaking, but so loathe wearing what's available that I put it off. I won't be a minute though."

"I shall wait in the parlor," Daniel said with a nod and turned into the room as Richard started up the stairs.

Christiana watched Richard jog lightly up the steps, and then glanced to the side when Suzette touched her arm.

"When do you want to start interviewing the staff?" her sister asked, glancing toward the parlor after Daniel.

"We will wait until everyone leaves," Christiana decided. "Why do you not go keep Daniel company? I want a word with Richard about how he wishes us to proceed with the staff anyway."

Suzette smiled and immediately slipped into the parlor. She also pulled the door closed, Christiana noted and briefly considered opening it and reminding her sister that unmarried ladies did not stay alone in a closed room with men. However, she simply let it go and turned to head upstairs. The two would be married soon enough.

She found Richard in the master dressing room, contemplating George's wardrobe with a less than pleased expression. Christiana supposed she could not blame him. George had dressed like a dandy and Richard just was not a dandyish man.

"Oh, Christiana," he said and smiled wryly when he noted her entrance. "Is something wrong?"

"No," she assured him quickly, running a hand absently over a pair of pink knee breeches. "I just wondered how you wished us to proceed with the interviews. I presume you don't wish us to give away what we are trying to learn?"

"You presume right." Richard frowned. "We don't want whoever hired them to realize we are on to them before we sort out who it is."

"No," she agreed.

"I suppose you and Suzette have the hardest task of the bunch of us. I'm sorry about that."

She smiled faintly and shrugged. "It will not be hard to carry out, just hard to succeed at. We might manage to be able to cross servants off the list, but I doubt we will learn exactly who could have poisoned the whiskey. It could have been put in at any time between the day he died and the last time he drank from it before that. George didn't allow anyone else to drink his special whiskey."

"True, which suggests there was no urgency to seeing him dead," he murmured thoughtfully. He shook his head, apparently unsure what that meant, and then held up a pale green cutaway frock coat. "This appears to be the best of the lot."

"Yes," she agreed and watched him shrug out of the dark coat to pull on the lighter one.

"Do I need to change my trousers?" he asked as he buttoned the coat over his cravat.

Christiana glanced to the buff trousers and hessian boots and shook her head. They went with pretty much everything. It was why the color was popular.

"Good." Richard sighed and started past her. "I had best go then."

"Before you do," Christiana said, catching his arm as he started to pass her.

He paused and glanced down at her in question.

Christiana hesitated and then blew out her breath and said, "I wanted to thank you for trusting me to interview the staff."

His eyebrows rose slightly, and then he frowned and took her by the shoulders to turn her until they faced each other. "I am not George, Christiana. I realize you are an intelligent woman capable of many things. You are also my wife and partner. Trust is important in such a relationship. We must learn to trust each other if we wish this marriage to succeed."

"Yes," she acknowledged. And while she knew it was true, it was just so hard. She had little confidence in her ability to inspire love after life with Dicky.

The thought made Christiana blink in surprise as she realized that it wasn't really that she worried Richard would change, but that she feared she wasn't worthy of love anymore. It was something she'd been confident of while growing up surrounded by family and friends who loved her. But somehow that foundation had been washed away, leaving her floating in a sea of uncertainty . . . because George hadn't loved her and she'd assumed it must be due to some flaw in her. If she'd just been smart enough, pretty enough, charming enough he would have loved her. In truth, she'd spent the last year trying to earn that love, and almost lost herself in the process.

"I should go," Richard murmured, peering at her worriedly. When she managed a smile and nod, he bent to press a quick kiss to her lips. At least, she suspected he'd intended it to be a quick parting kiss.

However, it didn't end up that way, because Christiana did what she'd wanted — and had been too afraid — to do that morning. The moment his lips met hers, she went up on her toes to wrap her arms around his neck, pressed her body against his and opened her mouth to him.

Richard stilled, obviously taken by surprise, but then his own arms slid around her back and he pulled her close and deepened the kiss. Christiana breathed a little sigh of relief into his mouth. She had followed her instincts and he had not rejected her, berating her for unladylike behavior. It was a small first step, but a step just the same, she thought and then let go of her worries and merely enjoyed the kiss as he caught her head in hand and tilted it to allow him more access as he tried to devour her with his mouth.

When he clasped her bottom through her skirt and lifted her to press her against the hardness growing between them, Christiana breathed a little moan and curled her fingers into his hair. Heat was already pooling in her lower belly and spreading outward to answer that hardness, but he then lowered her back to the floor and broke the kiss.

"Temptress," he growled, leaning his forehead against hers.

"Are you tempted?" she asked in a pleased whisper.

"You know I am," he said on a humorless laugh.

"Do you mind?" she asked next, holding her breath as she waited for the answer.

"Mind that my wife tempts me to take her in the dressing room amongst the hatboxes and breeches?" he asked with amusement. "No, I don't mind at all. But Daniel probably would if I succumbed."

"Suzette is with him." She slid one hand from around his shoulder and let it drift down to press against the proof of how she was affecting him. "I don't think he would mind a short wait."

Richard growled as she ran her hand over him through the cloth of his trousers. "Still, I should —"

His words died on a gasp as she suddenly slipped her hand inside his trousers and clasped him.

"Witch," he breathed and oddly enough it didn't sound like an insult. In the next moment he was kissing her again, his own hands beginning to move over her body through her gown, cupping and caressing her breasts, squeezing her behind and then dragging her skirt up to slip beneath and move over the skin of her outer leg and hip as she undid his trousers to be able to caress him more fully. Christiana had just got the last button undone and taken him in hand again when his own hand slid between her legs to press against the center of her. They groaned in unison into each other's mouths then, the sound and vibration merely adding to their excitement.

Christiana felt the dressing table press against the backs of her thighs through her dress and realized he'd backed her up, but was taken by surprise when he removed his hand from between her legs and suddenly lifted her to sit on the spindly legged piece of furniture. His hand returned to her then, caressing and urging her legs wider so that he could move between them. When he urged her hand away, she released him and clutched at his shoulders. Richard then took himself in hand and rubbed his shaft against her teasingly and Christiana gasped and wiggled her bottom to the edge of the table, her legs wrapping around his and urging him closer.

"Witch," he repeated, breaking their kiss, and then he clasped her bottom and pulled her even further forward on the tabletop and finally gave up his teasing to thrust himself into her.

Christiana cried out and clawed at his

shoulders, her heels pressing into his behind and urging him deeper. She lifted her face to his, seeking his lips again and then kissed him desperately. Richard withdrew, and then groaned as he plunged into her again, his tongue thrusting into her mouth at the same time. She was vaguely aware of a banging sound as he moved and realized the table was moving with them and hitting the wall with each thrust, but didn't care and simply held on as the sound became a rapid tattoo.

As fast as it had started, it ended just as swiftly, both of them crying out as one and clutching at each other as they were rocked by the explosion. Christiana then sagged back against the wall, taking Richard with her. He leaned his head against her shoulder for a moment and then gave a shaky laugh.

"What?" she murmured, raising one languid hand to brush the hair from his face in an effort to see his expression.

Richard raised his head and smiled at her wryly. "I was just thinking, whatever his faults, George had excellent taste when it came to choosing a wife," he admitted almost apologetically, and then cupped her face, pressed a gentle kiss to her lips, and whispered, "Thank you."

CHAPTER SIXTEEN

"That went well."

Richard settled back in the carriage and merely nodded. They had just finished making arrangements for the funds to pay the blackmailer. He was hoping that wouldn't be necessary, but was prepared if it was. Richard was glad to have the business out of the way. He'd spent the past hour constantly worrying that someone was going to stand up shouting, "Imposter!" He supposed that was foolish since he was the true Richard Fairgrave, Earl of Radnor. However, George had been impersonating him for over a year and it was he everyone was used to. Richard had been sure someone would notice something different about him, courtesy perhaps, or a less caustic attitude. He was actually surprised and even a little insulted that they hadn't. He liked to think he was different enough from his brother that someone would have noticed something, and couldn't help his slightly disgruntled tone as he commented, "No one seemed to notice anything amiss or different about me."

Daniel smiled wryly and shrugged. "People see what they expect to. Besides, while you were thanking the clerk for your tea I commented to Lord Sherwood that I was glad to see you finally shaking off the strange mood that had claimed you this last year since your twin's death," Daniel admitted. "He said he'd heard you were finally coming around and had even attended a ball. So I wouldn't worry too much. It appears everyone will just put down any oddity they notice to your finally getting over the grief that has supposedly plagued you this last year."

"Well, that's something anyway," Richard said wryly, tugging at the sleeve of his pale green coat and grimacing. He detested the color, but it had been the best of the lot. "I really need to improve my wardrobe."

"George always did have terrible taste in clothes," Daniel said dryly, eyeing his outfit. "Why do we not stop at the tailor's on the way back to the townhouse?"

Richard hesitated, his conscience making him feel that he should head right back to the townhouse and try to further their investigations. But he didn't want Christiana to think he didn't trust her to interview the staff, and he could hardly gain gossip on himself. There seemed little reason not to stop, so he nodded and ordered the driver to change direction.

"How are you finding marriage so far?" Daniel asked as Richard sat back in his seat.

"It has not even been a full day yet," he pointed out with amusement.

Daniel shrugged. "Christiana appears terribly wary. I think she fears you will suddenly begin criticizing and berating her as George apparently did."

Richard nodded, not surprised his friend had noted the wariness that often clouded Christiana's eyes. It was seldom missing. The only time it seemed to him that she managed to completely shed it was when he stirred her passions. Then she managed to forget everything but the pleasure they were enjoying together, and to trust him with at least her body. It gave him hope that eventually she would trust him with more and he said, "Time will help undo the damage George did. When she sees that I do not change and do not try to change her, she will relax and be more herself."

Daniel nodded and said with a grin, "She made a good start this morning racing Lisa downstairs barefoot."

Richard smiled at the memory. That had surprised him. Christiana had been so polite and stilted when she first awoke, the complete antithesis to the warm passionate woman he had made love to just hours earlier. In truth, he'd been disappointed when he'd kissed her that morning and she'd not kissed him back. It had made him worry about what it might indicate for their future together. Would she be one woman at night, a warm passionate lover in their bed, and then another woman, the cautious, wary proper lady during the daylight hours? Not that that would have been the worst thing in the world to deal with, many men were not even fortunate to have the passion. However, Richard wanted more from Christiana. He wanted her to trust him and to be as unguarded and warm with him all the time as she was in their bed. He wanted the easy affection he saw her shower on her sisters and even Robert. He wanted her as a friend as well as a lover.

Much to his relief, the episode in the dressing room before he and Daniel had left had gone a long way toward reassuring him, however. She hadn't been a proper lady then, and they hadn't been in their bed either, but in the closet in broad daylight.

Richard wasn't sure what had caused the difference in her, but was grateful for it. He was truly beginning to believe they would more than make a go of this marriage. They might actually have a sterling one like his own parents had enjoyed. Theirs had been a love match and while he'd never really thought about it before, Richard now decided he would like that for himself as well.

"Here we are."

Daniel's words drew his gaze out the window to see that they'd arrived on the street where the tailor was. A glance along the busy lane told him his driver wouldn't be able to find a spot close to the tailor's without some difficulty and he commented, "It looks as if we will have a bit of a walk to reach the tailor's."

"I don't mind," Daniel said. "After spending all yesterday and last night in a carriage, I shall enjoy the brief walk."

Nodding, Richard banged on the wall of the carriage. Moments later they were disembarking and making their way along the crowded walk toward the tailor's.

"You'll need a whole new wardrobe," Daniel commented as they swerved closer to the road to avoid a small party of women walking the opposite way.

"Yes," Richard agreed dryly. "Fashion is

one of many things George and I did not have in common."

"Did you have *anything* in common?" Daniel asked with amusement.

"Taste in women," Richard answered promptly.

"Ah." Daniel grinned. "I'll take that to mean you are not displeased to have Christiana for a wife."

"If Suzette is half the woman Christiana is, we can both count ourselves lucky men," Richard assured him.

"Hmm. Suzette mentioned that Christiana had followed you upstairs, and I did notice a certain spring in your step when you found me in the parlor *some time later.* I wonder what could have happened to cause that?"

"You can keep wondering," Richard said dryly and led the way into the tailor's.

As he'd hoped, his time with the tailor was short. The man was swift and efficient, taking Richard's measurements and his order with a speed that spoke of the years of experience he had. Much to Richard's relief, the man assured him he could have several of the items to him by week's end. He also did have a couple of cutaway coats, a pair of trousers and a pair of breeches available right away. One of the coats was a perfect fit and could be taken at once, the other items needed a bit of tailoring, but the man promised to fix them up right away and send all four items along to the town-house by the day's end.

"Well that went well too," Daniel commented as they stepped out of the tailor's and started up the walk in the direction of the Radnor carriage. "Perhaps we shall be lucky and arrive back at the townhouse to find that everyone has had such a successful day, and the identities of the blackmailer and poisoner have been discovered so that we need only round them up."

"We should be so lucky," Richard said wryly.

"Was it not you who said just as we entered the tailor's that we were both lucky men?" Daniel asked cheerfully.

Richard glanced around at Daniel's words and opened his mouth to respond, but froze as he spotted the carriage careening toward them. The first shout of warning went up then, but Richard was already grabbing Daniel's arm and throwing himself to the side, out of the way of the oncoming vehicle. They crashed to the ground amid a cacophony of screams and shouts as the people around them noted the danger and tried to get out of the way, and then there was a moment when the only sound Richard could hear was that of the horses' hooves and the trundle of the carriage's wheels as it raced past, the breeze of its passing telling how close they'd come to being trampled.

"Are you all right, my lord?"

Richard glanced around at that alarmed question and sighed when he spotted his driver just reaching and kneeling beside him. Nodding, he rolled onto his back to sit up, and then glanced toward Daniel, who was as of yet unmoving.

"Woodrow?" he asked with a frown.

Daniel groaned and pushed himself to a sitting position, but said, "Yes. Thanks to you."

"It was a yellow bounder, my lord," the Radnor driver said grimly, glaring in the direction the post chaise had gone. "Probably rented. The postillion didn't even try to steer clear of ye. In fact, it looked almost like he was aiming for the two of ye."

Richard grunted at the man's words, suspecting he was right. George had been murdered after all and they had expected the murderer to try again. He definitely had to be more careful in future.

Richard got to his feet even as Daniel did and then paused to brush down his clothes, frowning when something dripped down the side of his forehead.

"You're bleeding," Daniel said quietly. "You must have knocked your head as we fell."

Richard raised a hand to his forehead, grimacing when he felt the scrape there. Sighing, he wiped the blood away and started toward the carriage. Daniel and the driver followed.

"Where to now, my lord?" the driver asked solemnly as he held the carriage door for Richard and Daniel to get in.

"Home," Richard answered abruptly as he settled back in his seat.

Nodding, the man closed the door.

"What are we going to do now?" Daniel asked as he settled across from him.

"Find out who wants the Earl of Radnor dead, and fast. I should like to accomplish it before Christiana is made a widow . . . again."

"This is a waste of time," Suzette hissed with frustration as Christiana led her from the guest bedroom Robert and Daniel had shared the night before. They had gone there to have a little chat with the upstairs maid who had been making the bed and cleaning the room. The problem was that

380

was all it had been, a chat, Christiana acknowledged. They could hardly ask flat out if she had been paid to poison George's whiskey. They didn't want everyone on staff to know about George's attempt to kill Richard, his stint as his imposter and that George was now dead . . . again. That being the case, they couldn't ask much of anything useful really, and instead had been forced to ask each person general questions about how long they'd worked for Lord Fairgrave and where they'd worked previously, what their family situation was like and so on.

"It isn't a complete waste of time," she assured Suzette. "I am pretty sure we can cross most of the staff we've talked to off the list of suspects, and that is a good thing."

Suzette sighed with exasperation. "Why am I not surprised you are looking at the bright side?"

Christiana glanced at her in question. "What do you mean?"

"You have been Miss Bloody-Cheerful-and-Optimistic ever since *talking* to Richard upstairs before the men left," she said with disgust.

"And you have been Miss Glum-and-Pessimistic just as long," Christiana said wryly. Suzette had been surly and cross throughout the interviews.

"Aye, well I suspect that would be because I didn't find the same satisfaction you obviously did before Richard came into the parlor and interrupted us."

Christiana paused and whirled to gape at her. "By satisfaction you do not mean . . . ?"

Suzette rolled her eyes and urged her to keep moving toward the stairs. "Of course I do. Anyone could tell what the two of you had been up to. If the banging from upstairs hadn't given it away, then your wrinkled skirts, the smile on Richard's face, and your utterly replete relaxation and good cheer since would have."

Christiana felt herself color with embarrassment and glanced anxiously down at her skirt, self-consciously brushing at the wrinkles she hadn't noticed until now as they started down the steps.

"What was the banging by the way?" Suzette asked. "If it was your bed, you should have the servants shift it away from the wall, else no one will sleep tonight."

Christiana stiffened at the taunt, but rather than answer, narrowed her eyes on Suzette and asked, "What do you mean by the satisfaction *you didn't find* before Richard interrupted you?"

"Exactly what you think I mean," she assured her. However, despite Suzette's attempt to sound blasé about it, a pink flush stole up her cheeks.

Christiana gaped at her. "But you are —"

"An unmarried woman, pure and innocent and completely ignorant of what a man and woman do behind closed doors," Suzette said dryly, urging her to continue down the stairs. "Heavens, Christiana, this is the nineteenth century. Women need not go to the marriage bed completely ignorant."

"I did," she muttered, half embarrassed and half annoyed.

"You never read any of those books Lisa constantly has her nose in."

"And you did?" Christiana glanced at her with amazement as they stepped off the stairs and started along the hall. Suzette had never been much of a reader.

Suzette shrugged. "It gets a bit boring in the country now that you are not there. Lisa is always reading, and Robert has been in town the last year, while trying to discover what was going on with your marriage. There were days when I think I would have gone mad without something to read."

"But surely those horrid novels Lisa reads do not —"

"Nay, not most of them, but —" Suzette paused to glance around and then ushered her into the nearest room, Richard's office. She closed the door and urged Christiana over to the chairs by the fire before admitting, "Lisa received one recently that was about a young girl named Fanny who runs away to London and becomes a prostitute and it was . . . er . . . quite informative."

"And you and Lisa *read* this?" she cried with dismay. When Suzette reddened but nodded, she asked, "Does Father know?"

Suzette snorted. "No, of course not. He hasn't known much of anything ever since the first gambling incident. He has mostly stayed locked in his office, hiding from his shame since you left with Dicky the day after the wedding." She scowled briefly, but then glanced to Christiana and pleaded, "Don't say anything to him. And don't say anything to Lisa either. 'Tis a banned book, and she made me swear not to tell anyone about it."

"If 'tis banned, how did she get it?" Christiana asked grimly.

"I am not sure," Suzette admitted. "She won't tell me. But I think she got it from Mrs. Morgan."

Christiana didn't recognize the name. "Who is Mrs. Morgan?"

"A widow whose carriage broke down by the estate on her way to London," Suzette explained. "Father invited her in for tea while the men looked at it for her. Of course, then he left us to entertain her," she added bitterly.

"And this Mrs. Morgan gave Lisa the book then?" Christiana asked.

Suzette shook her head. "Her carriage was beyond the men's ability to repair and had to be taken into the village. Mrs. Morgan stayed at the inn for nearly a week while it was repaired and Lisa visited her there every day. They became quite friendly and I guess before she left for London, Mrs. Morgan gave her the book as a thank-you gift for keeping her company."

"Dear God," Christiana growled. "What kind of woman gives a banned book like that to an unmarried girl?"

"Mrs. Morgan is very forward thinking," Suzette said with a shrug. "She believes women should have more rights and freedoms of our own rather than be ruled by our fathers and husbands. Besides, Lisa is nearly twenty, Christiana. She is not a child anymore, and should already have had her debut and be settled with a husband and starting on children."

Christiana didn't argue the point. Their father had been lax in seeing to their future. But then she and her sisters hadn't been pushing to have their debuts. They'd all simply been content as they were, each uneager to leave their childhood home and loved ones for an unknown husband. Although, Christiana *had* been contemplating doing so more and more the last year before marrying Dicky. She had begun to think she wanted children, which meant a London season to choose a husband, and she probably would have soon broached the subject with her father had the supposed ruination at the gambling table not forced the marriage to Dicky.

That thought made her recall what Richard had said about the gaming hell and the rumors about what went on there and she asked, "Father has been punishing himself for what happened and my having to marry Dicky?"

"Yes, and so he should," Suzette said grimly. "I was actually feeling sorry for him, but then he went and did it again."

"That may not be true," Christiana said quietly. "He may not have gambled at all."

"What?" Suzette glanced at her sharply.

"Richard said there are rumors that Dicky had befriended a certain owner of a gaming hell reputed to drug its patrons and fleece them. He suspects it's possible that is what happened to Father."

Suzette's breath left her on a whoosh, making Christiana's eyebrows raise. Before she could ask what had caused it, Suzette said, "When we found him at the townhouse, Father kept saying he was sorry, and he didn't know how it had happened, that his memories were a jumble and he didn't even recall how he'd ended up at the gaming hell, just waking up there both times to learn he'd gambled us into ruin."

Christiana sighed. "He probably didn't gamble at all."

"Oh God," Suzette moaned and dropped back against the chair unhappily. "I was so cruel to him the morning we arrived in London. I said some awful things."

"It is understandable under the circumstances," Christiana said quietly. "How were you to know Dicky may have drugged him to bring about his downfall?"

"Damn Dicky," Suzette burst out furiously, sitting upright again. "If he weren't already dead, I think I'd kill him myself."

"Hmm," Christiana murmured, and then bit her lip and pointed out, "Although, if it weren't for Dicky and what he'd got up to I wouldn't now be married to Richard and you might never have met and proposed to Daniel."

"That's true." Suzette frowned, some of

her anger easing from her expression, and then she glanced to Christiana and asked, "So you are content with Richard?"

"I think we might have a good marriage," she said cautiously, and much to her surprise Suzette snorted at the tame words.

"Oh, give over," she said with disgust. "A *good* marriage? I've heard the moaning and groaning coming from your room, both the night Dicky died and last night as well. *Oh Richard, oh . . . oh . . . yes . . . ooooooh,*" she mimicked with amusement. "Then you scream like you're fit to die."

Christiana blushed furiously. "You could hear us?"

"I'm sure the whole house can hear you," she said dryly. "He roars like a lion, and you squeal like a stuck pig." She paused and then added thoughtfully, "Which I suppose is an apt description from what I read in Fanny's book. Did it hurt very much the first time he stuck his maypole in your tender parts?"

"His *maypole?*" Christiana gasped with disbelief.

"That's what Fanny called it. Well one of the things," she added thoughtfully, and then repeated, "Did it hurt?"

Christiana groaned and covered her face, mortified by the entire conversation.

"Well?" Suzette persisted.

"A little perhaps," Christiana said finally, forcing her hands away and straightening in her seat.

"Hmm, Fanny fainted from the pain," Suzette muttered. "And there was a great deal of blood, which suggests pain as well."

Christiana grimaced and decided a change of subject was in order. "Anyway, what happens in the bedroom is only a portion of marriage, Suzette. I must deal with him out of the bedroom as well and begin to think I may be able to."

Suzette glanced to her curiously. "He seems to treat you much more kindly than Dicky did. And he upheld the marriage to prevent us all from being cast into scandal. I thought at first that he avoided scandal as well, but Lisa is right, men do not suffer scandal like we women do and he probably did uphold it for your sake, which is really very chivalrous. Much more chivalrous than Daniel's marrying me for money."

Christiana frowned slightly. Suzette's last words sounded almost bitter and yet the girl had written the rules for this marriage herself, choosing to marry someone who needed money to ensure she was not trapped in a miserable marriage as Christiana had endured with Dicky. However, the

389

marriage might not be necessary at all now, she realized, and frowned over the fact that she couldn't say as much because she hadn't yet spoken to Richard about his promise to make everything right. She really must remember when he returned, Christiana told herself firmly. Until then, she couldn't say anything to Suzette, at least nothing certain.

A deep sigh drew her attention back to Suzette.

Seeing the dissatisfaction on her face, she asked quietly, "Are you having second thoughts about marrying Daniel?" Biting her lip, she added, "Perhaps Richard would be willing to cover Father's gambling debts. If we even need to cover them. If we prove he was drugged and didn't gamble at all —"

"Nay, 'tis fine," Suzette said quickly. "I doubt it would be that easy to prove and we have enough on our plate at the moment. Speaking of which, we should really get back to our task. Who have we not yet talked to?"

Christiana hesitated, but then decided to let her change the subject. They really did have to continue with their task. "I think we have spoken to all the maids and footmen. That leaves Haversham, Cook, Richard's valet —"

"I thought his valet died in the fire where Richard was supposed to have died?" Suzette interrupted.

"Yes, of course, I meant Dicky's valet. I guess he will have to be Richard's now though. Well, once he recovers from his illness."

"Are you sure that's a good idea?" Suzette asked.

"What do you mean?"

"Well, I'd like to think Georgina knows me well enough that she would know in an instant if someone tried to take my place, even if they were my twin."

"I'm sure Grace would realize at once too, if a twin tried to take my place, or at least rather quickly." She frowned. "In fact, that's why George ordered Richard's valet to be murdered. He feared the man would know that he wasn't Richard."

"Well there you are," Suzette said quietly. "It's just as likely that George's valet will notice something amiss with Richard and suspect he isn't the master he has served this last year."

"Twenty years," Christiana corrected and when Suzette raised her eyebrows in question, she explained thoughtfully, "Dicky once said that Freddy had been with him for twenty years, they pretty much grew up together."

"Hmm." Suzette grimaced. "Then Richard definitely wouldn't be able to fool him."

"No," she agreed grimly. "And George wouldn't have been able to fool him into thinking he was really Richard."

Suzette's eyes widened with realization. "Freddy had to know what George had done."

"Yes. He could be the blackmailer," she exclaimed with excitement, and then just as swiftly shook her head. "But he has been ill since the day you and Lisa arrived and hasn't been to assist Dicky-George since, so can't yet know he's now Richard again."

"Are you sure about that?" Suzette asked.

"That he's sick?" Christiana asked with surprise. "Haversham told us Freddy was ill when he caught us with Dicky in the rug. Why would he lie?"

"I'm not suggesting he lied," Suzette said. "But just because this Freddy is ill doesn't necessarily mean he has been confined to bed all this time. Maybe he has been up and saw or heard something that made him realize Richard was back and George gone."

Christiana sank back in her chair with a frown. What Suzette suggested was more than possible. Ill or not, Freddy would have to get up to eat and drink and tend to other functions. Cook was busy enough she probably wouldn't tend to him like an ill child unless he was at death's door, and Haversham had not suggested the ailment was that desperate. The man probably had been up and about and while it was most likely that he'd stuck to the back of the house, it was possible he had seen Richard at some point or other. He may even have gone in search of Dicky to explain his illness and seen him then, though Richard hadn't mentioned seeing the man. But then Freddy could have seen Richard without his even noticing. Servants, at least the good ones, could go about their business in an unobtrusive way that ensured their presence went without note.

Nodding, she stood up abruptly. "You're right, and it's certainly worth checking into at least. I will ask Haversham to send him to us. He will be our next interview."

Suzette nodded. "I have a good feeling about this."

Christiana too thought they may have struck on something with Freddy. She didn't think for a minute that he might be the servant who had poisoned Dicky-George. The man had always been obsequious and toadying with Dicky. But she was suddenly almost positive that he might be their blackmailer.

The hall was empty when Christiana stepped into it and she started toward the kitchen, glancing into each room in search of Haversham as she went. The man usually appeared the moment she stepped into the hall. Actually, she suspected he was usually hanging about listening at doors. It appeared he wasn't today, however, and she didn't see him in any of the main-floor rooms. Frowning, she made her way into the kitchen, but he wasn't there either.

Giving up on the man, she asked one of the kitchen girls where Freddy's room was and then went to fetch the man herself. She'd intended to simply knock on his door and request that he come join her and Suzette in the office, however when she arrived at the room she'd been directed to, she found the door ajar. After a hesitation, she pushed it open, calling out, "Freddy?"

There was no answer and no one in the room, she saw as the door swung open. The bed was also made with no sign that a sick man had just risen from it. Frowning, Christiana turned to leave, but paused with a start when she found the man in question standing behind her.

"Oh, Freddy! You gave me a start. I was

just going to ask you to come to the office for a minute," she said nervously, one hand at her throat.

"Yes, I know," Freddy said grimly, moving forward.

Christiana stepped back to avoid his running her down, but paused abruptly as she realized that she was moving further into the room. Not comfortable, she started to move around him then, suddenly desperate to get back out into the hall, but Freddy quickly blocked her exit, slammed the door closed and locked it with a definitive click.

CHAPTER SEVENTEEN

"Do you know that fellow?" Richard asked. They'd just pulled up in front of the townhouse and Richard had been about to open the door to get out when he'd noted a man pacing back and forth on the path leading to his front door. The gentleman would walk toward the house as if to seek entrance, stop, shake his head and walk away from it, only to pause halfway to the gate and turn back to approach the door again. The fellow was well dressed, with gray hair, and a hat and cane, but his noble appearance was belied by the fact that he appeared to be talking to himself as he repeated the bizarre behavior.

"He looks vaguely familiar," Daniel said, leaning to peer out the window as well. "He seems a little troubled about something."

"Grand." Richard sighed, opening the door to get out. "More trouble at my door."

"You do seem to attract it of late," Daniel

said dryly as he followed him out of the carriage.

"Hmmm," Richard muttered, and headed up the path. When he reached the fellow, the man had again approached the door and stopped to peer at it as if it were some insurmountable mountain he dearly wished to climb. Richard was about to tap him on the shoulder to get his attention, when the fellow shook his head again, muttered under his breath and turned abruptly, then leapt several steps back as he found Richard standing there. Richard raised his eyebrows, but asked politely, "Is there something I can assist you with, sir?"

"What?" the man asked with disbelief.

"I am Richard Fairgrave, Earl of Radnor," he offered, holding out one hand. "Can I be of assistance?"

The gentleman peered down at his hand as if it were a snake and then scowled at him grimly. "Surely you jest, my lord. After all you have cost me with your shady dealings, you think to act like you do not know me?"

Richard let his hand drop to his side, his eyes narrowing. This was obviously someone his brother had known and had dealings with. And someone not happy with those dealings, which put him on the list of suspects who might have wanted Dicky-George dead. So far it was a list of one, the man before him.

"Why do we not go inside and discuss this?" Richard suggested, moving past him to open the door.

"Why do you not go in there and fetch the girls back to me while your friend and I wait out here instead."

Richard glanced back to insist they go inside, but paused when he saw the man had moved up next to Daniel and now held a very large black-and-ivory pistol to his side. For his part, Woodrow looked somewhat startled, but not unduly alarmed. Richard, on the other hand, noted the fine tremor in the man's hand and was worried for him.

"Ha! Not so clever now are you, Dicky?" the man asked grimly. "Now give me my daughters. All of them. I'm not leaving a one of them here for you to abuse any longer."

"Your daughters?" Daniel asked with interest, half turning toward the man. Fortunately the action didn't get him shot; Richard had spoken at the same time, saying, "Lord Madison?" in an amazed tone and the old man appeared more interested in him than Daniel, though he kept the gun pointed at Woodrow.

"Save your games, my lord." The man said with dislike. "You have managed to fool me one too many times already. I know you have mistreated my Chrissy. Robert told me everything after the Landons' ball the other night. He said the girls told him that you've treated her terribly and I've sorted it all out from there. You never loved my gel, it was all an act to get your hands on her dower, and now you've somehow swindled me again hoping to force my Suzette into the same position. Well I won't have it, and I am not leaving my Chrissy in your hands either, marriage or no marriage. I'll have it annulled. I'll take it to the King himself if I have to. Now fetch me all three girls before I lose my patience."

"Father?"

All three men glanced to the woman hurrying up the path toward them: Lisa Madison with Robert Langley on her heels.

"Father, what are you doing pointing that pistol at Suzette's fiancé? Put that away before you hurt someone."

"Nay," Lord Madison said firmly, grabbing her arm with his free hand and urging her to the side to keep her out of harm's way as he dug the pistol more firmly into Daniel's stomach. "I'll not let Suzette marry this blackguard. No doubt he's a friend of that devil's there, which means he'll be as bad as Dicky. Now, be a good girl and fetch your sisters, gel. We are leaving here and going back to Madison. I've sold the townhouse to pay the debts. There is no need for Suzette to marry anyone."

"You sold your townhouse?" Daniel asked with alarm.

"Aye." He smiled meanly, his eyes darting from Daniel to Richard. "The two of you didn't think I'd do that, did you? But I'd sell the estate itself before I let you rope another one of my girls into a miserable marriage." He stood a little straighter and added, "And I will see Chrissy out of her marriage as well."

"Oh Father," Lisa said with a sigh. "That wasn't necessary at all. Daniel agreed to let Suzette keep half her dower to pay off the debt and use the rest as she wished. He is not the devil Dicky was."

"And actually, Richard here is not the villain you think he is," Robert added, moving to the man's side. Pausing, he leaned forward and whispered in the old man's ear, and whispered, and whispered. Really, while Richard knew it was quite a bit to explain, he thought Langley could have been a little more succinct. It seemed to take a very long time before Madison's mouth dropped and the hand holding the gun fell to his side.

"What?" he squawked with amazement.

Robert nodded solemnly. "Chrissy is very happy with the Earl of Radnor. *This* one," he added firmly. "And Daniel is a good and honorable man. He'll make Suzette a good husband."

"Only if he doesn't tell her he sold the damned townhouse to make good on his debts," Daniel muttered with disgust. "If she finds that out she is just contrary enough that she may very well not marry me."

"I'm sure Lord Madison will keep that information to himself for now," Richard said dryly.

"Why would I do that?" Lord Madison asked. "If Suzette doesn't wish to marry him, I will not let her be forced into it."

"Under normal circumstances I would agree with you," Richard said solemnly. "However, after what I interrupted in the parlor between the two of them this morning, honor demands he marry her, and as her brother-in-law I feel it my duty to ensure he does."

"Eh?" Madison's eyes shot to Daniel, who was suddenly grinning.

"I'd forgotten about that." He nodded

cheerfully. "Yes, she has to marry me to avoid ruin."

Madison's eyes narrowed and he turned to Robert. "You're sure he's a good and honorable man?"

"Positive," Robert assured him, obviously fighting a grin. "Truly, just look how eager he is to do the right thing. Besides, the fact that Suzie allowed him to take liberties with her proves she is not averse to the marriage. However, she can be contrary. It may be best to allow her to continue thinking for now that the marriage is necessary."

"Hmm." Madison grimaced. "Of the three of them she has always been the most stubborn and difficult." He glanced to Daniel. "Are you sure you know what you're getting yourself into? She won't make life easy."

"Perhaps not," Daniel said with unconcern. "But life shall certainly never be boring with her either."

Madison relaxed and nodded solemnly. "There is much to be said for that. She is like her mother and that woman had me hopping to keep up with her from the day we wed. Never regretted marrying her even for a moment."

"So you won't tell her that there is no need to marry?" Daniel asked hopefully.

Madison pursed his lips, his gaze moving

first to Lisa, who nodded solemnly, then to each of the men before he heaved a sigh. "I shall talk to her, and if Suzie doesn't seem averse to marrying you, I will keep the sale of the townhouse to myself for now."

Daniel relaxed and nodded. "Thank you."

Madison turned to Richard then, his gaze moving slowly over his features, and then he shook his head. "You look remarkably like Dicky."

"We were twins," he pointed out quietly.

"Aye, well, there is a difference in the eyes. When you looked into his they were usually empty or calculating. Yours . . ." He shook his head, apparently unable to come up with a way to describe the difference.

"Perhaps we should move inside now," Richard suggested, his gaze sliding to the road as a carriage passed.

"Aye. Let's go in. I could use a cup of tea nice and sweet. I got myself all wound up to come here and now feel quite worn out," Madison admitted.

"Tea it is, then," Richard said, opening the door and leading the small group into the house.

"What are you doing? Unlock that," Christiana snapped, trying to grab the key from Freddy, but he merely caught her hand with one of his own, while his other dropped the key in a pocket.

"Shut up and sit down while I figure out what to do," Freddy barked, pushing her toward the bed.

Christiana stumbled back under his push, landing in an ungraceful heap on the edge of the bed, but promptly sprang back to her feet. "I demand you unlock that door this instant and let me —" The rest of her words died as he slapped her face and pushed her down on the bed again.

"I said sit down and shut up," he growled, looming over her to prevent her rising again. "I need to think what to do."

Her hand clasped to the spot where he'd slapped her, Christiana stared at him for a moment, and then slowly let her hand slide away. "You are the blackmailer."

"Yes, and I want that money. I'm not going to spend the rest of my life as some lackey to the gentry, helping them pull on their drawers and pull off their boots."

"You knew what George had done to his brother from the start?" Christiana asked, though she was sure she already knew the answer to that.

"Yes, yes," he said on an impatient sigh. "I knew from the beginning and was paid well to keep my mouth shut. You and your sister had the right of it."

Christiana jerked back as the words struck her. "How do you know what my sister and I were talking about? You were listening?"

"I was in the office trying to find something when I heard your voices approaching the door. I slipped out through the French doors but left one cracked open to hear when you left so I could continue my search and instead heard a whole lot more." He grimaced with irritation, but went on, "The moment I realized you were heading to look for me I rushed around the house to try to get here before you, but was not quick enough."

He turned his back to her then and paced the floor a couple times. Christiana glanced around, hoping to see something to use as a weapon, but really the room was as sparse as a monk's cell. Glancing back to the man, she asked curiously, "What were you looking for in the office?"

He hesitated and then apparently decided there was no harm in telling her and admitted, "Your father's marker. Between that and the blackmail money, I can set myself up well in France or Spain. Have a good life as a man of means." He sighed at the thought.

"Why would Dicky have the marker?"

Christiana asked.

He scowled her way and then propped his hands on his hips. "Bloody women, always asking questions, just have to know everything. I suppose you won't shut up and give me a moment's peace until you know everything?"

"Probably not," she admitted unsympathetically.

His mouth twisted and he snapped, "Fine. I knew all from the start. I knew when George hired those men to kill his brother, I knew he then stepped into his shoes and pretended to be him, enjoying his wealth and title in his place. I knew when John Butterworth told George about the dowers for you and your sisters. I —"

"So it *was* all for the dowers," Christiana interrupted with disgust. While she'd suspected it for quite a while, actually hearing the words made her angrier than she'd expected.

"Oh, yes," Freddy said with amusement. "He drugged your father and dragged him to the gaming hell to make him think he'd gambled so deep he would accept an offer of marriage for you in exchange for George's supposedly paying off markers he already held. And he did the same again, this time to force Suzette to be married to one of his friends. The markers were to be George's payment for acting as procurer."

"Who was the friend who was supposed to marry Suzette?" Christiana asked curiously.

"Does it matter? She's set her mind on marrying that damned Woodrow," he pointed out dryly, and then shook his head. "Were George still alive he would have arranged an accident for the man or some other such thing, but the stupid bastard went and hired idiots to kill his brother. They failed him and now Richard is back and poisoned him to get his title back."

"Richard did not poison him," Christiana said firmly.

"Well someone did," Freddy snapped.

"Yes, but it wasn't Richard," she assured him and then tilted her head in question. "How did you know he was poisoned?"

"Because I saw him die," he said grimly. "He dragged me into his office the morning your sisters arrived to crow about the latest success of his plans. He was sure they were there about your father's latest apparent faux pas," he explained, and then continued, "Once assured I was properly impressed with his cleverness, George sent me for snuff. When I got back the whiskey was there, and he was clawing at his throat, then he died right there in front of me."

He grimaced. "Well, I know trouble when I see it and got myself out of there right quick. Told the cook I was unwell and his lordship had excused me to recover, then came in here to await the hue and cry that he was dead. *But there was none*," he added with exasperation. "When I finally ventured out it was to be told his lordship was feeling unwell and resting abed. I came back to my room to try to puzzle that one out. I knew damned right well the man was dead. So I waited until the servants were all abed and you were at the ball and then snuck upstairs to see for myself, but as I started up the hall your bedroom door opened. I ducked into the guest bedroom across from yours and watched through the cracked door as a man came out carrying George over his shoulder with a second man following. I recognized the one man as Lord Woodrow and while George's body obstructed my view of the other man's face, when Woodrow called him Richard I knew he wasn't dead after all."

"I stood there in that room for a long time that night, watching the comings and goings as a plan formed in my mind. I could blackmail Radnor about George's death, take the markers and force your father to pay his debts, and then head for the continent." He fell silent, his lips twisting with displeasure. "And it would have worked perfectly. By this time tomorrow I would have the blackmail money. The money for the gaming debt would have followed and then I'd be on my way."

"Except for Suzette and myself," she murmured.

"Aye," he agreed grimly, his gaze scouring her with displeasure.

"You realize she knows I went in search of you and will soon worry that I have not returned," Christiana pointed out quietly. "You may as well release me and just go. I promise if you do that no one will pursue you."

"I'm sure you think that a very kind offer," he said dryly. "However, I am not going anywhere without the money."

"Do you really expect my husband simply to pay, knowing it is you?"

"He doesn't know," Freddy pointed out. "And he will pay. In fact, I think I will just up the price now that I have an added bargaining chip in you."

"Me?" she asked with surprise.

"Aye. Judging by the caterwauling that's been coming from your room the last couple nights, I think it's safe to say he will pay handsomely for your safe return."

Christiana flushed and glanced away. She was definitely going to have to stuff a bit of cloth or something in her mouth when she and Richard were alone. It was too humiliating to know everyone could hear them.

A tearing sound caught her ear and she turned back, frowning when she saw that Freddy had retrieved an old shirt and was rending it into strips. Wariness creeping up her spine, she asked, "What is that for?"

"To bind and gag you. We cannot stay here and I want to find that marker, but I am not sneaking you around to the office until I am sure you will not scream and give us away."

Christiana stared at him wide-eyed, her mind working quickly. She was in a bit of a spot now, but if he bound and gagged her she would be helpless and she just didn't feel like allowing him to put her in that position. She needed to draw attention while she could. Drawing in a deep breath, she opened her mouth to scream, but all that came out was a moan as his fist suddenly slammed into the side of her head, sending her into unconsciousness.

"I thought I heard voices out here."

Richard glanced toward his office door as

Suzette stepped out into the hall. She pulled the door closed as she glanced over them. Her eyes widened with surprise when she spotted Lord Madison there and she started forward at once.

"Father, what are you doing here?"

"He came to rescue us," Lisa told her before anyone else could speak. "He even held Richard and Daniel at gunpoint until Robert and I explained the new situation to him."

"Oh, how sweet," Suzette said pausing before her father and hugging him, which seemed to leave the man a little startled. Apparently, he hadn't expected a warm greeting from her, but she said, "I am sorry I was so angry when we arrived in London, Father. You didn't deserve it." She pulled back and added, "Chrissy says the men think Dicky drugged you and just made you think you'd gambled the money away. It was all a trick to try to get our dowers."

When Lord Madison glanced his way in question, Richard nodded solemnly and said, "There are rumors that I, or Dicky really, had become quite chummy with the owner of a gaming hell famous for the trick."

Lord Madison sagged with relief and nodded. "I had begun to suspect as much. I have no recollection of gambling at all, and what recollections I do have of the gaming hell are quite fuzzy flashes of being led through it, people talking and laughing, being told to sign something . . ." He grimaced and shook his head. "I have never cared for gambling and don't even know how to play the games of chance in those places. Yet there was the marker with my signature on it."

Suzette patted his back and hugged him again.

"Well, now that that is all straightened out, why do we not sit down and hear what everyone has learned?" Daniel suggested, moving to Suzette's other side so that she stood between the two men.

Richard managed to restrain the grin of amusement that wanted to claim his lips. He knew Daniel's main concern was changing the subject before anyone could mention that Lord Madison had sold his townhouse to gain the money to pay off his debt without the need for Suzette's dower. The man was going to be itching to get Suzette to Gretna Green before someone spilled the beans. It seemed he'd definitely settled on the woman to wife, but wasn't sure she would willingly wed him in return were it not for the circumstances she had found herself in. Richard wasn't so sure Daniel had anything to worry about though. He had noted the way Suzette seemed always to track him with her eyes, and the way she tended to stick close to him. And then there was the scene he'd walked in on that morning after leaving Christiana to straighten her clothes. By his guess the pair had been a heartbeat away from anticipating their vows. He suspected Suzette's feelings for his friend were much deeper than anyone suspected.

"Yes, let's move into the parlor," Richard suggested and then glanced to Suzette to ask, "Where is Christiana?"

"Oh." She frowned and glanced along the hall. "I was just going in search of her. She was going to have Haversham fetch Freddy to us to interview, but has taken an awfully long time so I thought I'd best check on her."

"George's valet, Freddy?" Richard asked with a frown. Freddy had been his brother's valet for twenty years and, like Robbie, wouldn't have been fooled into believing George was Richard. The man must have known all along.

"Yes, George's valet," Suzette said now. "We realized that he might not have been fooled by the switch George made and if he somehow saw you the last day or two may realize you are not George. If so, he could be the blackmailer."

"Of course," Richard growled, and then glanced up the hall as Haversham came hurrying out of the kitchens, heading their way. He knew at once that there was trouble. Haversham was a proper English butler to the core of his being and simply never hurried anywhere. It was considered unseemly, and butlers were never unseemly. Still, Richard was more interested in Christiana's whereabouts than any small emergency the butler may be approaching about and asked, "Haversham, have you seen my wife? She apparently went looking for you to have you send Freddy to her."

"Actually, my lord, I was just coming to seek you out about that. It appears Lady Christiana was unable to find me and went in search of your valet herself and has now found herself in something of a fix."

"What kind of a fix?" Richard asked grimly.

"Well, I happened to be passing Freddy's room and overheard him saying that he intended to take her and force you to pay to get her back safely," he admitted grimly. "I believe he is planning to take her around to the office to try to find something first, however, so if we were to hide ourselves

414

away in there and wait for him to approach we may be able to take him by surprise and relieve him of Lady Christiana without her coming to harm."

"That's actually a good plan," Daniel said with some surprise and eyed the butler with a new respect. He then glanced to Richard and said, "We should move quickly though, I don't recall a lot of places in the office to hide."

Richard had already turned to head to his office when Robert announced, "I am coming too."

"And me," Lord Madison said firmly.

"Me too," Suzette announced.

Richard paused abruptly and glanced back to see that everyone was following, including Lisa and Haversham. Scowling, he shook his head. "There aren't enough hiding spaces for everyone. Robert and Daniel only will come. The rest of you need to get into the parlor and out of the hall so you don't scare Freddy off." His gaze slid to Lord Madison, who opened his mouth to protest, and forestalled him by adding, "I trust you are the only person here who could keep Suzette and Lisa in that parlor."

Lord Madison let his mouth close with a sigh and nodded.

Richard started to turn away then, but

paused and swung back to ask, "Might I borrow your pistol, my lord?"

"Of course." Madison held out the pistol and said grimly, "Keep her safe."

"I intend to," Richard assured him as he took the weapon. He then stepped back and waited as Christiana's father turned to take Suzette and Lisa each by an arm to lead them to the parlor. Both girls began to protest at once, but he merely said, "I am your father and you will go in the parlor and like it."

When Richard's gaze next slid to Haversham, the butler hesitated, but then nodded stiffly and turned to follow the others. Richard immediately turned and led Robert and Daniel to the office to seek out hiding spots and await the arrival of his wife and her captor.

Christiana groaned, or tried to, as consciousness returned to her. However, her groan was stifled by the gag in her mouth. She blinked her eyes open, and immediately wished she hadn't and closed them again. The sight of the ground moving by below was only her first hint that she was not in a position she wanted to be in. The pain of the shoulder lodged in her stomach was her second hint.

Freddy had obviously knocked her out, bound and gagged her and was now carting her about over his shoulder like a sack of wheat. Her head was dangling down his back and aching. Though she wasn't sure whether the aching was from the blow she'd taken to the head, her position, which had the blood pooling in that same abused head, or a combination of both. All Christiana really knew was that her head hurt, her stomach hurt from the jarring it was taking with each step, and the corners of her mouth hurt where the gag rubbed tightly against it. The inside of her mouth wasn't all that happy either; it was as dry as a bone thanks to the gag apparently soaking up every drop of liquid in there.

Basically, she was very uncomfortable, and growing very annoyed with Freddy for it. Christiana could hardly wait to fire the man, for those were going to be the first words out of her mouth once the gag was removed. She was sure it wouldn't upset him much, considering he'd planned to leave their employ and move to the continent. However, she would still enjoy saying the words.

Grimacing at her own thoughts, which truly were just an effort to distract herself from her discomfort, Christiana forced her eyes open again. The ground was still moving by below her, but now it was grass. They were outside. Lifting her head, she peered around to see that Freddy was carrying her along the house toward the French doors leading to the office. Christiana supposed he'd decided this was the safer approach and lowered her head, hoping that Suzette wasn't still in there. The only thing she could think of that would be worse than her being held for ransom was Suzette being caught and held with her.

Freddy slowed and she glanced around to see that they had nearly reached the French doors. He was creeping close to the house now, presumably approaching cautiously in case someone was inside.

Apparently, the room was empty. At least that was her guess when Freddy began to move faster again, opening the door to slip into the room with her still over his shoulder. He paused halfway through the door, tensing like a rabbit smelling a predator on the wind, and Christiana tried to glance around to see what had made him suddenly tense, but couldn't see past him to the room. She sagged against his back again, her gaze moving over the yard instead and it was then she glimpsed the man creeping up behind them along the back of the house. Haversham. The butler was moving with the silence and stealth of a thief as he approached. He also carried a rather wicked butcher knife in his hand.

Movement behind Haversham then drew her attention to the fact that there was another man following the butler. Christiana's eyes widened as she recognized her father. She had no idea what he was doing there, but there he was, face grim and eyes determined as he crept along in much the same manner as Haversham, a smaller knife in his own hand.

Christiana had barely taken note of that when she next spotted Suzette and Lisa tiptoeing along behind the two men. Her sisters were each armed as well, Suzette with a rolling pin and Lisa with a big, long two-tined cooking fork. It appeared the whole household intended to save her and had raided the kitchen to do it, she thought wryly, and then wondered where Richard and the men were. She supposed it was possible that they were not yet back from their own task of arranging for the blackmail money, but Lisa and Robert had been together so she knew he at least must be there somewhere, though she didn't see him yet. And then Freddy apparently got over whatever had spooked him and continued into the office and Christiana could no longer see her would-be rescuers.

CHAPTER EIGHTEEN

Richard felt his hands clench into fists when one of the French doors opened and he recognized George's valet entering with Christiana bound and gagged and unmoving over his shoulder. It was the unmoving part that worried and enraged him and the degree to which he was affected was almost startling to him. He wanted to rip Christiana from the man's back, assure himself she was alive and well, and then tear Freddy limb from limb for even daring to touch her let alone manhandling her so.

That rage was swiftly followed by terror when Freddy paused in the door and re-adjusted his hold on Christiana, revealing the short, wicked blade in one of his hands. Richard was not used to such depths of emotion. Even what George had done to him had not left him with this level of fear or rage, and he found it unsettling to feel that way now, but his mind was crowding with images of his time since returning home from America, and all of them were of Christiana, laughing, smiling, looking thoughtful and then vexed.

When Richard had left her in the dressing room that morning, he'd never imagined the next time he'd see her would be in a situation like this, with her life at risk and he uncertain he could save her, but desperate to do so. And he *was* desperate. Short though their time together had been, he already could not imagine life without her in it and didn't want to. Somehow she had managed to wiggle her way under his skin and into his heart and he wanted to keep her there.

Freddy had finished adjusting his hold, but stood a moment longer as if sensing danger before closing the French door partway. He left it a crack open, probably for a swift escape, Richard supposed, watching from his hiding place behind a suit of armor in the office corner furthest from the doors. Robert had suggested hiding behind the curtains, but Richard had pointed out that if Freddy came from the outside he would surely see them there and their advantage of surprise would be lost, so they'd all had to find alternate spots. Richard had chosen the suit of armor, Daniel had ducked behind a settee in another corner and Robert had taken the only place left — the knee cubby under the desk. He'd squeezed himself in there and then pulled the desk chair in behind him to help disguise his presence.

Richard imagined Robert was probably in the most uncomfortable spot, but wished he'd taken it himself. It would have put him closer. His hand tightened around Lord Madison's pistol as he waited for the man to put Christiana down to conduct his search. He would rather she was out of the way before he confronted the man. However, it soon became obvious the valet wasn't going to put her down. He was poking through the top side drawer of the desk, just inches from Robert, but with Christiana still firmly over his back.

Richard ground his teeth together. He didn't even want to aim the pistol at the man with Christiana acting as his shield and wished he'd thought to have one of them hide somewhere in the yard just in case something like this occurred. They could have crept up behind him then.

He'd barely had the thought when Richard noticed the French door easing slowly open behind Freddy. He held his breath briefly, and then recognized Haversham slipping into the room, a large butcher knife in hand.

Alarm coursing through him, Richard tightened his hand on the pistol he held and moved out from behind the suit of armor. It immediately drew Freddy's attention from the drawer he was rifling through and he froze. Leveling his weapon at the man, Richard started forward, saying, "I really think it would be in your best interests to put my wife down."

Panic crossed briefly over Freddy's face, but then was replaced by a calculating look. Straightening slowly from the desk he said, "You wouldn't shoot me. You might hit her."

"I won't let you leave here either unless it's in chains," Richard said grimly, continuing slowly forward as Lord Madison now slid into the room behind Haversham. Suzette and Lisa were behind him, hesitating in the door as they took in the situation.

Freddy took an unknowing step back toward Haversham and then glanced sharply toward Daniel as the other man rose from behind the settee and started forward as well. Beginning to look a little less sure of himself, Freddy shifted the knife he held, pressing it to Christiana's backside. "Stay back or I'll cut her."

"Ouch! That is my bottom," Christiana

squawked.

Richard felt a moment's relief at his first sign that she was alive and well, but growled, "Put her down."

"Go to hell!" Freddy yelled back in frustration and whirled to charge out of the room, only to come up short as he crashed into Haversham. No one moved for half a second and then Freddy began to fall back, taking Christiana with him. Richard saw Haversham and Lord Madison trying to grab for Christiana, even as he leapt the last few feet and caught at her himself as Freddy dropped. No one apparently thought to grab Freddy and save her from her fall that way, so it ended with all of them holding her up. Richard had her by the hips, Haversham had managed to grab one leg through her gown and Lord Madison had only managed to snatch a handful of skirt. Unfortunately, it left Christiana still hanging head down, her behind in the air and her skirt raised.

The men all exchanged a horrified glance and then Lord Madison quickly released his hold on her skirts, Haversham stepped back releasing his hold as well, and Richard set Christiana down and stepped back to allow her to straighten. However, she stayed bent over and murmured, "Oh dear."

Richard glanced down, noting then that she was peering at Freddy, or really at the large knife sticking out of his chest.

"He ran right into it, my lord," Haversham said calmly.

Richard nodded, but his thoughts were taken up with the fact that had Haversham been a little more to one side, the knife would now be sticking out of Christiana.

Christiana finally straightened and patted the butler on the arm. "Do not feel bad, Haversham. He wasn't a very good man."

"Yes, my lady," the butler murmured, and then cleared his throat and glanced to Richard. "Shall I send for the authorities, my lord?"

"Ah . . ." Richard scowled at Freddy, not pleased at the prospect of having to admit to the authorities that the man had been blackmailing them. They would have to explain what he was blackmailing them about and all their attempts to keep George's activities a secret would be for naught.

"He was trying to take Lady Christiana and hold her to ransom," Haversham pointed out quietly. "The authorities should really be informed of this and his death."

Richard relaxed and nodded. They would just stick to that and not mention the blackmail or anything else.

"Very good, my lord." The butler slid silently from the room and Richard turned to Christiana, only to find she had moved to speak to her father and sisters by the door. He started her way, eager to touch and hold her and reassure himself that she was well. In truth, he wanted to strip her naked, examine every inch of her to be sure she bore no wounds and then make love to her, but knew he would just have to be content to wait for that.

"Hello? Can someone get this chair out of the way? Hello?"

Richard glanced down at Robert's call to see that Freddy had fallen behind the chair, blocking it so that Langley couldn't push it out and unfold himself from the cubbyhole where he'd hidden.

"Problems, Langley?" Daniel asked with a laugh, coming around the desk to Richard's side.

"Move the damned chair, Woodrow," Robert barked. " 'Tis hot as hades down here and I think my leg is cramping."

Richard chuckled and together he and Daniel shifted Freddy's body around to the side of the desk. By the time they straightened, Robert was crawling out from under the desk.

"That was a damned stupid place to

hide," Langley muttered with self-disgust as he straightened. "Freddy was leaning against the chair while searching the desk and there wasn't a damned thing I could have done to help anyone while stuck under there."

"It wasn't like there were many hiding spots to choose from," Richard pointed out wryly as the man brushed himself down.

"Hmm." Robert glanced to Freddy's body. "Well, that is one problem taken care of anyway. The blackmail threat is over."

"Now we just need to figure out who poisoned George and is still trying to kill Richard," Daniel agreed dryly.

Robert frowned and shook his head. "Well, I'm afraid Lisa and I didn't find out anything of use today. I think people were reluctant to gossip about you with Lisa there. She is your sister-in-law, after all. Perhaps Christiana and Suzette were more successful at discovering what servant may have administered the poison."

"We should ask them," Richard murmured and turned to find that Christiana and her father were gone. "Where —"

"Father wished to speak to Christiana. They have stepped out into the garden," Suzette explained before he could finish his question.

Richard glanced toward the French doors,

spotting the two at the back of the garden, their heads together. Before he could decide whether to intrude or wait, the office door opened and Haversham led two men into the room; both wore the telltale red vest of Bow Street runners. The authorities had arrived.

"What is it, Father?" Christiana asked when he stopped walking but stared at his feet rather than bring up whatever it was he'd brought her outside to discuss. "If 'tis about this gambling business, you should know you didn't do it. We think George as Dicky drugged you and —"

"Yes, I know, Suzette told me," he interrupted, and then added, "I came here today to take you away."

"Take me away?" she asked with surprise.

Lord Madison nodded. "Robert had written, telling me how unhappy you seemed in your marriage and how Dicky treated you. It was why I came to London in the first place. I told the gels I needed to see the lawyer, but truly I was coming to see you."

"Thank you," she whispered, hugging him tightly.

Lord Madison hugged her back and said, "I can still take you away."

Startled, Christiana pulled back to peer at

him. "Has no one explained that George was Dicky and now I am married to Richard, the true —"

"Yes," he said solemnly, cutting her off. "Robert explained everything. He also said that Richard was a fine, honorable man who will treat you well and he hopes you will have a good life together. But you were tricked into marrying Dicky, and if you only married Richard to avoid scandal, I don't want you to feel trapped into it." He eyed her solemnly and then said, "Just say the word and I will take you home and we will figure out a way to get you out of this marriage."

Her eyes widened incredulously. "Father, the scandal would —"

"Scandal be damned," he growled. "We can weather that. 'Tis your happiness I care about, and the fact that your only protest is the possible scandal tells me you do not really wish to be in this marriage. Come." He caught her hand and started to drag her toward the house. "We shall collect your sisters and head straight for home. I am done with this damned town."

"No, wait!" Christiana cried, tugging at her hand as panic seized her at the thought of leaving Richard. "Please, Father, stop. I don't want to leave. Really. I love him."

Lord Madison paused at once and turned to peer at her in question. "Really? Do you love him?"

Christiana stared at him blankly, her mind in an uproar of confusion. She hadn't meant to say that, wasn't even sure where the words had come from. Surely she didn't mean them, her sensible side argued, but the idea of leaving him had struck such terror in her . . .

Taking a deep breath she tried to think clearly. The passion they shared was incredible, of course, but love was more than passion, and she hadn't known him long enough to — Christiana let that thought die in her head, because another part of her mind was arguing that she did know him. With Dicky-George Christiana had been constantly on edge, anxious over what he might say or do, and wary of his temper making an appearance and his lashing out at those around him. But Richard didn't seem to have the same unpredictability: he was courteous and respectful of everyone he encountered, even the lowliest servant. Richard was also honorable where George probably wouldn't have been able to even spell the word. And he had married her to save her and her sisters from scandal, which was as chivalrous as a man could get, really, she acknowledged and realized that Lisa was right, Richard was her hero, and she *had* come to love him for it. For that and so much else.

Straightening her shoulders, Christiana nodded solemnly. "I love Richard. I do not want to leave him."

Lord Madison nodded solemnly. "Very well."

"But thank you, Father," she added, hugging him.

Lord Madison patted her back, and then took her arm when she stepped back. "We should go back inside and join the others."

Christiana nodded in agreement and they turned to walk into the house, but both paused abruptly when they spotted Richard standing in the open French doors. Christiana bit her lip, worried about how long he'd been there and whether he'd heard her declaration, but her husband merely said, "The authorities have been and gone. We explained that Freddy had tried to take you to ransom and we all stopped him and they accepted our explanations and took him away."

"Oh," Christiana murmured. "They didn't wish to speak to me?"

"I told them you were upset. They accepted that and said there was no need to talk to you with so many other witnesses."

"Oh, good," she smiled crookedly, glad not to have to explain things. She really was a bad liar, even when it came to lies of omission and probably would have blurted out everything.

Her father urged her forward then and Christiana started to walk again. When they came abreast of Richard, he slid his arm around her waist, drawing her to a halt. Her father immediately released her arm and continued into the office, leaving her to smile nervously at her husband.

"Are you all right?" he asked solemnly. "Freddy didn't hurt you?"

"I have a slight headache and a lovely goose egg from when he knocked me out, but am otherwise fine," she assured him and glanced around the office as he led her inside. Her father, Daniel and Robert were there, but Suzette and Lisa were missing, as was Haversham. "Where — ?"

"Suzette took Lisa to the parlor while the runners were asking questions," Richard answered before she could finish the question. "Apparently Freddy's body lying here was distressing to her."

"It would be. Lisa doesn't care for the sight of blood. She will even faint if there is enough of it," Christiana murmured, and then frowned as she noted the scrape on his forehead. "What happened to your head?"

"It's nothing," Richard assured her. "Daniel and I stopped at the tailor's after arranging for the blackmail money and a carriage came after us. I got this as we jumped out of the way."

"As *he* jumped out of the way and dragged me with him," Daniel corrected dryly. "I didn't even see the thing until it was almost upon us."

"I suppose that wasn't Freddy," Christiana said with a sigh as she realized the worst was not over. While they had caught the blackmailer, they still had a murderer to find.

"No," Daniel said, looking doubtful. Still, he sounded hopeful when he asked, "Unless Freddy happened to confess to being the killer as well as the blackmailer?"

Christiana smiled apologetically. "Sorry. No. He thought Richard had killed him."

"Then who killed George?" Robert asked with a frown.

"I fear that would be me, Lord Langley."

Christiana turned toward the door, her eyes wide as she peered at Haversham. The butler stood in the open door, back straight and face as expressionless as ever. The perfect servant.

"Would you care to explain, Haversham?" Richard asked quietly after several moments of silence had passed.

"Of course," the man murmured. "I suspected quite soon after the fire that the man masquerading as the Earl was not you, my lord, but your brother, Master George. He quite simply did not act in a lordly manner as you have always seen fit to do. He was careless with his possessions, cruel to the staff, and both careless and cruel to Lady Christiana."

"Did you tell anyone of your suspicions?" Richard asked, and Christiana felt him tense beside her. She supposed he worried that if Haversham had told anyone his suspicions their worries wouldn't be over. But Haversham shook his head.

"No. All I had were suspicions. I could not prove anything and who would believe a servant over a member of gentry?"

"I see," Richard murmured, relaxing.

"I saw no choice but to allow the situation to progress as it would and hope for some proof to come to light. I was rather counting on Lord Woodrow becoming suspicious himself and looking into the matter. I would have come forward then with my own suspicions, of course. However, that never came to pass. Lord Woodrow disappeared from society the week of the townhouse fire and simply did not return."

"Er . . . yes. I'm afraid I was a bit distracted with matters at Woodrow," Daniel explained apologetically under the stern man's displeased eye.

"Yes," the butler said dryly. "So I was forced to simply stand by and wait, a witness to Master George's abuses of his position and shabby treatment of Lady Christiana, but unable to do anything about it."

"What made you stop waiting?" Christiana asked curiously, wondering that she'd had at least one ally all that time and hadn't even realized it.

"It was the morning your sisters arrived at the townhouse, my lady," he said solemnly. "Master George had been tense and expectant, almost buzzing with a certain excitement for the two weeks prior and I anticipated that he was up to something, but was unsure what until your sisters arrived with the news your father had apparently gambled again. I realized then that this must have been what Master George had been waiting for, and quite impatiently, I will add. From the conversation I chanced to overhear afterward, I gather he had expected them to come to you much sooner, or for your father to come pleading his case.

"However," Haversham continued, "After leaving you ladies in the parlor, Master George was quite cheerful and ordered me to bring his best whiskey to him in his office. Freddy appeared then, headed for the kitchens and Master George took him to the office, where I overheard his gleeful announcement that the plan was finally moving forward again. He was sure the sisters were there about the gambling, and that it would be no time before he had Suzette married off to one of his friends."

"Who?" Daniel asked sharply, making Christiana glance curiously his way. His expression suggested the answer was important to him, though she couldn't imagine why he cared. He and Suzette were marrying. Whoever the friend was, he was out of luck.

"I'm afraid he did not speak the proper name of his friend, but referred to him as Twiddly."

"Twiddly?" her father echoed with disbelief.

Haversham nodded, and then continued, "Apparently Master George was to get a good portion of the money supposedly owed to the gaming hell from this gentleman, Twiddly, for acting as broker. Then they merely had to wait for Lord Madison to come to town again, drug and drag him to the gaming hell for a third time and force Lady Lisa into marriage as well. Master George would gain a portion of her dower in that instance as well. The gaming hell only took a percentage to keep its mouth shut about the fact that no money was actually owing at all."

"I will see the place shut down," Robert growled furiously.

"No doubt you would be doing many unwary men a favor," Haversham assured him and then continued. "Once all three women were wed and fleeced of their dowers, the plan was to dispose of them all in one tragic carriage accident."

Haversham allowed a moment's silence and then added, "Once the women were dead, Master George already had his sights set on a certain young heiress who was too young to enter society yet, but should be on the verge of her debut by the time he was widowed. Master George was quite pleased with himself and his clever machinations," he added dryly.

"I considered warning lady Christiana," he admitted. "However, I fear I could not see how that would help. There was still no proof of the man's perfidy, and while she might be able to warn her father and prevent his going anywhere near Master George again, I worried it would force Master George to kill the whole lot of them earlier than intended, including perhaps Lord Madison since he would know what was going on and be suspicious of any accidents to befall the women. It seemed to me the only other option was to stop Master George myself, and so I dropped cyanide into his glass of whiskey before taking it in to him."

He sighed. "I expected Freddy to be there when I took the poisoned drink in to Master George, and had not yet decided how to handle the man. However, he was nowhere to be seen, so I simply left the master to enjoy his celebratory drink and waited for matters to develop. It wasn't long after that Freddy claimed he wasn't feeling well and Master George had excused him. For a short time I was quite concerned that he may have drunk the master's whiskey in his place. However, when I checked on Master George, he was quite dead. I quickly emptied and wiped the glass to remove any proof of what I'd done, then refilled the glass halfway and set it back before returning to the kitchens to await his discovery. But of course it never came. Lady Christiana eventually went into the office, her sisters followed, and they were in there quite a while, but there was no hue and cry. Instead, the three ladies came out some time later lugging the dead George about in a rug."

"You knew he was in there?" Christiana asked with surprise.

"My lady, you really were not gifted with a talent for subterfuge," Haversham said kindly.

Christiana flushed as she recalled that her first words on running into Haversham had been *We're just taking Dicky up to warm the rug.* Honestly, she didn't lie well at all.

"And then of course there were his fingers," Haversham added.

"His fingers?" Christiana echoed with confusion.

Haversham nodded. "The three of you apparently rolled up Master George with his arms stretched above his head?"

"We thought the rug would seem less lumpy that way," Christiana admitted with a frown.

"I'm sure it did. However, his fingers were sticking out the top end and waving at me the entire time as you struggled to hold the thing and lie about what the three of you were doing. It was most distracting."

"Oh dear," Christiana murmured.

Haversham smiled at her gently and

continued, "I realized at once that you were going to hide the death in the hopes of finding a husband for Lady Suzette and so ordered the staff to stay away from that wing of the house for the time being. Of course, later that night I nearly had an attack of apoplexy when the Earl — the true Earl —" he added firmly, eyeing Richard, "came rushing out of his office as I was coming up the hall. I thought I had failed after all and that Master George was still alive. However, the moment his lordship spoke I recognized that it was he."

"How?" Richard asked with surprise.

"You said 'excuse me,' " Haversham said simply.

"And from that you knew it was him?" Daniel asked with amusement.

Haversham nodded solemnly. "His lordship treats everyone from the lowliest servant to the highest nobleman with a certain respect that was sadly missing in his brother. George never would have troubled to excuse himself, not even to the King."

"Ah." Daniel nodded and the butler continued.

"After that the events in the house became rather confusing to me," Haversham admitted. "I felt a draft as I passed the library, opened the door to see that the French

441

doors were wide open, went in to close them and saw something lying on the lawn. Realizing it was Master George half wrapped in a blanket, I looked up and saw Lord Woodrow and Lady Suzette in the window in a passionate embrace."

Everyone turned to peer at Daniel. He shifted and murmured an uncomfortable, "Erm." And then Haversham drew the attention back to himself, saying, "I left Master George as I found him and started upstairs, but heard Lady Lisa and Lord Richard talking and realized that she — and I therefore assumed everyone else — believed Lord Richard was Dicky. It appeared to me then that he was simply going to remove George's body and step back into his life and all would be well. I nearly left then to —"

"Left?" Christiana interrupted with surprise.

"I am a murderer, my lady, leaving did seem wise," he said gently. "However, I decided I should wait to be sure the transition went without difficulty. Besides, there was still Freddy to worry about. He would surely realize that Richard was not George, and I thought I had best see how he decided to handle it. If he just pretended he didn't know and carried on I would have slipped

442

quietly away and retired. However, if he didn't and caused trouble I wished to be on the scene to help right things.

"That is done now," he added on a small sigh. "And I feel quite certain all will be well from here on in, so if no one protests, I shall collect my things and begin my retirement . . . on the continent."

Much to Christiana's relief, Richard slipped past her and moved to the man. At least she was relieved at first, but much to her dismay he merely shook the man's hand and thanked him for everything and then walked him out of the room.

"He isn't going to let him leave, is he?" she whispered with dismay.

"It would appear he is," Daniel murmured, and then moved toward the door as well, saying, "I should go tell Suzette everything is resolved and we can head for Gretna Green."

"Wait for me," Robert said, hurrying after him.

Christiana watched them go with a frown, but then glanced to her father as he moved to her side.

"Are you all right?" he asked with concern.

"I — Yes," she sighed and then said, "I need to talk to Richard."

Her father nodded, not appearing surprised. "I shall go check on the girls then."

Christiana walked with him to the door, but as he continued on to the parlor, she turned toward the front door, relieved when she spotted Richard and Haversham there, speaking quietly.

"Richard, you can't let him go like this," she protested rushing to join them, but paused with surprise when she saw the small chest and bag waiting to the side of the front door. The butler was already packed and ready to go. Frowning at that, she turned to Richard and added, "He only killed George to save my sisters and me."

"This is for the best, Christiana," Richard said quietly, slipping his arm around her waist and drawing her against his side.

"He is right, my lady. Besides I wish it this way. I am getting far too old to perform my duties as I should. It is time I retired," Haversham said, opening the door before bending to pick up his chest and bag. Straightening, he turned back and added, "I wish you both a happy and healthy life together." Then he turned and strode out the door.

"Richard," Christiana begged, trying to pull free and go after the man.

"Let him go, Christiana," Richard said quietly. "It really is for the best."

"Why? Killing George was a spur of the moment, desperate effort to save my sisters and me. He —"

"He used cyanide, Christiana," Richard said quietly. "That is not something a person typically keeps sitting about the house. It suggests premeditation."

Her eyes widened as she realized what he said was true and then she turned to watch Haversham get into a carriage waiting on the road. The man had planned his exit down to the last detail.

"You don't really think it was premeditated do you?" she asked with a frown.

Richard hesitated and then said, "Haversham plans everything. He is a very careful man and always has been. I suspect he intended to kill George eventually, probably as punishment for his killing me, but also to rid you of the man and the miserable marriage he'd trapped you into. I suspect Haversham had been planning it for some time before actually doing it. He was most likely just waiting in the hopes that you would produce an heir."

When Christiana glanced at him with surprise, he shrugged.

"Haversham is traditional. He would see the continuing of the family line as important," he explained. "No doubt by the time

445

he overheard George talking to Freddy, he'd realized that George never visited your room and there would be no heir. There was no longer a reason to wait, so he killed him."

Richard closed the door as the carriage pulled away. "He knows I would realize all this, and that the only way my conscience would allow me to stay mum on the murder was if he was gone and beyond the reaches of English law."

"Surely you wouldn't have turned him in?" she asked with amazement. "Everything would have had to be revealed then, what George did, that we weren't legally married . . . everything."

"I realize that, and I don't know if I would have actually turned him in knowing the outcome," he admitted quietly. "But I would have wrestled with the decision. Haversham knows me well enough to know that, which is — I think — why he said he was going to retire to the continent. He will be beyond English law and revealing what he did would accomplish nothing but cause trouble and pain for those I love. Now I don't have to wrestle with the decision."

"I see," she murmured.

"Is everyone still in the office?" Richard asked.

"No, Daniel went to tell Suzette — Oh,"

she breathed suddenly.

"What?" He glanced at her with concern.

"I just realized. Suzette doesn't have to marry Daniel now. The markers are in the office somewhere and —"

"I think you might want to keep that bit of information to yourself for a bit," Richard interrupted.

Christiana's eyebrows rose. "Why?"

"Because Daniel really wants to marry Suzette, and I think she wants to marry him too, but Daniel thinks she needs the markers as an excuse or may become difficult."

She considered that solemnly. The conversation she'd had with Suzette today had made her suspect her sister really did care for Daniel. In fact, she'd seemed quite disgruntled over the idea that Daniel was only marrying her for the dower which made her ask, "Does he want her for her dower?"

Richard grinned and shook his head. "He's almost as rich as I."

Her eyes widened incredulously. "Then why — ?"

"She fascinates him and he wants her. In truth, I think he's half in love with her."

"I think she may be falling in love with him too," Christiana said quietly. "Why do we not just tell them and —"

"Daniel believes, and your father concurred, that Suzette is just contrary enough to refuse to marry him despite her feelings if she finds out she doesn't have to. He also thinks that your year of marriage with George has put her off the idea of marriage altogether." He raised an eyebrow. "What do you think?"

Christiana grimaced. "I think he knows her very well."

"Then perhaps we can just keep the information about the markers to ourselves until we see how things go," he suggested, and then smiled wryly. " 'Tis a bit of good fortune for Daniel that Suzette wasn't in the room to hear all that business."

"Yes, I suppose," Christiana murmured, thinking she would wait a bit, but she would tell Suzette before she and Daniel married. Her conscience wouldn't allow her to do otherwise. She changed the subject then, asking, "If Haversham killed George, does that mean the carriage accident was just that, an accident?"

Richard frowned. "It could have been, I suppose. It was only George's murder combined with the fact that three spokes on the carriage wheel seemed relatively straight that made us think otherwise. I guess they could have simply broken that way as the wheel collapsed. Stranger things have happened."

"But what about the post chaise that nearly ran you down today?" she pointed out.

He frowned and considered, but then sighed and said, "Accidents do happen and drivers lose control of carriages. It's possible it was just an accident and we put it down as a murder attempt because George was poisoned."

Christiana frowned, not convinced. "We shall have to be careful and alert for a while until we are sure."

Richard smiled and drew her against his chest with a sigh. "I love you too."

Christiana glanced up sharply. "What?"

Taking her face in both hands, he said firmly, "I said, I love you too."

"You do?" Christiana breathed with wonder, and then realized he'd said I love you *too* and smiled wryly. "You did hear what I said to Father outside then?"

Richard nodded and then asked, "You did mean it, didn't you? You weren't just saying it to ease your father's worries and — ?"

"I meant it," she interrupted, covering his hands with her own.

"Thank God," he breathed, and lowered his head to kiss her.

Christiana sighed, her body melting against his and arms sliding up around his neck. She did love his kisses, they stirred her like nothing she'd ever before experienced, and apparently stirred him too, she realized as she felt him hardening against her.

"Richard?" she whispered, tearing her mouth from his.

"Yes?" he murmured, kissing her ear in lieu of her lips.

"Why do we not go upstairs?"

"Upstairs?" He stopped kissing her to pull back and peer at her face uncertainly.

Christiana nodded, pressed more tightly against his growing erection, and murmured, "I should like to discuss our feelings further . . . in the bedroom," she added shyly in case he was misunderstanding her meaning.

Richard's eyebrows flew up, and then he caught her hand and turned to start toward the stairs, only to pause abruptly as the parlor door suddenly burst open and Daniel and the others hurried out.

"Richard," Daniel said spying them by the stairs and heading their way. "Now that the blackmailer is caught and the identity of the murderer found there is no reason to delay. We are heading for Gretna Green at once."

Christiana heard Richard groan, and could have groaned with him, but then he suddenly straightened and said, "Certainly, we shall leave first thing in the morning."

"The morning?" Daniel frowned.

"Well, the women will have to pack and —" he began, but Suzette interrupted him.

"The chests are still packed from this morning. At least mine is," she added with a frown and glanced to Lisa in question.

"Mine too," Lisa said.

Suzette glanced to Christiana next and she hesitated briefly, but then nodded. "So is mine."

Richard ducked his head to her ear and muttered, "You could have lied."

"I am a terrible liar. Besides, all is not lost. Trust me," she whispered back.

"Richard, is your carriage still out front?" Daniel asked. "I don't recall you sending it to the stables."

"I didn't," Richard answered. "I wasn't sure we wouldn't need it again."

"Mine is still out front as well," Robert announced. "They just need to be loaded."

"Excellent." Daniel clapped his hands with satisfaction. "Then we merely need to have mine prepared and brought around, load them up and we can — Damn," Daniel interrupted himself, and muttered, "I forgot my carriage is presently out of commission. I will have to rent one."

"We can use mine," Lord Madison offered at once. "It is out front."

"Perfect," Christiana breathed.

"Why is it perfect?" Richard asked under his breath.

"The Madison carriage is a coach. Five or even more can ride in it comfortably."

He appeared perplexed as to how that could be perfect, but Christiana just grabbed his hand, gave it a squeeze and drew him with her as she backed toward the front door. "Lisa, will you see that Grace and the chest holding Richard's and my clothes aren't forgotten?"

"Of course," she said with surprise. "But where will you be?"

Christiana reached behind her for the door. "We are going to head out at once. We have something to do. We shall wait for you at Stevenage," she announced and then before anyone could protest or ask further questions, Christiana pulled the door open and hurried out, tugging Richard with her.

"What is the something we have to do?" he asked as they hurried to the Radnor carriage.

"I shall explain in the carriage," she assured him and moved to the door while he moved to speak to the driver. By the time he entered, she had closed the small curtains at the windows. Richard eyed them with surprise as he sank on the bench opposite her.

"What — ?" he began, and then swallowed the rest of his question when she tugged the sleeves of her gown off her shoulders and then shimmied her arms out of it. His breath then came out on a long, "Ohhhh," as the material dropped to pool around her waist.

Reaching across the space between them, Richard caught her by the waist and promptly pulled her from her seat to straddle his lap.

Christiana sighed with relief as she slid her arms around his neck. She was trying to be as brazen as she wanted and not allow fear to hold her back, but truly, she'd felt terribly vulnerable baring herself like that so was glad not to feel so on display anymore.

"So this is the something we had to do?" Richard asked, his hands moving over her back in circles.

Christiana nodded. "I seemed to recall from our last journey to Gretna that we could . . . *discuss our feelings* almost as well in the carriage as in our room," she whispered, pressing a kiss to the scrape on his forehead. "So I thought perhaps . . ." The words died on a gasp as his hands found her breasts and squeezed gently. When he then used his hold to urge her up, Christiana obeyed and rose on her knees until her chest was in front of his face. Richard immediately took one hardening nipple into his mouth, rasping it with his tongue and then suckling briefly, before releasing it to peer up at her.

"Have I told you how brilliant I think you are?" he asked solemnly.

She blinked in surprise, but shook her head.

"Well I do, and you are," he assured her, his hands moving over her hips and then down to slip under her skirts. "I find you lovely." He pressed a kiss to the spot between her breasts. "Intelligent." His hands glided up the outside of her legs. "Resourceful." He licked one nipple, nipped at it, then suckled briefly, before releasing it to say, "Amusing." His mouth dipped to the other breast, attending that nipple as one hand closed around her hip and the other slipped between her legs. "Charming."

"Richard," Christiana gasped as his fingers found her core.

"Hush," he murmured against her breast.

"I am discussing my feelings." And then he paused, his hands stilling as he raised his head to ask. "Or have you heard enough? Shall I stop?"

Christiana shook her head at once. "No, husband. Pray continue."

A slow smiled claimed his lips and he allowed his fingers to strum over her again as he said solemnly, "I fear it could take a very long time for me to tell you all of them."

"Then perhaps you should just show me," she suggested breathlessly, and bit her lip as his fingers slid across her damp skin.

"It would be my pleasure," he assured her, and proceeded to do so.

ABOUT THE AUTHOR

Lynsay Sands is the nationally bestselling author of the Argeneau vampire series as well as more than thirty historical novels and anthologies known for their humorous edge.

Visit her official website at *www.lynsay sands.net.*